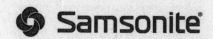

THE ART OF LOST LUGGAGE

AMANDA MURPHY

POOLBEG

This novel is entirely a work of fiction. The names,
characters and incidents portrayed in it are the work of the
author's imagination. Any resemblance to actual persons,
living or dead, events or localities is entirely coincidental.

Published 2002
by Poolbeg Press Ltd.
123 Grange Hill, Baldoyle,
Dublin 13, Ireland
Email: poolbeg@poolbeg.com
www.poolbeg.com

©Amanda Murphy 2002

The moral right of the author has been asserted.

Copyright for typesetting, layout, design
© Poolbeg Group Services Ltd.

1 3 5 7 9 10 8 6 4 2

A catalogue record for this book is available from the British Library.

ISBN 1 84223 055 7

Cover Designed by DW Design
Typeset by Patricia Hope in Goudy 11/14.5
Printed by
Cox & Wyman Ltd.,
Reading, Berkshire

About the Author

Amanda Murphy writes in a tiny office in her house. Her sitcom "A Whole Nother Story" was transmitted on Radio 4 in September 2001. This is her first novel.

She lives in Salford and, to her mother's utter dismay, she is still unmarried – she hasn't even got any cats!

Quotes

"I couldn't put it down." – My Grandmother

"I never said that!" – My Mother

"I'll sue." – My Best Friend

"Am I in it?" – My Brother

Acknowledgements

Thanks first and foremost to Gaye Shortland, who is a treasure, a love and utterly spectacular as an editor. Thanks to all at Poolbeg for giving me the chance to show off and say, "I'm having a novel published!"

To Mr Meadows and the other surgeons at North Manchester General Hospital, it seems slight to simply say thank you – seeing as you did save my life and all – but thanks all the same. To the nurses (Michelle, Jackie, Damon, Eileen, Kay and Gill) on Ward 15 – you made hospital fun. I'm sorry I was such a pain! And to my physios (Steff, Chris, Louise, Lyndsay, and Graham) for all their hard work getting me to walk again.

To my brother Dave, friends Allison Brimble and Annette Ractliffe – for reading every chapter and making me write more – this book would not have been the same without you. To Tracey Wilkinson, who reminded me that it was fun. To Sandra and Mark – see, it's a book now, you have to read it! To my Dad because he's my Dad.

Big huge I-love-you to my Mum, for patiently typing in the commas. Don't you wish I'd put them in as I went along?

Thanks to the airlines for screwing up my luggage so badly I had to write about it. (Amanda D, it wasn't your fault, I know.)

And finally . . . to Carl Cooper, my muse, my friend and the funniest guy I know.

To Paula Nunn,
Who loved books.

Chapter One

"Where is it?"

The Finland Air clerk looked over at the increasingly red face of the chubby person in front of her, winced at the volume of the voice and thought to herself that chubby people were meant to be jolly, like Santa Claus, not venting steam from their ears, with nostrils flaring in a most unattractive way. She looked directly into the woman's green eyes and was certain she could see sparks.

"Well, Mrs Yordan, it seems to be in Manchester, but we cannot be certain of this fact." She sniffed the air suspiciously. Although her straight blonde hair was tied back, a little had escaped onto her forehead and she attempted to move it by blowing at it out of the corner of her mouth rather than removing her hands from the keyboard in front of her.

"Look . . ." Sam peered over at the name tag on the clerk's jacket, "Jaane, it's Jordan, J as in Jumpy-woman-standing-in-front-of-you-needing-her-luggage, not Y as in

You'd-better-tell-me-pretty-soon-where-it-is-before-I-get-really-agitated." Sam looked at Jaane and smiled, which only served to make Jaane feel more nervous, her attempts at blowing her hair becoming more frequent as the pressure on her increased.

"I'll try and find out for you, Mrs –"

"Ms," Sam interrupted.

"Ms Jordan."

"OK then. I'll go outside for a cigarette, but by the time I get back, I really had better know where it is!"

Sam stomped off outside the main airport doors. She took a sharp involuntary breath as the cold hit her like a sheet of ice smashing over her head. She turned up her fake-fur collar and searched in her pockets for her gloves. Typical, she thought. I've forgotten my gloves – it's minus twenty and I leave my gloves on the radiator at home! She huffed angrily and chuntered like a displeased camel. She looked up at the ink-black sky and was once more utterly amazed at how dark Finland could get at that time of year – in England it was spring, but this country was still in the grip of winter. She made her way carefully to the ashtray, trying not to lose her footing on the thick layers of ice and mumbling under her breath. "Bloody Airlines, they should be strung up the lot of them. I'd like to get all the managing directors together, line them up against a wall and . . . "

The person we have left plotting the collective deaths of all managing directors of all airlines is Samantha Jordan, Management Consultant and Trainer for Martti Saari Consultancy OY. What we have experienced is her arrival in Turku, Finland, to start work. Unfortunately her luggage has once more been misplaced at any one of the three airports through which she has already passed this evening. Once you get to know her, you'll discover that this is a regular occurrence. Her inability to fly between any two points and arrive at the same point as her luggage is legendary and not achieved without having had some major argument with Lady Luck in a previous life. She's not normally this bad-tempered but, given the situation she once more finds herself in, a little latitude would be appreciated in any evaluation of her character at this juncture.

" . . . wouldn't that be fun!" Sam looked up to see Jaane walking tentatively towards her, her blonde hair now perfectly in place and clipped back with two large, blue, airline-regulation hairgrips for extra reinforcement.

"Ms Jordan, I-I-I've f-f-f-found out where it is," she stammered. "Your suitcase has been located in Helsinki and it should be here on the next flight."

"What time?" Sam asked in a tone suggesting that she was more resigned than angry.

"Well, the next flight arrives at seven thirty so the good news is that you should have your luggage by 8am." Jaane briefly smiled and rushed on, "I have arranged for an airport taxi to take you to your hotel – here is an overnight pack and four hundred Finnish marks for the inconvenience – I'll just need the name of your hotel and your signature on this."

Jaane exhaled in a rush. She'd obviously been able to carry out the extraordinary feat of talking whilst holding her breath. She waved a yellow form in front of Sam, looking a bit like Chamberlain coming back from his meeting with Hitler, with the same lack of conviction. Sam stared at this woman, utterly at a loss for words and wondering why the fact that her suitcase would arrive in, she looked at her watch, eight hours, should be good news.

3

An awful thought hit her. If her suitcase was arriving at eight o'clock in the morning and she had to leave for the company at seven thirty . . . She looked down at her legs. Jeans. She had a flashback to herself at home, getting ready to leave, spilling her coffee down her jumper and hurriedly grabbing a sweatshirt from her wash basket because the taxi was waiting. She sniffed her armpits and made a sound akin to a cat being strangled. She took a deep breath and tried to compose herself.

She appeared to be, rather unnervingly for Jaane, serenely calm, which, as most of her friends know, is either the prelude to screams or tears. But knowing that, in Finland, any form of ranting and raving would get her precisely nowhere, she gave in, signed the form, picked up her handbag and said, "Send it to the Cumulus Hotel." She felt the tears welling up, but held them back.

She got into the front seat of the waiting taxi next to the driver and surveyed her possessions. One DKNY handbag, slightly worn, one Finnish-designed briefcase complete with mobile-phone holder, one Finland Air Overnight Pack (containing: T-shirt – size M, toothbrush, toothpaste, hairbrush and selected Elizabeth Arden skincare products) and a Manchester Airport Duty Free carrier bag, containing two hundred cigarettes.

"Well, at least I can smoke myself to death if I get really desperate," she muttered.

Sam smokes when she is angry, anxious, sad, happy and especially after a particularly good meal. I suppose you could say she smokes quite a bit, pretty much all the time. However, her time for doing so is slowly running out, as she promised her mother that she would quit on her thirtieth birthday. Her birthday happens to coincide with the date that the EU have decided to stop duty free, so it works pretty well all round really.

She picked up her mobile and dialled a number.

"Corporate Finance," said a familiar voice.

"Well, it's happened again, Lexi. I'm sitting in a taxi going to my hotel, without any means of sleeping peacefully. You know how much I hate sleeping in the nude and they still haven't implemented my suggestion that they put in T-shirts which might successfully cover up more than Kate Moss's breasts, which I see that she's got out again on the cover of some mag. By the way, why on earth do they call them Supermodels? What's so super about standing around having your photo taken? Maybe it refers to their unparalleled ability to imbibe narcotics whilst sticking their fingers down their throats. What do you think? Anyway I digress. I've had it with these bloody airlines, Lexi."

"Sam, do you ever take a breath?" Alex paused, checking to see whether her boss was watching her. "OK, tell me all about it."

The person to whom Sam is at this moment pouring out her frustrations is Alex Spencer, her best friend. They met each other while studying in Munich and have been best friends throughout the ten years since.

Sam had been at the welcome meeting for a student house that she was to share with two other people. She'd checked out her fellow house occupants and evaluated their appearance. One was mousy-haired, with a pale and pallid complexion, and as Sam had been told that there was another English student sharing, she decided that that sort of pallor could only be achieved by the total lack of sunshine that the UK provides. The second occupant was blonde, and blue-almost-violet-eyed, textbook

German, or so Sam thought. All three were being bombarded by rule after rule, which was accompanied, in typical German style, by page after page of laminated Commandments, which they were expected to display prominently on their walls at all times.

Thou shalt not use the kitchen after 00:00 hours, unless the majority of the house are present, in which case this time shall be extended to 01:00 hours. Thou shalt not play loud music at any time, unless the majority of the house are present, in which case this is restricted to between 10:00 hours and 22:00 hours (21:00 on Sundays). By the time they got to the using-the-washing-machine rule, Sam had completely given up trying to listen and had mumbled, "Fuck this for a lark. I'm off down the pub."

She was unbelievably surprised when the other 'new tenant', the one Sam had assessed as being an undoubtedly, one-hundred-per cent, blonde-haired, blue-eyed German answered, "There's one down the hill, I think – let's go". They made their excuses and ran off together giggling. The inauspicious start of a beautiful friendship. Together they managed to negotiate the minefield which was the 'year abroad' in Germany. When they returned to England, their friendship grew to the point that they could understand each other with the minimum of effort. This is not to say that they don't have disagreements, of course they do, but they have both learnt to accept and in some ways love the quirks and inadequacies of the other person.

Alex now works for Citibank in London, as a bilingual secretary in the Corporate Finance division. Even though it is almost ten o'clock in the evening in London, Alex is still at work. Her rather austere boss frowns upon extended personal telephone calls. In fact he frowns upon any personal telephone calls at all. Both Sam and Alex are well used to interrupting conversations and restarting after Alex's boss has left the room. Sam is quite *used to being called Mr Smith as a way of averting the boss's suspicion. Who knows what would happen if he ever realised that none of his clients were actually called by this name. As Sam is speaking, Alex continues to type a PowerPoint presentation. Since she has heard this story many many times before, she is fully aware that it will be some time before Sam takes her next breath. Keeping one eye out for her boss and the other on her computer screen, she settles in to listen to the unfolding tale.*

"So here I am in the taxi, wearing nothing but my jeans and a smelly sweatshirt. I knew I shouldn't have had that garlic pizza last night. It was so hot on board, I'm practically sweating garlic. I've got to go to work like this tomorrow. Do you know how embarrassing it is turning up at a company wearing a fetching jeans/sweatshirt combo and smelling of garlic? Especially when they're expecting a strait-laced English consultant. Are you listening to me?"

"Of course I'm listening to you, but I would have thought that, by now, you'd expect this to happen. You've been working in Finland for two years and you go there practically every other week. What is it now? Six times this year and it's only," she glanced briefly at the calendar on her desk, "April sixth. I know it's going to happen, everyone you know knows it's going to happen – what's wrong with *you*?"

"I don't know, I keep hoping they'll get it right, I guess, and I keep forgetting to travel in something I can work in the next day. You know how I hate lugging stuff around airports and there's only so much you can put in carry-on luggage and I have my computer with me, so the bitch at check-in wouldn't let me take my trolley case on as hand luggage. Apparently it's one and a half inches too long. I mean, what's the point of being a gold card holder, a record-breaking gold card holder, by the way –"

"Yeah, yeah, Sam, I know. The quickest accumulation of plus points in the history of the airline. But –"

"Are you taking the mick? This is a disaster. A total disaster. Garlic sweatshirt! Just think of the effort involved in trying to make these people over here understand that I don't normally smell like this. Usually I'm fragrant, you know like that MP's wife, Whatsherface." Sam moaned again, realising that she was going way off track, but somehow unable to stop herself.

"What's a politician's wife got to do with anything, Sam?"

"I dunno, it's just so . . ." Sam racked her brains to think of the appropriate word, "irritating."

"That's it, Samantha Jordan! I've heard enough."

"Well, I've had enough, so we make a good pair."

"Why can't you just accept the fact that you are not meant to do the air-travel thing and get yourself a job where you stay in one place and while you're at it, move down to London. I'll never understand why you insist on living in that awful place anyway –"

"Don't start that again, Alex – this is not the time for a tourist information broadcast on London. This is a crisis situation."

"Yeah, it always is," Alex mumbled, resigned to the fact that Sam was determined to have her full moan.

"Anyway, Manchester is not awful. I love it there." Sam would defend Manchester, for all its faults – after all, it was home. Although sometimes, Sam also had trouble remembering why and how she ended up there. It seemed like one minute she was taking on a six-month project assuring all and sundry that it was just a breather to get herself together after HIM, while she decided what she wanted to do. Then after all the of-course-I'm-moving-back-to-London's and the I-could-never-stay-here's, suddenly eighteen months later she woke up at home in Manchester.

"Don't change the subject – either change jobs, or accept it." Alex looked up to see her boss walking towards her. "Got to go. I'll call later."

"OK, bye."

Sam clicked her mobile shut and leant back in the seat. She toyed briefly with the idea of attempting conversation with the taxi driver, but decided against it. Instead she decided to rest her eyes.

"Seems like you've been experiencing an interesting welcome to my country," said a low voice from the back seat of the cab. "Let's hope it is not prejudicial."

Sam's eyes flew open and she turned to see that there was someone else in the taxi. She replayed her discussion with Jaane, remembering too late that she had said "airport taxi". Airport taxis were an interesting concept that Sam had only encountered in Finland. The idea was that you could get a taxi to and from the airport for a fixed fee, usually a third of the price of the normal taxi fare, as long as you didn't mind sharing the taxi with one or sometimes two other people going in approximately the same direction. Sam had been too incensed to notice that the taxi already contained another passenger. In any case, the usual taxi companions in Finland were shy and unable to speak any English at all. Hearing the slight American accent in the voice, it finally sank into Sam's brain that she'd been sharing her laundry problems with more than Alex.

"Personally, I like the smell of garlic. I've spent quite a few holidays in France. It's very good for you, apparently," the voice uttered.

"Good for the blood, but not the nose, I'm afraid."

"Well, don't worry. My nose isn't that badly off at the moment."

"You'll be glad of that because I perspire more when I'm angry." Sam had run out of steam – maybe a little chit-chat would do her good. "So, were you in France much then?"

"A while. Although, I have spent most of my time in America, recently."

"Oh, were you there long then? I mean, you speak English very well for a . . ." Just in time, Sam stopped herself from making a potentially rude remark about the linguistic prowess of the Finnish race and realised that he was waiting for the rest of her sentence, "erm . . . for a . . . um . . . man, I mean."

"Or indeed for a Finn, maybe?"

"Maybe," Sam mumbled. "So, do you come here often?" The last question emerged as more of a squeak than anything else. This was turning into more of a disaster than the entire luggage affair.

"Fairly often. I do live here. And pardon me for returning to the original discussion, but are you angry often?"

"Whenever I come to this country I am."

"And I suppose England does nothing to displease you?"

"Oh, England does plenty, but as soon as I arrive here it's . . . oh, I don't know how to explain it. It's like stepping into a parallel universe. You know, like going through the

Looking-Glass, only worse, because it's real. And there's no helpful little white rabbit to show me around." She wondered if he would get the reference.

"Maybe one day something may make you feel different about my country."

"I doubt anything could make me feel different about this particular country. Sorry."

"I shall remember that."

From the rich warm timbre of the voice, Sam sensed that he had been teasing her all along. Sam turned round to attempt to see the owner of the voice. Unfortunately it was so dark that she could only make out a silhouette. Luckily it was also too dark for him to see her blushing furiously. Nice voice though, she reflected.

The taxi stopped outside her hotel. Sam said her goodbyes to the voice, paid the driver and went inside.

The first thing she did was check out how Sirpa, the hotel receptionist, had done her hair. Over the previous year, Sam had noticed a direct correlation between Sirpa's long curly hair and her mood. If her hair was pulled tightly back, Sirpa would almost certainly be in a bad mood and therefore unwilling to indulge in small talk. Today however, Sirpa's ebony hair was clipped loosely at the sides which usually meant that she was in a playful mood. She did look a little tired however, which wasn't surprising as it was way way past midnight and she'd probably been working since breakfast. Sirpa looked up as Sam walked towards her, her blue eyes ringed in a dark grey colour that seemed out of place in her creamy complexion. The smile on her face more than made up for the bags under her eyes and Sam felt herself relaxing.

"Good evening, Ms Jordan. Nice to see you back again – no luggage, I see." Sirpa grimaced sympathetically at Sam. "You need your kit for emergencies, yes?"

Her emergency kit contained a few bare essentials that she had left in the hotel after the last visit. Customer Service was a totally unknown concept in Finland and it had taken quite a few negotiations to achieve this. The hotel frowned upon guests leaving articles of clothing behind and eventually they'd made an exception for Sam, but had restricted her to a small bag so as not to seem like total pushovers. But, after all, she was a valued customer.

Sam nodded, breathing a sigh of relief that she would at least have clean underwear and make-up for the next day.

"I already have put it in your room, as usual."

"Isn't it about time for your holiday? You normally go around this time of year."

"No, this year my holiday is cancel. We get new computer system, soon. I must stay until it installed – I take holiday then."

"They really work you hard, don't they?"

"Yes, we look for more persons, not easy in Turku. Staff who speak English difficult to find. Have pleasant stay, Ms Jordan."

"Thank you, Sirpa." Sam picked up her room key and started to walk away. She turned back. "My bag should be –"

"Arriving on the morning flight and I'll make it sure to be in your room, as soon as it arrives." Sirpa paused and then added, "As usual."

Sam turned back towards the lift and sighed. Maybe Alex is right. Everyone expects it to happen. I should just accept it, she thought to herself. It's my lot in life to be forever luggage-less. I seem to be the living embodiment of Murphy's Law. Whatever I did in my last incarnation, it must have been spectacularly bad. While waiting for the lift she pondered on her problem. Had it really been six times since the New Year? She decided there must be something going on. Paranoia was beginning to set in. Someone at some airport somewhere must have something against her. It had happened too many times for it to be simply bad luck, but what to do? What could she do? Airlines were a law unto themselves and the last time she'd asked for an investigation, she'd been fobbed off with 'a computer failure' as explanation. She needed to think about how she was going to approach this problem.

In her room she took her laptop computer from its pouch in her briefcase. She booted it up and clicked on the icon to access her talking journal. She took out the tiny microphone, lay back on her bed and spoke to her computer. As she spoke, the words appeared in the window on her desktop.

What she's doing now is chatting to her talking journal. She tells it everything and, as you probably realise, she talks quite a bit, so it contains absolutely everything about her, and most of her friends too, not that they know anything about it, of course. She's been threatening to write a book about her life for ages now but has never got around to it.

Sam is twenty-nine years old and, in her words, sliding inevitably towards that pit of despair which is the big Three – Zero. She is extremely pretty, in a plump kind of way, with unusual coloured eyes. Most of the time, they are a greeny-hazel mix, but when she gets emotional they turn into a deep emerald colour. Her family discovered many years ago that it is best not

13

to attempt to cajole her into losing weight as she can be pretty lethal when deprived of sugar for any great length of time. She's not your usual nearly thirty-something however and she's definitely not what you could call neurotic. Although, knowing her life, neurosis is probably her best option.

She is either 'independent and opinionated' or 'a bit of a stroppy cow', depending on which female member of her family you ask, and is currently single. She is a mass of contradictions, exceedingly efficient at work, but highly disorganised in her personal life. Effervescent, but likes her solitude on occasion. Forthright and straight-talking, but tends to babble when nervous. What most people don't realise is that Sam is much more sensitive than people give her credit for. She is a tough cookie with an extremely soft centre, but ever since HIM she doesn't let anyone close enough to see it. She would never admit this out loud, but Sam is a 'blubber' – she cries copiously at films and they don't even have to be sad ones. Luckily, being a contact-lens wearer, she can often pass these tearful moments off as a 'dust under the lens' problem.

The mobile rang sharply, interrupting Sam's flow.

"Hello?"

"Where are you? I've left three messages for you at home already."

"Mother, what day is it?"

"Tuesday, why?"

"Well, when I rang you yesterday, what day did I say I was going to work?"

"Tuesd- oh, I see! Well, I just wanted to ask you if you were going to come and visit this weekend. Although, I suppose not, seeing as you're over there. Chelsea wants to have a word, hold on . . . "

There was a brief scuffle to be heard and the urging voice of her mother saying "Go on" in the background.

"Hello, Auntie Sammy."

"Hi, Chelsea. How are you?"

"Mummy said p'jamas Spaceship game with Nanny."

"That's lovely, darling. Can I speak to Nanny now?"

"'kay."

More scuffling noises occurred at the other end, then, "Sam –"

"Mother, I wish you wouldn't do that – this phone call is probably costing the GDP of a small South American country, just so a three-year-old can tell me some utter nonsense. What's she doing up at this time of night anyway?"

"Oh, hush up. Why are you such a grouch? Lost your bags again? Anyway, she's in bed with me – we thought we'd give you a ring. She wouldn't go to sleep until she'd talked to her favourite auntie. Oh and I have some news for you. Do you remember Debbie, your little friend from school? Well, I met her mother in the Co-op today and Debbie's getting married, to a man, dear, an optician, and if it wasn't for the fact that you have a glamorous-sounding job, I wouldn't have known what to tell her when she asked about you. All puffed up and proud, she was. It's so embarrassing! Thirty and unmarried, the shame of it . . ." Her mother let out an agonised noise.

"I'm twenty-nine, mother, as you well know – you were there after all."

"Well, what was the point? If I'd have known you were going to be such a disappointment –"

"What, mother? What? You wouldn't have had me?"

15

"No, nothing like that, dear – I should never have bought you that toolkit, when you were six – I knew it was a mistake. I told your father that it was a mistake – I know what mistakes are. I'm the one who stopped you making one with You-know-who."

"Actually, mother, if memory serves me right, you're the one who thought You-know-who would make the perfect husband."

The You-know-who in question is Sam's ex-fiancé Phillipe, a rather vain and arrogant French photographer, with whom Sam lived for six years. Somehow he'd managed to confuse her normal filter of good character judgement. They had met when Sam was organising the marketing for a French company.

In her previous life, Sam had worked for an international management consultancy, working with blue-chip companies throughout Europe. She had been supervising the photo shoot for their new brochure, when she quite literally bumped into him. It started out very well; he was romantic and she was swept off her feet.

He would buy her gifts of clothes and jewellery. He would accompany her everywhere and would telephone many times during the day, if they had to be apart. At first Sam found it wonderful that he wanted to be with her all the time. Eventually, however, she realised it was more to do with him wanting to know her every move than any real concern or feelings for her. After the first year, she began to notice a pattern emerging. He told her what to wear, controlled what she did and rarely let her out of his sight, almost forcing her into giving up her job. And his insane jealousy almost drove her to breaking point on many occasions. Once, he even raised his hand to hit her, but stopped himself just in time. He knew exactly how to manipulate her, pushing her just so far before withdrawing into the obligatory "I'm sorry. It's only because I love you so much" phase, where Sam found it impossible to be angry at him. Over the years, his controlling ways nearly succeeded in changing Samantha from a vivacious, fun-loving and confident young woman into a nervous and anxious mouse. Though he never actually hit her, the threat was always there, lurking behind his interrogations and accusations. Luckily, after many long-distance telephone calls to Alex, and the discovery of one or two of his secrets, Sam had come to her senses and left him before her self-esteem was completely eroded, leaving us with the person we have in front of us today: outwardly cynical hard shell jealously protecting the woman within.

Her mother usually describes her as 'sadly intelligent' because Sam seems to know what's good for her and she realises that this probably means that Sam will never produce a grandchild to complement the adorable Chelsea. But as every mother of a single twenty-nine-nearly-thirty-something professional knows, there is still time.

It's not that Sam is totally against babies and marriage, it's just that she can't seem to reconcile these with her life at the moment. She loves her job and simply cannot see how the 'family/kids' thing would ever fit in with her flying around Europe every other week. Sam refers to her mother as her 'Biological Timekeeper', as she never fails to remind Sam that her biological clock is ticking away and soon it'll be too late.

"Look, mother, it's getting late over here so just send me an e-mail outlining all the pertinent points of your embarrassment and I'll try and address them when I get back. OK?"

"All right, dear, don't work too hard – you know, you always work too hard. How will you ever meet a man, working all hours God sends in a frozen country halfway to the North Pole? You're there so often I can't understand why you don't at least attempt to find yourself a nice Finnish man."

"Have you seen Finnish men?"

"What's wrong with Finnish men?"

"Do the words 'Quasimodo is the more attractive option' give you a clue?"

"Quasi-who?" Her mother sounded confused.

"Well, put it this way, mother. In the two years I've been travelling to Finland, I've yet to encounter a Finnish man who wouldn't scare the socks off me on a dark and dingy night." Sam was exaggerating wildly to make quite sure that her mother understood her reservations. "And in the light of day, I'd probably be blinded by the glare off his slaphead."

"Socks? Someone your age should never wear socks! In your case, I'd stick to stockings anyway. Use anything that might give you an edge, darling."

"Mother!" Sam was exasperated.

"And what exactly is a slaphead when it's at home?"

"A nice shiny bald head, mother, just perfect for being slapped."

"Bald heads aren't that bad. Those sort of men are supposed to be very virile."

"That's a myth perpetuated by balding advertising executives, I'm afraid, mother."

"Still, maybe your expectations are too high. I mean what with your being so big-boned and all . . . "

"I shouldn't be too fussy," Sam finished for her.

"Exactly. The more homely type of man would be more likely to be faithful anyway."

"Next you'll be talking about mantelpieces and poking fires."

"Mantelpieces? Fires? What are you talking about? I don't know, young girls these days. In my day –"

"I'm going now!" Sam hoped to head off the 'in my day' lecture. It seemed that in this case, she'd succeeded.

"At least give them a try, eh, Samantha? Keep your options open."

"OK, mother. I'll keep my eyes peeled," Sam acquiesced.

"Speaking of eyes, they are your best feature. God knows you don't have many. Remember, you never know when you might meet someone, so make sure that you wear some make-up. Even a little mascara is better than nothing, just to perk up your eyes. Maybe a little eyeliner and even –"

"Bye, mother," Sam exhaled and switched off her phone, leaving her mother to continue the make-up lesson alone.

Chapter Two

Sam was knackered. Not simply tired – she was absolutely ready-to-fall-into-her-hotel-bed-and-get-comatose knackered. She had a hell of a day behind her and could hardly think straight.

She'd been tossing and turning all the previous night and by the time the wake-up call came that morning, she had decided to call Finland Air and demand that this entire luggage problem be investigated. Jaane still sounded a little nervous, but managed to assure Sam that she'd call as soon as arrangements had been made.

Sam had spent the day consulting a small Finnish company. Her work, although mainly training, also involved assisting small and medium-sized companies in their efforts to export to the UK. Mostly she loved her job. She enjoyed the fact that she got to meet many different types of people. The usual Finland trip was a pleasant mix of training and consultancy. The training days tended to be particularly tiring and often she could only describe the consulting days as trying. She'd been working in Finland for two years, but she knew that she'd never really get the hang of the Finns, no matter how long she worked there. They were a curious breed of people. Sam hadn't quite managed to work out whether they were naïve or so incredibly intelligent that they only appeared naïve. They were collectively the most stubborn people that she had ever encountered. They even had a word for it: *sisu*. This had no real English translation. It described the idea that if Finns came up to a door that opened inwards, they could through sheer force of will make the door open outwards. Saying that, they were collectively the nicest people she'd ever met, which rather lent weight to the intelligent theory.

Luckily her work that morning had consisted mainly of working through the company's books in a little room on her own. This meant that she could avoid anyone noticing the increasingly pungent stench of garlic which emanated from her sweatshirt. At lunch, she gladly ate as much garlic as she could stand, in order to pass her pungency off as a recent occurrence.

The company was called Turun Puu Oy, which translated into English meant Turku Wood Ltd and Sam had spent the better part of the afternoon sitting in the Managing Director's office attempting to persuade him that, in order to be successful, they would have to change their name.

"Sorry, Pekka, but the name just won't work in the UK."

"But, Samantha, it is our trademark. We have even translated our stamp into English, so now all of our products are clearly marked, *Made with Turun Puu*."

"Pekka, it's 'made by', not 'made with' and that just

makes matters worse." She tried a different tack. "I understand that *puu* in Finnish means wood, and that over here, you are Turku Wood Ltd, but puu sounds like 'poo' and in the UK, 'poo' means, for want of a better word, crap." She shrugged apologetically and smiled sweetly at Pekka. "You don't want British suppliers thinking your products are crap, now do you?"

"I don't, but –"

"No, so you can't send your products over to the UK with *Made with Turku Crap* stamped all over them."

"I see what you mean. Let me think about it."

So that was how it was left, an entire day of consulting used up and the MD still didn't want to commit to a name-change. The word stubborn certainly didn't seem strong enough to describe these people.

That wasn't even the worst part of the day. She'd been summoned into the office by Martti Saari, her boss and owner of the consultancy. He'd been approached by an old friend who needed help in his company. Apparently the son was in the process of expanding the company's interests abroad and had requested 'the English consultant'. He hadn't actually asked for her by name, but as good as. This meant that she'd be staying an extra day to visit their office.

Sam sighed at the thought and sat down on her hotel bed. That was all she needed, another crazy Finnish managing director. What was wrong with them? Didn't they fancy exporting to France, so that the French consultant could deal with them? Why did they all want to export to England? From her discussions with her German colleagues, it seemed that all the sane managing directors were happy to export to Germany, leaving all the mad ones for her to deal with. Something else was worrying her as well: Martti had been very careful not to mention the company's name. In her experience this usually meant the worst. Martti was obviously trying to hide something. She wondered what delights this company's name had in store for her. One day she'd have a company with a nice normal name – at least she fervently hoped so.

It was four thirty in the afternoon and she was feeling isolated and lonely. This, she thought, is what people don't realise when they think of my so-called 'glamorous' life. Being stuck in a hotel room in a freezing country where it is too cold to go out is no fun. Even if she did go out, she didn't know anyone. Plus there was no way that she'd be able to strike up a conversation with someone in a restaurant. The Finns were so unforthcoming. Not once in the entire time she'd been working there had anyone other than waiting staff ever talked to her – well, apart from that unusual guy in the airport taxi. And the waiting staff only did it because they had to. Sam was certain that the restaurant workers were just waiting for an effective push-button method of food ordering, in order to be able to pass their entire shifts without having to utter a word. She missed the UK. Oh well, it looked like another night in front of the television. In any case, she was exhausted.

She picked up the remote and pointed it at the television. Nothing happened. She fiddled around with it and discovered that in order for it to work, she had to go through a series of strange contortions involving holding on to the battery compartment and pressing the buttons in a certain order. The television came to life and she flipped through the channels.

"Finnish stuff . . . Finnish stuff . . . *Family Ties* re-run . . . Finnish stuff . . . OK. MTV it is."

Now, it is a well-known fact that there is only so much MTV anyone can take before they go screaming mad. Sam had it on good authority that some terrorist groups used it as their preferred form of torture based on the speed with which it is able to bring sane people to their knees. It seemed also to have the opposite effect. She'd heard that some cost-conscious sanatoriums preferred it to electric-shock therapy, as it cured even the toughest of tough cases, quickly bringing them to their senses long enough to politely (or not so politely) request that the channel be changed. It called for rather less electricity than the electric-shock therapy and proved the point that their inmates might be mad, but they weren't stupid. So, after grumbling about how refreshing it would be if one day the video jockeys actually looked like normal people rather than clones from the 'presenter factory' where all youth programmes get theirs from, Sam switched off the television and turned to her suitcase.

After arranging her clothes in the wardrobe, she began hanging up her blouses in the bathroom, turning on the shower to its hottest setting. This was as close as Sam came to actually ironing, but it seemed to do the job every time.

After her short bout of housekeeping, she sat down on her bed and switched on her laptop. This was probably a good time to check her e-mails, she thought. There were a couple of work-related ones, which were easy to deal with. She found one from Pekka asking her if she was completely certain about the pronunciation of *puu*, adding that everyone makes mistakes. To which she replied that although mistakes do occur from time to time, the fact that she'd been speaking the English language as her mother tongue for nearly three decades rather indicated that she was unlikely to be mistaken on this occasion. That should shut him up, she thought. Checking the rest of her e-mails, she found one from her sister, accusing her of neglecting her niece (she wrote back with a promise to visit as soon as she possibly could) and finally, there were two other large-sized files from her mother, which she decided to delete rather than deal with.

"Job's a good 'un," she said out loud to no one in particular, which was lucky because her attempts at a Mancunian accent left lots to be desired. She yawned once, moved over to her bed, lifted up the covers and slipped in between the cool hotel-white sheets. As she drifted off to sleep she wondered dreamily how on earth hotels managed to keep their sheets so white, when her one set of white sheets were a funny pinky-grey colour after the first wash . . .

It's not that Sam was a total disaster in domestic matters. It was just that she'd had too many years of hotel rooms, where, by the time you'd returned in the evening, you'd find the room vacuumed, the bathroom cleaned and your pyjamas folded neatly on your pillow, as if by magic. When she first bought her house, she was surprised when her mother informed her that someone actually had to do these things. So she gamely attempted to get into the swing of housework, but after a few major calamities involving a bottle of bleach and a carrot, she had come to realise that household chores are not her forte and best left to professionals if at all possible. Unfortunately, finding a professional in the household chore sector was a task which involved patience and plenty of time – two things that Sam was sorely lacking. Knowing that she functioned best under pressure, she had set herself a deadline and was determined to find a cleaner by December. Until then, Sam's home would continue to look 'disorganised' as she euphemistically calls it. Another reason why she was happy living alone – there was no one else around to witness her shameful lack of neatness.

She was in the middle of turning down Brad Pitt's invitation for dinner because she had already said yes to Jeremy Paxman, when the phone rang.

"Leave it, Brad. I'm talking to you," she mumbled. "Jennifer doesn't even have to know that I'm here."

The phone was persistent and after a while she realised that it wasn't ringing in her dream – it was her hotel phone ringing in her room.

"Damn," she grumbled and got up to answer it.

"Mrs Yordan?"

"Look, my name is Samantha Jordan, Ms not Mrs, J not Y and it is, um," she glanced at the clock, "7.30pm. What are you doing calling me at such an ungodly hour? Who is this?"

"Ms Jordan, it's Jaane at Finland Air. Sorry to bother you at this, um, late, um, hour, but if you remember, you asked me this morning to get someone to find out why you keep losing your luggage."

"Yes?" Sam said grumpily.

"Erm, yes, well, I have been in touch with our Manchester office and you will be met on your return to Manchester by Anne Mansfield, who will outline the measures we have arranged for you." She paused for effect. "I hope this is OK? You did say that we should call you as soon as we had sorted something out."

"Yeah, all right. That's fine, thanks."

Putting down the phone, Sam crawled back into bed and picked up where she had left off. Unfortunately by the time she got back to her dream, Jennifer Aniston had turned up and everything was turning slightly nasty.

"Damn!" she said and rolled over.

* * *

She woke up grumpily the next morning. As usual on her first full night in Finland, despite her exhaustion she'd had a restless night. Unable to get into a comfortable position, she'd tossed and turned, finally falling into a deep sleep at close to five o'clock in the morning only to be buzzed awake by the hotel wake-up service at half past six. Unfortunately, no matter how wretched she felt, she was always forced to be polite. Automated services did not exist in her hotel and on the other end of a wake-up call was a living and breathing person, to whom Sam had to croak her thanks for bringing her into unwelcome consciousness, as if they'd been doing her some sort of favour.

Sam really wasn't a nice person in the mornings, and the intensity of her grumpiness escalated when she was in Finland. She managed to grunt unhappily at every perceived slight that Finland caused her. The room was too cold, grunt. The water took more than five seconds to warm up, grunt. The shower gel wouldn't lather properly, grunt. She froze getting out of the shower, grunt. Even her ever-so-slightly squeaking bathroom door caused a grunt.

Finnish hotels are the strangest of places. Because of the extreme cold, every hotel is equipped with a fully functional heating system, which by law has to circulate and replenish the air every five minutes. The upshot is that there is a constant draught. The ever-

moving atmosphere made her shiver every morning. Especially when stepping out of the 'hotter than hot' shower that she needed just to get her body to function effectively. She'd tried everything. She'd even used extra quilts, but they'd only caused her to sweat, thus making her shiver when the air touched her damp skin.

In most countries this would not cause too much of a problem as most countries had four seasons. Finland also had four. Unfortunately their four seasons were winter, cold winter, freezing winter and for a very brief two weeks in July, summer. Nowadays, Sirpa made sure that from October until May, Sam had two extra electric heaters in her room.

Finally dressed and ready, Sam went down to breakfast. It was coming up to seven o'clock and in most English hotels this would be the slow period for breakfasting. However, Sam was in the geographical equivalent of the 'Twilight Zone' and she had to queue for a seat at a table. She finally managed to stake her claim to a seat opposite a man who was talking avidly on his mobile phone. She made the internationally understood head gesture, which indicated, 'I'm going to get something. Can you make sure no one steals my seat'. Having received the reciprocal nodded reply of 'I suppose I could look after it', she went in search of orange juice. Walking past table after table of large coffee urns, she was struck, as usual, by the propensity of the average Finn to consume copious amounts of extremely strong coffee. She surmised that, apart from the lack of a signal on a mobile phone, the only thing guaranteed to make Finns riot would be a coffee shortage. Having eventually found the orange juice, she returned to the table to find the man still chatting on his phone. Not only that, but she also saw that her supposedly 'saved' seat had been occupied by a woman, who was also deeply absorbed in a call on her mobile.

The man gave Sam the internationally recognised shrug, which meant 'Sorry, she was better-looking than you, and I wasn't going to turn her down'. Sam felt like showing him the international sign for 'Go forth and multiply, you git' but she restrained herself. Irritated and more than a little uncomfortable, she propped herself against a nearby wall and attempted to balance her drink, coat and briefcase. In an effort to tune out of the situation she found herself in, she turned her thoughts to the day ahead, indignant that she still had to be in the country at all.

* * *

"Markku, he in factory, he say make comfortable in office. He happy you enter company," the secretary in the company explained falteringly, while showing Sam into a large room containing a huge mahogany desk. She pointed to a chair and said rather startlingly, "Sit."

Sam was going to mention that although she didn't look her best this morning, she wasn't in fact a dog, but she was, by this time, in a better mood, so she let the imperious command wash over her. "Thank you."

In her company's office, she'd found the instructions of how to get to her consultancy job. With a sigh of relief, she'd noted that the company had a nice solid English-effect name. It was called 'Fintec Technologies' and she was to meet the owner's son, Markku Nieminen. As usual with Finnish names, she was practising the pronunciation aloud, when a voice came from behind her.

"Call me Mark. The Americans found it easier to pronounce."

Sam froze. She recognised the American twang in the voice. It was the silhouette. The mystery man from the taxi.

29

It couldn't be a coincidence. Could it? She turned around to see a tall brown-haired man, whose face was taken over by a huge grin. Sam wasn't quite sure what she'd expected, but looking at him once more, this certainly wasn't it. She'd grown so used to seeing what one could euphemistically call 'less than attractive' people in Finland that to see a decent-looking male was the equivalent of seeing Robert Redford walking down Deansgate in Manchester.

"So we meet again," he smiled. "You must be . . ." he looked down at the papers in his hand, "Samantha Jordan?"

"Sam, yes, I mean, call me, um . . . Sam, Sam . . . er . . . Jordan, that's me right enough . . . erm . . ." her voice trailed off. She was babbling again. A warm feeling started in her stomach and proceeded to move rapidly up her face until it stopped on her forehead, just above her green eyes. She was in danger of winning a 'spot the beetroot' competition.

"Pleased to meet you." He held out his hand.

"Yes . . . um . . . me too. Pleased to meet you, I mean." She tried to focus on her hand which was being gripped in a strong-but-not-too-strong grasp.

"Sit down. Sit down. Would you like a coffee?"

"No, I'm fine." Sam started rifling around in her briefcase to avoid his gaze and buy some time in which to pull herself together.

"I didn't mean to startle you."

"No, no, it's all right. I wasn't expecting . . . er . . . "

"Me?"

"Quite."

"So did you steer clear of the garlic last night?" He smiled a broad beam of a smile at her, which only caused her to blush even more furiously.

Pulling herself together she managed, "I thought you liked garlic?"

"I do, I do, but I don't want you feeling uncomfortable. I see they've returned your luggage. I was half expecting you to be in that rather fetching – how did you describe it?"

"Er . . . jeans/sweatshirt combo."

"Yes, that's right." Mark laughed.

"So, what a coincidence, eh?"

"Well, I must admit, it's not completely a coincidence. You see, I had a feeling that you might work for Martti. I mean, it's not often foreigners come all the way over here at this time of year and, from the conversation which I overheard last night, I presumed that you weren't a tourist."

"No, I suppose not."

"I simply asked around. You were with Pekka yesterday, weren't you?"

"Yes. Pekka, that's right," Sam murmured. "Americans?"

"Excuse me?"

"Yes, you said the Americans found it easier."

"So I did, yes. I did my MBA out in Boston."

"Boston. Oh yes, America, you mentioned it in the taxi, I forgot –"

"I worked there for a while also. I made quite a few friends out there. I try to get back as often as I can. Just to keep my English up to date."

"American," Sam said automatically.

"All right then, my American English. I'd forgotten how snobbish you English can be." Markku laughed and continued, "I usually manage to get over there about two to three times a year."

"Oh, yes, right. How did you know I was with Pekka yesterday?"

"It's a small place. Word gets around," he shrugged. "I thought you might be able to help. You see, we have a slight problem . . . "

Sam was grateful for his business problem as it gave her a chance to listen absent-mindedly whilst getting a good look at him.

He was in his mid-thirties, she guessed. It was obvious, judging by the expensive and surprisingly well-fitting suit, that he'd had business experience outside Finland, Finnish managers preferring a more casual approach to the working day. It wasn't uncommon for her to meet a Finnish manager who was dressed in a shell suit and trainers. Looking at Mark, she noted that he had beautifully cut brown hair, which, later, by the time she got around to describing him to Alex, had turned into a deep chestnut colour. He had a warm, kind face, smiling blue eyes and astoundingly, yes, there was no doubt that he was rather nice-looking. Not exactly 'tall, dark and handsome', but definitely a cut above your average Finn. And judging by the scale of the problem he was describing, they'd be seeing quite a lot of each other.

Inwardly, Sam smiled so broadly that she could have taught a Cheshire cat a thing or two about teeth exposure. Things are looking up, Mother, she thought.

* * *

The day flew past. For the first time in all her years in Finland, she was having fun in a manager's office. It was absolute heaven not having to explain the four P's of Marketing. Price, Product, Place and Promotion. Normally this explanation could last an entire consulting day, more if each word necessitated a five-minute frantic search through a Finnish/English dictionary as was often the case.

The best and most wonderful part of the day was just before lunch when Mark said, "I think I can handle the Price, Place and Product parts, but I would definitely need your help on the Promotion side of it, in England especially. I suppose you could say I'm too Americanised to really get to grasp with the British."

"Get to grips with the British," she immediately corrected and realised that that was the first time that she'd had to do so. It was strange, she could sit down with someone who made fifteen mistakes per sentence and after a few minutes, she would no longer notice them. But when an excellent speaker of English or American, especially one with a good accent like Mark (American or otherwise) made one single slip-up, it seemed like a huge glaring error.

"Would you like another coffee before we go for lunch?"

"Why not? I think I've only had about twenty today – I'm probably caffeine-deprived as far as you Finnish are concerned."

Mark smiled, "Do I detect a little leg-pulling by my UK consultant? You should watch that – I may retaliate and start discussing the details of British cuisine. What do you have? Fish and chips? Definitely a cordon bleu dish if ever I saw one!"

"At least we don't eat salmon every day at every meal. I swear, after a two-week Finland trip, I'm so sick of it that I heave if I see anything vaguely pink-coloured."

They began shouting foods as insults, Mark started it all off with, "Roast beef!"

"Trout!" Sam threw back at him.

"Jellied eels!" Mark parried.

When she got to 'Frozen cranberries and hot caramel sauce,' Sam gave in. "Actually, I really like that one. OK, I give up. You win. British food is rubbish, but we have the best Indian restaurants in the world."

Mark laughed – how could he argue with such logic? "This whole talk has made me peckish – would you like some pastries with your coffee?"

"Only if they're Danish."

Together they chuckled until the coffee arrived.

* * *

"What are you thinking?" Mark looked over at Sam curiously. They'd been discussing marketing ideas and suddenly she had started gazing out of the window.

She motioned for him to be quiet, "I'm getting something!"

Mark waited patiently while she scribbled furiously on the pad in front of her.

Finally, she raised her head and said, "Right, I've got it."

"You've definitely got something," Mark smiled. "Don't ask me what it is."

"Shush," Sam dismissed.

"Oh shush, is it? And who's paying your wages?" he said cheekily.

"You are, which is precisely why you should shush and let me stun you with my brilliance."

"Go on then. Amaze me."

"We have a product, but the product is intensely boring –"

Mark immediately interrupted, "I wouldn't exactly call it –"

Sam glared at him, "Trust me, it's remarkably tedious. Do you want to hear this or shall we get another, less able consultant in here?"

"God forbid. Do go on – apologies."

"So, we have a ridiculously boring product, with no real value in marketing terms –" she immediately raised her hand to prevent further interruption, "– apart from the extreme utility. Basically, it works well. So what we have to do is run a campaign which totally ignores the product. We run with the company. The company name is good, Fintec Technologies – it conjures up so much imagery, the product doesn't matter. All we need to do is convince people that they want it and more to the point, we need to convince people that they want it from us."

Mark smiled at the use of 'us'. It showed that Sam was fully committed to the project and he liked the sound of it. "OK, I buy that, but how?"

"Well, that, Mr You-pay-my-wages, I don't know, but we have time to come up with something. I'll do some research when I get home and I'll be in touch."

"Great."

"And that about wraps up our day, Mark, my old chap."

"Are you this familiar with all your clients?"

"No, just the cute ones." Sam's hand flew to her mouth.

What the hell was she playing at? She was flirting! With one of her clients. She risked a glance at Mark. He was busy tidying up and had seemed not to notice. She stamped her foot silently and gave herself a good talking to. You will not flirt with or even attempt to chat up a client. You've never ever slept with a client. This in turn shocked her – was she thinking about sleeping with him already? What was wrong with her? Well, it's not going to happen, not on my watch, she promised herself.

Mark looked up at Sam, hearing her mumbling under her breath about watches. "Yes, it is time to go. It's been a good day. Thank you, Samantha."

"Sam, please."

"Sam. I look forward to our next meeting."

"Yeah, I'll ring you next week though, once I've done some research."

"Great."

"Goodbye, Mark."

"Goodbye, Sam."

Outside in a taxi, Sam thought about the day. It had been a good day, hadn't it?

Chapter Three

"Ladies and gentlemen, we are now making our descent into Manchester Airport. Please ensure that your seatbacks are in the upright position and that your tray-tables are safely stowed away. Please fasten your seatbelts. The local time is eleven o'clock, two hours behind Finnish time – please adjust your watches accordingly. The weather in Manchester is a little wet, surprisingly. The ground temperature is around ten degrees. On behalf of the Captain and her crew, we hope you have had a pleasant journey with Finland Air and look forward to welcoming you on board in the near future."

Sam looked up from her book and saw one of the female cabin crew rushing to the back of the plane to have a word with her colleague who was making the announcements.

"Sorry to bother you again, ladies and gentlemen, but I forgot to mention to the gentleman in seat 23C that the police are waiting at the gate to speak to you about the sexual harassment that you have inflicted upon our cabin crew this afternoon. You didn't think you'd get away with it, did you? Thank you, ladies and gentlemen, and have a nice day."

The slightly creepy guy who was sitting in the aisle seat opposite Sam looked up horrified and after going bright red seemed to sink lower in his seat, shielding his face. Sam smiled, as he'd been giving her slimy looks throughout the flight. She was also convinced that when he opened the locker halfway through the flight, he had tried to look down her, admittedly low-cut, blouse.

Sam's bosom can only be described as ample and therefore she is susceptible to the occasional glance or double take from the odd (sometimes, really odd) guy. Sam is, as her mother describes her, 'pretty but solid'. Her sister, Michelle, describes her as simply 'fat' and, as Michelle is blessed with the same no-nonsense bluntness gene as Sam, her description is probably the more accurate. Sam has no hang-ups about her weight at all; she is mostly content. Although sometimes, when the mood takes her, she does look over at her sit-up machine, which sits accusingly in the corner of her living-room, and thinks about working out. When it comes down to it, in the larger scheme of things, Sam has decided that life is too short to concern herself with diets, gym memberships that you never use and skipping dessert. Sod society. She'd rather be fat and content than skinny and constantly hungry.

Landing at Manchester Airport was always a pleasure for Sam, as it usually meant that in less than thirty minutes she could be tucked up in her bed, sleeping off the effects of Finland. Thirty minutes give or take the 'occasional' luggage deficiency which could take any amount of time to rectify.

Getting off the plane last, as was her custom, she overheard the cabin crew giggling about 23C's face as he got off to indeed find a transport policeman waiting at the gate. Apparently he fainted and had to be helped into the terminal by three of the ground crew.

"He didn't know that my new boyfriend was waiting for me, did he?" chuckled the one with slightly less make-up than the others, who apparently, Sam found out a bit later in the conversation, was called Shell.

Sam was somewhat miffed that she had missed the spectacle, but continued on her way. She was met at the door by a smart-looking middle-aged woman. Sam thought that she looked quite Finnish with her obligatory blonde hair pulled very very tight, in an attempt, Sam supposed, to mimic a home facelift. This had the obvious drawback that she almost looked Chinese. Sam chuckled to herself.

"Ms Jordan?" the woman enquired.

"Yes?" Sam enquired right back at her, thinking, why should she make this easy for her?

"I'm Anne Mansfield. I'm the Manchester Customer Service Representative for Finland Air." She made an attempt to smile, but what with the hair and everything, it ended up looking like she'd just stubbed her toe. "I'm here to tell you what we have planned for you."

She had pronounced her name Ann-e with emphasis on the 'e', confirming for Sam that she was indeed Finnish, and with her surname, possibly married to an Englishman.

"This I've got to hear," replied Sam.

"Let's go to my office." Anne offered briefly to take one of Sam's bags but, before Sam could take her up on the offer, started striding in the opposite direction to Baggage Claim.

"Don't worry about collecting your suitcase. It's still in Helsinki."

"Oh," Sam said and followed at a trot, irked at her flippant tone.

Following Anne to the office, Sam had the opportunity to examine the woman, from behind at least. She was quite tall, taller than Sam anyway. She had that slim athletic build that Sam had recognised to be a Finnish characteristic. She'd not actually seen a single overweight Finnish person, the whole time she'd been working there. It must be something to do with all that striding through snow, Sam mused.

Not long into her trips to Finland, Sam had come up with a theory as to why the Finnish were so brisk with their walking and also with their speech. It was all due to the inhospitable weather conditions. In the southern countries, people tend to wander rather than walk and a basic conversation could take anything upwards of an hour. This is because the weather is warm and welcoming. In Finland, if you stand still for longer than five minutes you are more likely to resemble an ice sculpture. Therefore the people had learned to limit their speech to basic greetings and not much else and to walk as fast as they could just to ensure that their blood didn't freeze in their veins. More often than not, Sam felt that in this day and age, with all the modern clothing and heating, they could afford to be slightly more forthcoming – but they obviously liked their way and who was she to complain?

Sam was beginning to flag, so she was inordinately pleased to see Anne stop in front of what presumably was her office door.

Anne turned to the gasping figure behind her and held the door open. She looked disapprovingly at Sam in that you-should-get-yourself-off-to-a-gym-immediately-fatso way that skinny people always use when confronted by someone of Sam's proportions.

Once inside, Sam sat down and looked around. It was a large office, tastefully furnished with Scandinavian-looking furniture, all wood and glass with curvy edges. The table was in the same style as the gift that her last group had given her, as an end-of-course 'thank you' present. Usually the participants gave her something small, like a bookmark or something, but on this occasion they'd presented her with a stool, which had been designed by a Finnish designer, whose name Sam could never remember.

"It's Alvar Aalto," Anne explained while hunting around for Sam's file. "He's a famous Finnish designer."

Sam didn't know how to respond, so she made an interested sound and continued to examine the room. The walls were filled with customer-service awards and some official-looking certificates. There were piles of paper and files on the desk, but curiously no family photos. There were cardboard boxes on the floor and she wondered if Anne had recently moved into the office.

"I've just moved office," Anne stated.

Sam stared at Anne incredulously. What was she, a mind reader? Just to make sure that she wasn't, Sam looked out the window and concentrated on the thought that Anne seemed to be as much fun as a wet weekend in Blackpool. Although that seemed to be a little unfair to Blackpool – after all, it did have 'The Big One'.

" . . . the big one?"

Sam's eyes flew to meet Anne's. Surely not? She couldn't be!

Anne was looking at her questioningly. She had

obviously been talking to her. "Sorry?" Sam managed to croak.

"Could you pass me the file over there by your right arm? The big one."

"Oh, yes, of course." Sam breathed a sigh of relief. She lifted up a huge file, bulging with papers, which was at least three inches thick, and passed it over to Anne. "There you go."

Opening the file Anne asked, "So your troubles started in April last year?" She looked at Sam for confirmation.

"Yes, I started working in Finland in February of last year and for the first few months everything was fine. Then, in April, my luggage went missing three times, once on the outward to Helsinki and twice on the return to Manchester." She looked over at Anne, who nodded for her to continue. "Well, ever since then it has been happening on a fairly regular basis, although strangely it stopped between July and December."

"I see. Well, I have all the notes here of the exact instances and their reasons, but I agree, it is most unusual. I see that your suitcase always seems to turn up in the end. That's something, I suppose." She attempted to smile sympathetically at Sam and continued. "I understand that you have had this investigated in the past?"

"Yes, but all they could come up with was a computer fault. That was just before July. So I thought it had all been sorted out when it stopped and then it started again in earnest in January. In fact, it's happened six times since New Year. I know that if it happens on the way out to Finland, chances are that it will happen on the return. As you can imagine, I've just about had enough with the whole thing. I even considered giving up my job, just to be free of all the hassle."

"I don't think there's any need for such drastic action, do you?" Anne looked at Sam and left her in no doubt that she thought she was being overly dramatic.

Sam desperately wanted to shout, 'I'd like to see you deal with it week after week, you supercilious old cow,' but thought that that might not aid their working relationship, so instead she murmured, "Suppose not."

"Well, you may be glad to hear that I have been looking for a pattern in the occurrences and I have come to the conclusion that your problem is in London Heathrow."

"How did you work that out?"

"Well, it was fairly simple, really." Looking quite smug, Anne looked directly at Sam. "It always seems to happen when you connect to your international sector at Heathrow. For some reason, your luggage gets mixed up there and misses the international flight and the same thing on your return."

"So all I have to do is?"

"Avoid Heathrow and you'll get your luggage, yes." Anne smiled triumphantly. "I understand that you already have your bookings for your next trip, so if you would like to give me the details, I'll make sure that they get through Heathrow for you and then you can book another route for the next ones. Looking at the schedules, your best bet would be through Brussels or Amsterdam, but we'll sort that out later." She smiled again politely and continued, "I'll be in touch before your next flight."

Sam gave her the details and was elated. Did this mean that she'd be able to travel without that nagging anxiety?

She could hardly believe that her luggage problem was so easily solved. Why hadn't she insisted on this investigation before? She could have saved a year of annoyance and ill-fated optimism. She felt a weight lift from her shoulders. Upon leaving Anne's office, she was suddenly full of energy and thought to herself that she deserved a treat.

On her way to the taxi rank, she got out her mobile.

"Hairs & Graces, Louise speaking."

"Louise, hi, it's Sam – listen. I've just got back from Finland. Could you fit me in today? I feel like going for a new style."

"Now, Sam, you know I don't like to cut your hair when you've just got back from there. The luggage thing always makes you do strange things. Remember last time?" Louise warned.

Sam remembered the 'cut it all off and dye it purple' incident. "I know, I know, but this time I'm in such a good mood. Just don't let me cut too much off, and I think I might go fiery mahogany as well."

"Well, OK," Louise offered uncertainly, "but I'll make you sign something before I do it this time."

Chapter Four

Sam woke up in a glorious mood. The weight on her shoulders had lifted and for the moment she couldn't quite remember why. She smiled to herself. It was Sunday. She loved Sundays more than any other day of the week. The sun was shining, which in Manchester is quite a rare occurrence. There's nothing better than being woken up by the sun shining through your windows. She got up to go to have a shower, still having that niggling feeling that she'd forgotten something. As she walked past the full-length mirror on her landing, her Subconscious started to nudge her Conscious Mind.

"Hey, Consciousness," it said, "there's something you didn't spot."

"What?" said Sam's Conscious Mind. "Can't you see I have lots to do today? I still have loads of things to remind her – I have a list as long as her arm and I'm running late with some of them."

"Well, if you're going to be like that, I won't say."

"Oh for goodness sakes, stop messing about! I'm too busy for that," said her Conscious Mind testily.

"Nope, won't tell," said her Subconscious in a sulk,

"All right then, I'm sorry. Dear Subconscious, tell me what I missed."

"Make her go back to the mirror and you'll see."

Sam turned – she'd forgotten her bathrobe, which was hanging on the back of her bedroom door. As she passed the mirror again she stopped.

"Oh, my God!" she exclaimed in terror. "Fiery mahogany!"

Her hair was in fact a very bright scarlet colour, with some copper highlights. Suddenly it all came flooding back: the meeting with Anne, the phone call to Louise, the euphoric decision to go this colour and the subsequent celebration meal complete with too many bottles of red wine. Finally, her Conscious Mind reached number five on its list (which was hangover) and her head began to pound.

"Oh well, at least I woke up alone."

A noise filtered into her brain: the sound of music. There was someone downstairs. She sniffed. They'd made coffee. Her Conscious Mind ticked off numbers six and seven and felt glad that it had finally caught up.

She resigned herself to another one of those 'morning after' situations: the embarrassed meeting of two people who were too drunk the night before to remember what each other looked like. Well, she thought, I'm not facing whoever it is looking like this. So, this decided, she stepped under the shower. Then she heard George Michael music floating up through the floorboards and the rushing water. Her Conscious Mind ticked off number eight and she relaxed, knowing that it wasn't a stray man who was prowling around her lounge.

She dressed in her usual Sunday attire of sweatshirt and jogging bottoms and finally she felt ready to face the world, at least she would if only her head would stop pounding. She walked gingerly back to the bathroom, found the paracetamol, swallowed two with difficulty and carried the bottle downstairs. She knew that if she'd evaluated all the sounds correctly, Alex would be downstairs, probably scrunching her tall frame into the small armchair in an attempt to get into the foetal position. Her long blonde hair would probably be in a ponytail, uncombed of course – it was Sunday after all. As always, Sam was struck by the thought that Alex could easily be mistaken for a model. On this occasion, a model who'd had a particularly stressful night behind her.

"Hi, Alex, playing George Michael? It must be Sunday morning and you must have a hangover." Sam smiled and gave her a big hug. Noting her watery violet eyes with dark bags under them, Sam passed her the paracetamol. "Excuse me for asking, but what are you doing here?"

"Don't you remember ringing me yesterday? 'Lexi, Lexi, please come up, I have wonderful news!' You promised me three bottles of wine if I did it in under three hours." Alex laughed, winced and then sat down unsteadily on the sofa. "Two hours, thirty-five minutes, a personal best, but I doubt my car's going anywhere for a while."

Sam glanced out of her front window to see Alex's battered old Ford Fiesta sitting in her drive, visibly sagging with fatigue.

"By the way, that's very, very bright hair. I actually think that particular shade of scarlet is more intense in the daylight." Alex got up and disappeared off into the kitchen.

"It's fiery mahogany!" Sam shouted at her disappearing back.

What had in fact taken place was a feat of unsurpassed friendship. Alex, after taking that manic call, found herself worrying about Sam, in the way only a good friend would. She thought that a euphoric Sam would only get into trouble if she wasn't there to guide her. She was in such a frenzy that she forced her car up to ninety on the M6. She'd been through all this before. Sam had the wacky ideas and Alex usually sorted out the mess. In return, Sam would sort out Alex's personal relationships, which were usually messier than anything Sam could conjure up. Alex wasn't quite sure who got the better deal in this exchange, but one thing she did know was that when it came down to the final analysis, Sam was probably ahead of her for 'Friend of the Year'. Although the Phillipe mess probably earned Alex bonus points.

Alex returned, juggling with two mugs, a milk-jug and the coffee-pot. "I've made coffee. I want to hear all about what's been going on. Properly this time and without the giggles and the 'chat-up' breaks. By the way, I have three phone numbers here for you: a Brian, a James and a Dominic. You gave them to me to look after – I think your exact words were 'Hey Lexi, keep hold of these. I can hardly see straight!' not that I was any better of course . . ." Alex trailed off, massaging her temples.

"I remember James and I think I remember Brian, but Dominic?" Sam looked puzzled, held her cooling palm to her forehead and continued, "Oh yes, I remember now, I was sitting in the hairdresser's . . . "

The following story turned out to be a long one with many sidetracks. Including a discussion why Evans' clothes were so expensive (more material) and a really long detour on the fact that in Sam's opinion most men really did prefer a woman with meat on her bones, as her tally of suitors proved the night before. Essentially the story was this: while waiting in the hairdresser's, Sam had received a phone call from Anne, who informed her that she had organised for her new assistant to accompany Sam and her luggage through her next journey via Heathrow. She had given Sam his number and asked her to call on Monday to discuss the arrangements. Anne had also explained that Sam would need to change her suitcase and, out of their own goodwill, Finland Air would provide her with a suitable one. Apparently the fluorescent green and bright purple of her current suitcase was throwing off the computers at Heathrow and therefore they were finding it difficult to read the computerised tag. She would be able to pick up her new suitcase upon her return to Manchester, next time. It was at this point that Sam had made the final decision to go fiery mahogany and had telephoned Alex.

"That explains Dominic then," Alex noted, looking at the slip of paper containing the phone number on one side and 'Mrs Frisk 3pm, for wash and blow-dry' on the other.

They sat in companionable silence for a little while, each nursing their respective headaches and drinking coffe, until finally Sam got up to take her weekly constitutional.

This consisted mainly of walking the three hundred metres to the newspaper shop, buying The Sunday Times *and the* Sunday Mirror *and strolling back to her house. This was usually followed by retiring to her bedroom to read them thoroughly.*

If anything was proof that Sam had a romantic side, then it was her bedroom. It was her favourite room in the house. Painted lilac, with deep purple around the edges, it was plain and simple. It wasn't a large room and was, therefore, completely dominated by her four-poster bed, covered in lilac muslin. It was custom-made for her in France and was, theoretically, wide enough for at least four people to lie in comfortably, not that Sam had ever attempted to prove this particular theory. Basically, her bedroom reminded all those who entered of a scene from the Arabian Nights minus the flying carpets, lamps and mysterious Persian women in veils.

By the time Sam returned, straining under the weight of the Sunday papers, Alex had already prepared 'The Breakfast Tray', with coffee, orange juice and croissants. They both went upstairs in the manner of boarding-school girls having a midnight feast.

As usual, Alex was poring over the property section, imagining herself living in one of the multi-million-pound homes, when she said, "Jemima and Rupert."

Sam was a bit taken aback, "Jemima and Rupert? What on earth . . ." She trailed off remembering Alex's bad habit of trying out children's names, as she was determined that when she eventually had children, the names would be perfect.

"But Rupert will be the oldest, so actually, it would be Rupert and Jemima." She looked over at Sam for approval.

"You're not serious." Sam looked astonished. "You can't call them after children's television characters, I mean, Rupert the Bear and, what was the programme with the dolls and the windows?"

"*Playschool.*"

"That's it, *Playschool.* Jemima was that ugly doll."

"That was Hamble – Jemima was the ragdoll."

"Either way you look at it, Lexi, it's stupid." Sam looked at Alex and shook her head sadly.

Sam knew what was coming. She also knew that eventually it would involve her making a late-night dash down the motorway to London, many many boxes of tissues, copious amounts of mashed potatoes and a *Sleepless in Seattle* video.

Alex had been going out with Duncan for six months. As an interested third party, Sam had noticed that there was a pattern in all of Alex's relationships. Phase One: attempt to spend every moment of every day with him, ignoring all phone calls from friends and family. Phase Two: introduce him to friends, but only after telling them how 'unsexy' and 'uninteresting' he is in order to reduce expectation levels. Phase Three: the interesting phase, where the low self-esteem kicked in. Begin to question why he is with 'someone like her' and become convinced he will leave. Phase Four: turn into a passive puppet, fulfilling his every whim in order to keep him. Phase Five: decide that, as he's still around, he must want to get married. Phase Six: begin plans for happily married life, investigate children's names and potential marital homes. By this stage, the man, who has been pottering along quite nicely, begins to wonder who this person is and that surely it's not the same woman he first met. Eventually deciding to make a run for it, he disappears, customarily leaving a blunt razor in the bathroom and the odd sock under the bed. Which is where Sam usually comes in with her special 'get Lexi back out into the world again' routine. Her job, essentially, is to agree with everything Alex says, feed her mashed potato and pass her tissues, whilst persuading her that any man would be glad to have her.

When Sam first met Alex, this process would be spread over a twelve-month period, but since Alex's twenty-seventh birthday, the phases had been condensed into six months. Alex had read somewhere, probably in Cosmopolitan, that if you hadn't met

51

your potential mate by age twenty-eight, you were unlikely to get married at all. This threw her into turmoil, as, up until this point, she had been quite happy to be 'Ms Career Woman'. Lately, aged thirty, she has turned into 'Miss Frantically Searching'. Sam also had her doubts about Duncan. He was a trader in the city and, as far as she could see, was completely wrong for Alex. It's not that he was a bad person, quite the opposite. Sam really liked him. He was twenty-four and, after moving down from Newcastle, was experiencing his freedom and large amounts of money for the first time. Sam tried very hard to see him settling down and living the Country Life lifestyle, and from what she'd gathered from their brief discussions, the only question on his mind was whether to go for the Porsche or the Mercedes. Plus, she hated the fact that Alex always turned into a complete whimpering simpleton every time he went near her. Sam knew Alex well enough to know that this particular love affair was doomed to failure. Good friends as they were, Sam didn't see any point in even attempting to suggest this to Alex. She knew that all she could do was wait for it all to implode. Another thing Sam could never understand was why Alex was so passive with these men, when she could be as stern as a headmistress with her. What Alex needed was a responsible, intelligent, attractive man who would take care of her. Unfortunately, all women were searching for the same thing and there just didn't seem to be enough of that thing to go around.

"Lexi, you know I love you more than my Samsonite, don't you?" Sam ventured. Alex looked up and smiled. "Well, I'll only say this once and then I'll not mention it again. OK?"

"OK." Alex wondered where this was going, but was busy pondering over the merits of Annabel as a suitable name.

"Well, can we *not* plan the wedding, just yet? I think it

might be better to wait until he actually asks you. Remember what we said before, one day at a time and all that?" She glanced at Alex, who was clearly not listening. "Lexi, love."

"What?" Alex said rather crossly, having discarded Jason as a prospect.

"Repeat after me. 'One day at a time. I will not force the issue. I will let things take their course' – go on, say it for me," Sam urged.

Alex stared at her blankly and Sam gave up.

* * *

"Sam?" Alex called up the stairs.

"What?"

"Exactly why is it that you have a freezer filled to bursting with ice lollies and frozen cherry pies, and your fridge is conspicuously absent of anything other than raspberry pavlovas and orange juice?"

"It's a long story," Sam offered as explanation, suddenly appearing in the kitchen.

"Go on then."

"Well, you know the shop, *Iceland?*" Alex nodded and Sam continued, "Well, they've just started a new Internet shopping service."

"Yeah, so?"

"I was in the lounge in Helsinki and I saw that they had a computer linked up to the Internet. I was a bit bored so I thought I'd have a look, and for a bit of a lark, I decided to get some shopping in. It really is amazing what you can do these days. It was waiting for me when I arrived."

"That still doesn't explain the fridge."

"Yeah well, when you're going through the dessert section it's easy to get carried away. You know how much I like cherry pies and they had a 'buy one get one free' offer on Magnums – you can never have too many Magnums."

"I'll accept that, but what's with the pavlovas?"

"Oh that, I typed in ten instead of one and OK'd it before I noticed the mistake and I couldn't change it because they were 'Last Call-ing' my flight." Alex looked pointedly at the eight cartons of fruit juice, "Don't ask me, Alex. I have no idea what happened there."

"Do you actually have anything in your house that contains less than a week's worth of calories? Or something that could possibly, after a short time cooking in the oven, resemble a Sunday lunch?"

"Erm . . ." Sam preceeded to hunt around in the freezer and found a stray frozen Yorkshire pudding. Turning to Alex, she held it aloft victoriously.

* * *

Sitting in the pub waiting for their food to arrive, Sam decided to find out more about the state of play in Alex's relationship with Duncan.

"So how's Duncan? Did he mind you disappearing for the weekend?"

"No, not really, he's been a bit . . ." Alex tried to find the word, "distant."

"Distant? How distant?"

"Maybe not distant. More distracted."

"Distracted?"

"Or maybe he's aloof. I was never good at the describing thing."

"You detect a slight cooling of his ardour, perhaps?" Sam said trying to help.

"No, there's nothing wrong with his ardour. That is pretty much performing satisfactorily. He's still showing his ardour at least three times a night if you get what I mean!" She leered and giggled. "When he's around, that is."

"Three times? It's been a long time since I saw that much ardour."

"OK, Sam, I give in. That's the third time in fifteen minutes that you've, ever so subtly, mentioned your current shortage of bonks. Spill."

"I'm sure I have absolutely no idea what you are talking about," Sam dismissed.

"Spill now or lose your life." Alex held her extremely blunt knife up to Sam's throat. "It'll hurt. I promise."

"It's nothing."

"So humour me," Alex cajoled. "Last night you turned down two perfectly decent and presentable shags. There's obviously something, or should I say someone, in the pipeline. And don't be thinking of lying to me. You know I know what you're like when you lie."

"Sorry to disappoint you, Lexi, but there's nothing. Honest."

Alex, unwilling to let things lie, simply raised her eyebrows.

"There was this one guy . . . "

"A-ha, now we're talking!" She rubbed her hands with glee and settled down for a long discussion.

"Say, hypothetically speaking, I was to meet an OK-enough-looking guy and he, just for the sake of the discussion, turned out to be Finnish. Do you think I should go for it? If there was anything to go for, of course."

"Finnish?" Alex tutted with disappointment and tossed her blonde hair over her shoulder. "Scratch that idea then."

Unlike Sam's mother, Alex had actually visited Helsinki and was well aware of the remarkable lack of talent that Finland represents. When Sam first started working in Finland, Alex, thinking that it would be the perfect answer to her husband-finding plan, had invited herself over on one of Sam's longer two-week trips. Needless to say she was extremely disappointed with the available talent, or lack of it.

"It's easier for a rich man to enter a camel's behind on a needle than it is to find some 'Hot 'n' Sexy Beef Action' in this Nordic country. You're welcome to it," she was heard to mutter as she went through customs on her way home.

"Actually, he's not that bad."

Alex, who was by this time totally uninterested, muttered, "You don't say."

"Yes. He has the sexiest voice you could imagine and he's got a great personality."

"Sam, stop. You're embarrassing yourself. You've as much as admitted that he's a hideous swamp creature."

"No, I did not!"

"You did. You just said that he's got a great personality. You might as well have just held up a sign that said 'UGLY MAN AHEAD'."

"He's not ugly. He has these really cute dimples and these little lines around his eyes."

"Yeah, they're called wrinkles."

"No, laughter lines, like he's always smiling or something."

"I thought you said that Finns don't do that."

"Do what?"

"The smiling thing."

"Well, they don't normally, but he seems different. They may not be the bluest eyes I've ever seen, but they really seem to sparkle when he talks."

"All right, I'll admit, when you describe him like that he sounds interesting." Somehow her voice managed to convey the absolute opposite of her words.

Ignoring the undertones in Alex's voice, Sam continued, "See. Oh, and he's got the loveliest hands. Really big and strong. He's probably got muscly arms as well – it wasn't easy to tell under the suit, but I tell you what –"

"What?"

"The whole time he was talking, I was wishing he'd take me in his arms, throw me over the desk and . . ." Sam realised that she'd gone too far when she noticed Alex rolling her eyes and pretending to stick her fingers down her throat.

"How long's it been, then?"

"How long's what been?" Sam said innocently.

"I bet it's been about six months since you last had sex."

"Five months, twenty-three days and about six hours, not that I'm counting, why?"

"You are so predictable."

"No, I'm not," Sam protested.

"OK, if you're not predictable, how did I know that it's been six months?"

"Lucky guess, that's all."

"You're probably not sleeping at all, are you?"

"I'm sleeping fine, thank you very much," Sam lied unconvincingly.

"I bet you he's totally untouchable. Probably on one of your courses."

"A-ha no! He's one of my consulting jobs."

"See what I mean. Untouchable! You're going to obsess and obsess until you get laid." Alex pronounced so loudly that the two elderly women drinking sherries opposite started to choke on their drinks. "And you have the added bonus of knowing it's doomed from the start and there's no chance of a real relationship. You know, you're never going to find a real relationship unless you allow yourself to. I was reading in 'Men Who Love Women Who Would Love Men To Commit To Commitment' –"

Sam groaned inwardly. This was going to be another one of Alex's self-help-book pick-me-up speeches. Alex possessed more self-help books than any other woman on the planet. As long as it had the words 'men' and 'women' in the title and was written by some American guru who promised that it would help you find your ideal mate, Alex bought it and read it. She'd follow it until she realised that it didn't actually lead to her ideal man, then she'd 'discover' another one.

" . . . love is a gift that you give yourself."

"You mean, vibrators are a gift that you give yourself."

"Sam!"

"What does that mean anyway? Love is a gift you give yourself? Utter tosh."

"It means, Miss Unbeliever, that you have to allow yourself to be loved. You have to believe that you are worthy of being loved. That's what it means."

"And you think I don't?"

"To be honest, no, I don't. I detect definite phases in your 'so-called relationships' since You-know-who."

This entire conversation was starting to rankle with

Sam. It was strange how Alex had all the insights into Sam's life, but not once had she managed to turn all this insight onto her own. "Could we change the subject, please?"

"If we must, but I didn't realise things were that desperate though."

"What d'you mean by that?"

"You know, scraping the Finnish barrel."

"Shut up, Alex."

"Ooh, listen to 'Little Miss Shirty' getting all uptight," Alex mocked. "You're just pissed off cos I'm right."

They sat in silence for a few minutes, lingering over their drinks. Finally, in her own version of an apology, Alex got up, pointed at Sam's glass and said, "Same again?"

"Yeah, thanks."

Luckily, by the time Alex returned, their meals had arrived and Sam could begin a neutral topic of conversation.

"What's your lasagne like?"

"Oh, your average pasta goopy sludge." She lifted her fork for Sam to get a good look. "What about your scampi?"

"Not bad, quite crispy, but there are never enough." Sam settled into easy banter once more.

The food was part of a ritual that they'd begun upon their return to England from Germany. While in Germany, they had missed the typical English 'Pub Grub' and vowed when they got back the first thing they would have was a pub lunch. From that point on, this was their favoured Sunday lunch activity. Alex always ordered the lasagne and complained about the stodginess. Sam more often than not ordered the scampi (with chips and peas) and complained of the lack of value for money.

"Look," Sam pointed at her plate, "six pieces of scampi and it's like, six fifty. That's about a pound a piece."

They continued to eat, engulfed in an amiable silence. "Whose turn is it?"

"That would be you." Alex began her explanation. "I sprung for dinner at *Mezzo*, the last time you graced the Big Smoke with your presence."

"Ah yes, but I cooked Mexican for you the last time you came up."

"Your freezer is full of Magnums. Need I say more?"

Sam's face showed a lack of concern that Alex found extremely brave under the circumstances. She obviously needed reminding.

"I could always mention the lack of nutritional food the next time I chat to your mother. You'll be inundated with care packages containing nothing but healthy food for weeks and weeks, not to mention her making a mercy dash to Manchester to care for her little –"

"OK, OK, I get the picture. When you blackmail so beautifully, how can I possibly say no?" Sam laughed. "Don't order dessert though."

"Why not?"

"You promised to eat one of the pavlovas when we got back. Remember?"

"So I did," Alex smiled.

They sat again in an easy silence each imagining eating an entire raspberry pavlova, until Alex shook her head and said sadly, "A Finnish bloke, I don't know . . . "

Chapter Five

"Dominic should be here in a moment. I just have a few questions to ask about your luggage." Anne started looking around her desk, presumably trying to find Sam's file.

Sam looked over at her trusty Samsonite suitcase, remembering the rush she had had that morning to get herself packed. "One of these days," she mumbled, "I'll actually manage to pack the night before."

"Here we go." Anne looked up at Sam and, mistaking the distressed look on her face for apprehension, she soothed her. "Just a few short ones, I promise it won't be too painful."

"It's OK, really," reassured Sam.

"Firstly, we need to know if you would prefer a combination case or a case with padlocks," Anne continued. "I personally would go for the padlocks, much safer in my opinion."

"Fine, padlocks it is then."

Anne ticked a box. "Would you prefer a soft case or a

hard one? Many people swear by the hard-shell cases. The soft one is lighter, but the hard one protects the contents much better."

Sam began to drift off into thought. She looked over at Anne – her hair looked as if it had been pulled even tighter, but Sam wasn't sure that it was possible. She stared at her, and tried to decide if she was wearing that much make-up the last time they met. The airlines must give these women make-up lessons – it takes skill to apply that much sludge, Sam thought sarcastically. She was brought out of her reverie by a delicate cough and realised that Anne was waiting for her to say something. She really had to stop doing that. There must be something about this office that made her drift off into the world of daydream.

"Erm, yes," she took a wild guess.

"Yes, hard or yes, soft?"

"Yes, hard?" Sam was left desperately trying to work out what the question was.

"Lastly, we need to know if you have made a decision regarding your future connecting airport – the choice is basically between Amsterdam and Brussels." She paused briefly and added, "Although, realistically, Amsterdam offers a shorter waiting time."

"I think Amsterdam would be best, but my company normally makes the arrangements."

"Actually I wanted to have a word about that, as that might be another reason why you're having problems. Often tickets purchased abroad for travel from this country can cause them. I can get in touch with your company and assist them . . ."

Actually this was about as much as Sam heard, because

at that moment a vision walked into the room. Sam entered 'Romantic Novel Dreamland' and everything started moving in slow motion. He was tall, in a definitely-over-six-foot-tall kind of way. His hair could have been called blond but that would have been far too ordinary a colour, Sam mused – it was more like gold. He had the most stunning green eyes that she had ever seen. He stood in the doorway, looking like an Adonis. A stray sunbeam glinted off his hair, making it flare briefly as if it were a golden firework. He was wearing the navy blue uniform of Finland Air, with a blue and white striped shirt, his muscles rippling underneath. He moved with the stealth and grace of a lion, and radiated an aura of pure strength. Sam also noticed that his shoes were highly polished and gleaming like jewels. Every single part of him seemed to be perfect in every way.

Anne followed Sam's eyes towards the door. "Ah Dominic, this is Ms Jordan. You will be accompanying her to Finland today."

That was Dominic! Sam gasped inwardly.

She wasn't quite sure what happened next, but one minute he was walking manfully towards her and the next he was sprawled at her feet.

"Er . . . sorry . . . I didn't see your suitcase there," he stuttered as he was pulling himself upright with the help of the desk.

Sam glanced at her fluorescent green and purple case. "Yes, it's a bit hard to miss," she simpered.

Anne snorted. "For goodness sakes, Dominic, could you just get yourself together and take Ms Jordan's case to the check-in. She will be with you shortly." She watched him leave with Sam's case, stumbling as he left the office. "I'm sorry about that – he seems a bit hopeless, but he's quite capable, at least that's what the London office tell me. Why they sent him up here, I'll never know. Well, Ms Jordan, have a good trip and fingers crossed, eh?"

Sam mumbled something in response, but couldn't really focus. It was like being struck by lightning, she mused. As she left the office, she had already begun to pull herself together. To tell the truth, she was annoyed at herself for turning into a wimp as soon as she was confronted with a good-looking guy. A great-looking guy, she corrected. "You are a strong confident woman," she told herself. "You do not turn to jelly in front of men – that's Alex's speciality."

By the time she got to the check-in, she was back to her old self, determined that she would treat this man with the contempt he deserved. Apparently they would be sitting next to each other on the flight. She really ought to put her professional head on – she might be able to swing a few free flights for pain and suffering. If she handled him properly of course.

"Ms Jordan," Dominic started.

Sam looked up at him and melted once more, "Look, we're going to be with each other for the next eight or so hours – you might as well call me Sam." She smiled and privately kicked herself for not sticking to contempt.

"Sam, I've checked in your suitcase, but . . . um . . . I would need to take a quick look at your . . . um . . . passport."

She handed over her passport and was convinced that he smirked briefly when he found the picture page. Sam remembered that the photo was taken in her 'cut it off and dye it purple' phase, due to a situation involving an expired passport and an emergency application – and is unfortunately something she will be stuck with until well into the next millennium.

"Damn," she thought, but said nothing, bristling at his attitude. No one has a good passport photo, she reasoned. The machines are deliberately set up to take unflattering photographs, just to give the customs people something to laugh at. She snatched her passport back and began striding towards the lounge.

"Ms Jord . . . I mean, Sam . . . ?" Dominic called after her. Sam ignored him and continued walking. He caught her up with one manly stride and tapped her on the shoulder. "You seem to have forgotten your computer bag."

Sam stopped abruptly, grabbed her bag from him and stomped off, cursing under her breath. By the time she reached the lounge, she was hotly embarrassed and more than a little flushed. She poured herself a double vodka, took a long sip, which was more of a gulp really, and sat down heavily on the nearest sofa. She ran a flustered hand through her scarlet hair, leant back in the seat and closed her eyes.

She first became aware that someone was standing next to her when she caught a whiff of *Obsession for Men*. It was her favourite men's cologne and she inhaled deeply. She opened her eyes to see Dominic standing in front of her.

"It figures," she mumbled.

"Sorry?"

Sam shook her head and he continued, "I just wanted to explain what I'm going to do on the journey."

"This should be good. Go ahead."

"Well, basically, now you're all checked in, I'll take your baggage tag and go down to the luggage department. All I'm going to do there is follow your bag through, making sure that it gets on the plane and taking notes if anything goes amiss."

"That sounds fairly simple. Will you be sitting near me?" Sam told herself that she was only asking out of curiosity, but really she just wanted the opportunity to get to know him. She'd never in her life been that close to such a sexy guy.

"I'll be sitting next to you."

Sam let out a brief involuntary squeal, but managed to change it into a strange-sounding cough.

"Are you OK?"

"Yeah, I'm fine. Just a little frog in my er –"

"Yes, well. As you're making a short trip this time, I'll be attending to some things in our Helsinki office and I'll be able to meet you for your return journey."

"So, if anything goes wrong, I know you're to blame," Sam joked.

Dominic was having none of it – he seemed to be content to be po-faced and strictly professional. "That's right, although I can assure you that nothing will go wrong."

"You're confident! I still think something will go wrong. Maybe, this time, I'll go missing for a few days," she sniggered.

"Don't worry, I'll make sure you arrive in . . ." he looked down at his notes, "Turku, with your bag."

"Thanks. Although I don't think you know what you're letting yourself in for."

"Fear not. I can pretty much manage most things." He grinned. "Well, I'd better check things out now – I'll see you on the plane."

As he left the lounge, she saw the younger of the two women on the reception desk look at him and giggle. After he had left, she turned to the older one and began to tell an animated story. This caused much mirth and at one stage the older woman laughed so much she started to choke, forcing the younger one to slap her on the back rather roughly. This entire scene intrigued Sam. There was obviously a story behind Dominic, one which Sam was determined to investigate between Manchester and London.

Dominic was the last to board the plane, prompting Sam to assume that there had been problems with her bag. He sat down next to her and reading the expression on her face said, "It's OK. We found it."

Seeing as Sam didn't know it had been lost in the first place, she was prompted to ask, "Sorry?"

"Well, it went missing for about half an hour, but one of the lads found it and brought it to the plane, just as the doors were closing. It seems that it had fallen off the conveyor belt."

Sam didn't know quite what to say at this point so let out a simple "Hmmmmm".

After take-off, she turned to Dominic and gave him her most radiant smile, determined to find out what all the laughter in the lounge had been about.

"So Dominic," she ventured, "what's a good-looking . . . er . . . I mean an intelligent and not at all sexy in any gorgeous way whatsoever guy like you doing working in Manchester?" She was babbling like an idiot. Get a grip, she told herself silently.

"Sorry?"

"What brings you to Manchester?"

"Head Office felt that they needed someone of my background working in the regions."

"Have you been working for the airline . . . er . . . long?" her voice trailed off as she realised that she was beginning to sound like a sad, desperate person in a singles bar.

Luckily, Dominic seemed not to notice, "A while."

She wasn't sure where to go from there, so she simply uttered, "Do you like it?"

"Yes, it's good. I meet lots of people. Some jobs are better than others though."

"Oh," said Sam – well, that told her, didn't it?

"Oh, I didn't mean that this is necessarily a bad job. I mean, I didn't mean to say that –"

"It's OK, really." Sam helped him out. "So do you like Manchester then?"

"Not bad."

He was still not very forthcoming and Sam realised that he was going to be a tough nut to crack. She needed time to think up a strategy. "I think I'll nip to the loo."

There was a fairly long queue and, while waiting, she overheard the cabin crew in the galley chatting about one of the passengers.

"Is that definitely him then?" asked a Geordie voice.

"I'm certain of it," said a Cockney voice.

"So what exactly did he do?"

"Remember two months ago, when we were doing the Helsinki route – you know, when they had that 'fire' in Head Office and all the computers went down for the entire day?"

"Oh yes, that was the day when we missed all our Air Traffic Control slots."

"Yeah well, he caused it."

"How?"

"A cup of coffee!"

"What!" Geordie Woman gave a shout of laughter.

"No lie. He tripped over a cable and threw a cup of coffee over the mainframe in the computer room and shorted the entire system out." Cockney Voice began to cackle like a witch.

"I don't believe you," Geordie Voice said, in between giggles.

"Honest, my mate in IT spent the whole day with three of his mates, trying to get the system back up. They told everyone that there had been a fire."

"Why didn't they get rid of him? I mean, if I did that I'd be out on my ear before I could say sorry."

"Apparently he knows someone at the top, so they sent him to Manchester instead. He's a bit accident-prone, so who knows what he could get up to here!"

Sam chuckled and returned to her seat, arriving just as the breakfast was being served. Then the cabin crew came round with coffee. As they reached his seat Dominic held up his cup and said, "Coffee, please."

The stewardess recognised him and Sam looked down to see her laptop computer sitting, in its case, between the seats directly below Dominic's cup. "No!" Sam and the stewardess screamed simultaneously.

"Sorry?" said Dominic, confused, as he looked between Sam and the stewardess.

"I'm sorry, sir, but I seem to have run out of coffee."

"I'm allergic to coffee. I can't stand the smell." Both explanations came at once, leaving Dominic even more confused.

"He'll have orange juice," Sam decided for him, while moving her laptop.

The rest of the flight passed uneventfully. After much probing and prodding, Dominic finally started to warm up. They chatted about their backgrounds, life in general and the overwhelming evidence pointing towards global warming, but mainly they talked about popular culture. The discussion became almost animated with Sam and Dominic discovering that they had a passion for American sitcoms in common.

"Your favourite *Friends* episode then?" Dominic asked animatedly.

"Hmm . . . Chandler in –" Sam began

"A box!" Dominic finished. "Mine too."

"Favourite *Seinfeld*, then?"

"The Pez dispenser," he offered.

"Nah, 'The Muffin Tops' was much better."

"Ooh, ooh," he said excitedly "the one where it goes backwards, that's the best, what's it called?"

"'The Betrayal,'" Sam said chuckling at the memory. She was really enjoying their discussion and was disappointed when the captain announced their descent into Heathrow. Then she remembered the three-hour flight to Helsinki and smiled broadly.

"What's up?"

"Oh, nothing. Will you be sorting out my luggage here then?"

"Yes, I'll meet you in the lounge."

* * *

Sam was sitting in her taxi on her way to the hotel. She had had the most fantastic flight, sitting next to the gorgeous

Dominic. She pondered on their discussions and picked up her mobile phone.

"Corporate Finance."

"So there I was, sitting in a plane next to the sexiest man alive, talking about . . . "

"Sam, at the risk of interrupting your flow, but just when did this sentence start? I mean have you ever considered starting with, I dunno, maybe 'Hi' or 'How are you'?" Alex sounded a little irritated.

Sam was concerned. "So what's up, Grouchy Face? Problems with Duncan? How long has it been now?"

"Nearly six months. I'm not sure what's wrong. I probably just didn't get enough sleep last night – so tell me, who was the guy?"

Sam was unconvinced, and thought that Alex and Duncan were entering stage six rather early. She made a mental note to buy potatoes. "Well, I met the famous Dominic and I'll tell you, he's gorgeous. Remember your Tim?"

Alex remembered her boyfriend before last, a professional footballer. Tall, well-built and sexy, all brooding looks and muscles. He had modelled for Ralph Lauren, just before he dumped her. "Of course I remember Tim – he was my one great love."

"No, Lexi dear, he was great love number thirty-two and he was gay. Don't tell me you've forgotten walking in and finding him in bed with his chiropodist? Anyway, Dominic is just like Tim, but with blond hair and straight. I don't mean straight blond hair obviously, I meant he's straight and has blond hair. He could stun a woman at twenty paces, with a smile and a twinkle of his eyes."

"What am I hearing? Could it be that Samantha Jordan

is experiencing thoughts of an amorous nature about a member of the opposite sex? I don't believe it, could this be . . . LOVE!" Alex gasped theatrically.

"It's not love."

"Well, it sounds that way to me," Alex smiled. "So what's he like then? And how do you know he's not gay? You can never tell, you know. Tim was always so deliciously macho."

"Listen, Lexi, he's very much straight, and I think he likes me. We talked for hours about everything and nothing. He's thirty-one and never been married, but I think there's a story there. I can't work it out though. He comes across as self-assured one minute, but then is really clumsy the next. He looks like an athlete. I don't know, but I think there's more to Mr Stewart than he's willing to let on."

"What makes you think that?" Alex was definitely curious now and, despite the denials, she knew that Sam was seriously interested. "Did he say something?"

"Well, there might be something. We were on the plane and I was getting his life story out of him, then he said, after he finished his degree, he joined the . . . er . . . airline."

"What? He joined the what airline? I'm confused."

"He hesitated as if he was going to say something else: 'joined the . . . er . . . airline'. Now I'm not sure if it was just a slip or something, but I didn't get a chance to interrogate him because he accidentally knocked over my orange juice and tipped up my tray trying to clean it up. Anyway, apart from that he's lovely."

"So when are you seeing him again then?"

"Well, he's going to stay at the Finland Air offices in Helsinki for the next three days and he'll meet me at the airport on Thursday for my return leg. By the way, Lexi, I have my luggage with me."

"Oh my God, really? Did he do that? Marry him. Marry him now!" Alex urged. "Anyone who can save your luggage is definitely a keeper!"

"My thinking exactly." Alex seemed stunned into silence by this and Sam added hastily, "Joke, Lexi. Joke."

"So what about Mr Finland then?"

"Who?"

"Mr Finland. You remember. The guy you told me about. The one with the wrinkles."

"Laughter lines."

"All right, laughter lines."

"I'd forgotten all about him."

"Aren't you seeing him tomorrow?"

"Yeah, I am. I don't really know . . . "

"Oops. Boss. Got to go."

With that the phone call was at an end. Sam sat back in the taxi and waited for it to arrive at her destination. Of course she allowed herself a little smile.

* * *

Dominic was smiling. He was still bemused, but he was smiling. He thought about Sam and he grinned stupidly.

"Mr Stewart, there is something wrong?"

Dominic snapped to attention. "I'm sorry, Mika. What did you say?"

"I just wondered if there was a problem – you had strange look on your face."

"Mika, I know that these things are rare in Finland, but it was actually a grin."

"A grin, this is smile, yes?" Mika looked confused.

"Yes, it's what you do when you are happy." Dominic added, "Or what Finns do in the summer."

Mika wandered off into the other office, shaking his head and mumbling about an office not being place of fun.

Dominic stared after him and returned to his musings. Sam had such energy and vigour. Never before had he enjoyed talking to a woman that much. She seemed so intelligent, but still retained a keen sense of fun. He was acutely aware of the circumstances of their meeting, her being a client and everything, but he still allowed himself an optimistic smile. Even though he'd tried to keep his distance on the plane, she'd still managed to get behind some of his defences. She was a very persuasive woman and someone he wished he could get to know a lot better. If only they'd met under different circumstances. Still, he remembered a word his grandmother used to use, to his supreme embarrassment, whenever his friends were around. He raised his eyes to the heaven and said, "She definitely has spunk, grandmother."

Chapter Six

"Good evening, Sirpa." Sam looked at the receptionist and smiled whilst taking off her hat, coat and gloves.

Due to the sheer volume of clothing worn during the winter in Finland, the disrobing process upon entering a building can often take anything up to five minutes. Sam always complained that it is impossible to look glamorous in a country where you need at least six layers of clothing merely to survive the temperatures outside. As she was more susceptible to the cold than most, sometimes she was forced to wear so many layers that the congregation of clothing at her armpits meant that she couldn't put her arms down at her sides. Being quite chubby anyway, Sam was known to do a very passable impression of a Michelin man.

"Ms Jordan, nice to be welcoming you again." Sirpa took a room card from the board in front of her and looked up at Sam. She did a visible double-take and stammered, "Ms Jordan, you do something different this time. Your hair it very red . . . um . . . nice?"

Sam smoothed down her scarlet hair self-consciously. "Thank you, I think."

"Yes . . . I've put you in the room 238 tonight. We have, how do you say? Building fixings on fifth floor. I have put your emergency kit in your –"

Sam was already shaking her head and pointing at her suitcase.

Sirpa was taken aback. She was almost speechless but managed to utter, "You have luggage? Suitcase not lost?"

"Yes, wonders will never cease. I have my bag and I won't be needing the emergency kit. My problem has been sorted out. Finished, no more losing of the bag." Sam grabbed her room card and strode off confidently.

"Ms Jordan!" Sirpa called from her desk. "You seem to have left your computer bag."

"Damn," Sam muttered under her breath. "Why do I keep doing that?"

Up in her room, Sam began doing something that she hadn't done on arrival in Finland for many months. She began to unpack. Just as she opened her suitcase, her mobile phone rang. She searched around in her handbag until she found the loudly buzzing phone.

"Hello?"

"Samantha, dear, they're going to the Maldives on their honeymoon!"

Sam was confused. "Mother, is that you? Who's going to the Maldives? What are you talking about?"

"Debbie, dear. Debbie's going to the Maldives on her honeymoon. I bumped into that awful woman again. I say bumped. I'm sure she went out of her way to knock my trolley into the beginning of next week. Anyway, she was grinning like a Cheshire cat when she told me. So I told her that you were doing some work for the Finnish government, just to shut her up, and I told her that you had a new man friend. I thought that sounded like something you might possibly have by now. Are you there, Sam?"

"Yes, mother, I'm listening. I just wasn't sure whether my input was required in this monologue. You seemed to be having such fun."

"Sam, is there something wrong? Why are you so perky?" Her mother was suspicious. "You are in Finland, aren't you?"

"Yes, mother."

"You did fly out today, didn't you?"

"Your point, mother?"

"It doesn't matter. Where was I? Oh yes, your new boyfriend. Before you say it, I know I shouldn't make things up, but she annoyed me so much that I had to say something. Is there any possibility that I'm even vaguely psychic?" Her mother stopped, expecting an angry tirade to come shooting down the telephone line.

"It's all right. Under that sort of pressure, a mother's got to do what a mother's got to do."

"That's just what I was going to say . . ." her mother trailed off, confused by Sam's unusual reluctance to tell her to mind her own business. "Sam, are you sure you're all right?"

"Look Mother, I'm fine. I was just about to unpack, so I'd better go, early start and all that. Bye then."

"Bye, dear." As Sam hung up she thought she heard her mother utter bewilderedly, "Unpack?"

Sam walked over to her open suitcase and peered at it. Something was wrong.

"Hey, Consciousness, there's something strange here and I bet you can't guess what," pointed out Sam's Subconscious.

"Sorry," said the Conscious Mind irritably, dreaming about Dominic's firm, flat stomach. "What is it? Hold on, I'll guess. She has her bag?"

"That's not it."

"Her clothes are badly folded?"

"No, you're warm though. Go back to when she packed."

"OK, she was in a rush, her alarm didn't go off, and so she threw her stuff in her case."

"Yeah, you're getting warmer."

"She had forgotten her pyjamas, so she went into the spare room to fetch a clean pair."

"Colder."

"This is stupid. Can't you just tell me and stop this messing around?"

"No, carry on."

"OK, she put the pyjamas in the bag and snapped the elastic strap closed."

"Ooh, hot, hot!"

"She looked at her bed, saw her book and decided to pop it on top of the elastic strap. Then she closed the case."

"Boiling!" her Subconscious shouted gleefully.

Sam stared at her case as if it were a murder suspect. What's different? What's different? she repeated.

"Boiling! Under the strap," she mumbled to no one in particular and undid the elastic strap. "My book is under the strap!" she exclaimed and her Subconscious gave her Conscious Mind the thumbs up.

How did that get there? She wondered if it could have moved under during the flight. No, that was impossible –

her suitcase was much fuller than it usually was due to the unruly packing.

She picked up her mobile phone and dialled.

"Hello," said a male voice.

"Oh, hi, Duncan, How's tricks?"

"Fine, we're getting pretty close to bonuses so things are a bit hectic at work. How about you? Still having luggage deficits?"

"Yeah, 'fraid so."

"That's bordering on harassment now, isn't it? How many times is it exactly?"

"I'm not quite sure of the exact number." Sam was perplexed. Duncan never usually paid her this much attention – normally he'd call Alex as soon as he heard her voice.

"It must be well above the average. You'll let me know if you're thinking of going public, won't you?"

"Why?"

"The share price is bound to take a dip – if you kicked up a stink, that is."

"Oh," Sam said knowingly – no wonder he was so interested. "You'll be the first to know. Is Lexi there?"

"Yeah, but she's acting a bit weird. I'll get her for you."

"Thanks." While waiting for Duncan to fetch Alex, Sam started pacing the room.

"Hi, Sam, what's up?"

"Not my brain-cell count anyway. I think I'm going mad."

"I thought that years ago, when you said that you liked living in Manchester."

"Ha, ha, very funny. Thank God I'm not pregnant."

"What's that got to do with the price of fish on a bank holiday?"

"Nothing, it's just that I read in a magazine that pregnant women lose about two thousand brain cells per day or per hour or something."

"Really?"

"Yes, really. I just don't think I can deal with such wastage at the moment."

"So are you pregnant?"

"No."

"I'm sorry. You've lost me."

"I was just . . . oh I don't know what I was doing," Sam said in exasperation.

"Vitamin E, that's good for brain power, isn't it? Or is it vitamin B12? Then again we all have squillions of them, anyway, so I don't suppose it matters much."

"All the vitamins in the world won't help. You can't replace brain cells, Lexi," Sam warmed to her topic. "Also, did you know that every time you bump or jolt your head, you lose thousands of them?"

"OK, so you've explained my mother and why my moronic, ex-heavy-metal-loving brother is so dense. Is that it or do you want to try and explain why my dad is obsessed with gardening, or is that too much for one night?" Alex giggled.

"I think that's enough for one night."

"So, was there something special you wanted to talk about?"

"There was something, but I've forgotten what it was. It was really important."

"Yeah, it always is," Alex muttered.

"No, no. I mean really important." Sam's mind wandered in an attempt to remember why she phoned.

"As I said before . . . ooh, did you hear that Debbie's getting married? Her hubby-to-be is a contact-lens salesman."

"I heard he was an optician," said Sam.

"Nah, definitely a salesman. I saw Debbie in town. She was buying luggage for their honeymoon. She was dragging this huge suitcase behind her. It looked hilarious. I started telling her about your problems. She said to say hi by the way."

"Suitcase?" Sam mused. "Yes, that's it. Someone's been in my suitcase."

"What do you mean someone's been in your suitcase? How do you know?"

"Well, I put my book on top of the elastic strap when I packed it and when I unpacked it the book was under the strap."

"Don't the customs guys open them from time to time?"

"Yes, but they have to put a letter in, saying that they've opened it," Sam explained.

"And there's . . ." Alex began.

"No, there's no letter, but then again, they have been known not to bother. You can never be sure." Sam paused. "Dominic was with it the whole time."

"Dominic? You don't think it could have been him, do you?"

"It couldn't have been," Sam faltered. "I mean, he wouldn't do such a thing, would he? Why would he? No, I don't think it was him. I mean, he might have had to open it at some point because of his 'suitcase-minding duties', Oh, I don't know. He would have said something."

"Well, ring him and tell him about it then – maybe he took one look at your hair-colour and forgot to tell you."

The phone began beeping at Sam. "Hold on, Lexi, that's my Call Waiting," she swapped the calls. "Hello?"

"Ms Jordan? Sam? It's Dominic."

"Hi, Dominic, hold on. I'm on the other line." Sam switched back. "Lexi, it's Dominic, I'll ring you tomorrow."

Sam cut Alex off to the strains of 'Go on then, dump your best friend for a six-pack himbo, why don't you?' and swapped back to Dominic. "Sorry about that, what can I do for you?"

"I just wanted to tell you that I will be able to accompany you back to Manchester and we could meet up in the Helsinki Lounge at say 6.30pm." Dominic said this in a rush – he seemed nervous.

"Thanks for that. I do appreciate your taking all this trouble."

"It's no problem. Is everything all right?"

"Yes, everything is fine this end. Were there any problems while you were suitcase-sitting?" Sam enquired as nonchalantly as she could.

"Not apart from the falling-off-the-belt incident, no. Why do you ask?"

"It's nothing really. I just wondered if it, you know, burst open when it fell, or something like that," Sam said hopefully.

"No, it just fell off – it didn't open, I'm sure of it."

"Oh, all right then."

"Well, if everything's OK, I'll see you on Thursday."

"OK, bye."

Sam hung up and stared at her phone for a while, lost in thought.

Why didn't Sam tell Dominic about her suspicions? Well, she was thinking about what Alex had said to her and realised that it might in fact have been Dominic who had been through her case. She didn't really know him, did she? After all, four hours of discussion on planes did not a soul mate make. Also, if he had opened it in his official capacity, he deliberately didn't tell her. She'd given him a chance after all. If he wouldn't talk to her, she wouldn't talk to him. He might be one of those people that like rooting around in people's clothing, a 'knicker-sniffer' or something pervy like that. If that were true, she had made a fool of herself again. Fancying herself 'in like' with another attractive man. Letting herself be interested, just to find out that he'd been tampering with her undies. Lowering her defences, even a little, might have proven to be the wrong move. They always show their true colours in the end, she thought . . . Maybe her mother was right, she should steer clear of the stunningly gorgeous Dominic types and make do with the average, but mesmerising ones like Mark. She then entertained the possibility that that was probably why he phoned, just to check that she hadn't noticed anything strange.

"Damn," she thought.

* * *

At that moment in time, Dominic, sitting in his hotel room in Helsinki, was pondering over Sam. He was glad he'd called her, just to make sure. He had needed to check up on her. At that moment his phone rang.

"Dominic Stewart."

"So?" said a deep voice.

"The suitcase arrived."

"Good. So does she suspect?"

"No, sir, not a thing."

"Good work, Mr Stewart."

"Thank you, sir," Dominic said, but the man had already broken the connection.

* * *

Sam waited at the bus stop, looking out for Mark's car. She looked at her watch again. He was late. Ten minutes late to be precise. She would never get used to Finnish punctuality (or the lack of it). Even the more well-travelled businessmen seemed totally incapable of being on time. It's not too much to ask, is it? she thought. She stamped her feet and rubbed her hands together in an attempt to keep warm. It was minus 15 degrees Celsius at the very least and it wasn't the type of morning that any Brit in their right mind would consider being out in. She tried to pull her hat even further over her ears.

How on earth did I get talked into this? Sam remembered the choice she'd been given. Either drive one of the company cars or take the bus and be picked up by Mark at the bus stop. The thought of driving a left-hand drive car was in itself not too daunting. She was well practised in driving them. It was the thought of driving when the roads have six inches of snow on top of ice five inches thick which made her blood freeze. At least it matched the rest of her. Luggage loss is one thing; standing on a street corner doing a fairly accurate impression of an ice-cube is a completely different matter.

"That's it. As soon as I get back to the office this afternoon, I'm quitting. My notice will be handed in and I'll be free of this goddamned country once and for all. I mean it this time," she complained bitterly. "That's if I survive that long."

While she was mentally composing her letter of resignation, a car pulled up in front of her. The passenger door opened.

"Do you mind if I don't get out?" It was that gorgeous voice again. "There's no stopping allowed on this street."

Sam didn't really know how to respond, so she picked up her briefcase, wrapped her coat around her and lowered herself into the passenger seat. As soon as she sank into the surprisingly warm, soft leather, heat spread from her chilled bottom into her lower back and crept upwards to her shoulders. She almost purred with pleasure.

"That's lovely," she murmured.

"That's heated seats," Mark pointed out. "An invaluable asset in Swedish cars, especially in wintertime."

"This is a Swedish car?" Sam was surprised as Finnish people liked the Swedes almost as much as the British liked the French.

"Yes. Unfortunately Finland doesn't produce cars."

"Oh."

She took off her hat and combed her fingers through her hair. Mark glanced at her and stabbed the brakes in shock. "Samantha, your hair. It's very . . . um . . . red!"

"Yes, I had it done when I got home." She had just about had it with these people – hadn't they ever seen dyed hair before? This won't do at all, she thought. She made a mental note to book an appointment with Louise to have it toned down.

"I like it. It grows on you," he decided, nodding his head.

Sam giggled at the unintentionally funny comment.

"I'm glad to see you're well kitted out for the Finnish winter."

Sam considered this for a split second and remembered that she was angry at his tardiness. "Whatever happened to 'Sorry I'm late, Sam. Can you forgive me'?"

"Sorry I'm late, Sam. Can you forgive me?" Mark said obligingly.

"That's OK, Mark. These things happen," Sam parroted the expected response sarcastically.

"Sorry, Samantha. I forgot how anal you Brits can be about punctuality," Mark smiled.

"Anal?" Sam knew immediately that she shouldn't have asked.

"Yes, anally retentive – you know, all uptight and obsessive."

"How dare you!" she yelped.

"Admit it. I can almost feel your feathers ruffling as I speak. You've probably been thinking up ways to get out of such a backward country, haven't you? And all because I was a few minutes late."

"A few minutes?" Sam was incensed. "Over eleven minutes to be exact."

"See, what did I tell you – anal!" Mark chuckled to himself.

"You might call attention to time 'anal', but I assure you, where I come from, it's considered good manners." Sam went in for the kill. "Something you Finnish people obviously know nothing about. I mean, you haven't even got a word for 'please' in your language. How ill-mannered is that?"

"Ouch. And a good morning to you too."

Sam was about to burst forth with an angry tirade of particularly nasty swearwords when she remembered that he was her client and they were officially into 'his time'. As he was paying rather a lot of money for the privilege, she decided to radiate 'pissed-off-ness' instead.

"Look, don't sit there in a huff. I'm only joking with you."

"Well, it's your time we're using up. What do I care?" she grumbled.

Mark looked over at Sam, "I *am* sorry. Can we start from the beginning again? Pretend I was on time."

His eyes sparkled and Sam was fixed in his gaze, like a reindeer in headlights. She could feel her indignation thawing along with her body temperature.

Mark tried a different tack, "Did you get the information I sent to you?"

"I did."

"Well . . . ?"

"Well, the translator you hired obviously had no idea about English grammar. I bet you used some English guy that a friend of a friend's cousin's sister knows."

"You might be right on that one."

"Yes, I thought so. Let me ask you a question. If you were in charge of the Sistine chapel, would you have asked the local house-painter to do it?"

"No, but what's that got to do with the brochure?"

"It's all about technical skill. Just because someone knows which end of a brush to use, it doesn't mean they're Michelangelo, does it? It's the same with translation. Just because someone can speak two foreign languages, it doesn't mean they can necessarily do a good job of translating between them." Sam was warming to her theme, determined to make him pay. Anal, indeed! "A professional translator has the skill and requisite knowledge of grammar and linguistics. They understand nuance in a language and are able to get the same level of nuance into the other language. The ordinary 'Joe Bloggs' has no idea how to translate properly." She rooted in her briefcase to find the brochure they were discussing. "Take a look at this, two spelling mistakes on the first page alone. And the product description doesn't even make sense. I bet you paid thousands of Finnish marks for the printing of these brochures, didn't you?"

"Very possibly."

"Well, did it not occur to you to get a professional to at least check the spelling?" She wasn't going to let him speak until she'd served the final blow. "It's simple business sense to decide where to spend money and where not. What's the point of having a colour brochure with beautiful pictures when there are two spelling mistakes on the front page? You might as well have written it on the back of a fag packet, photocopied it badly and then spilt coffee all over it." There! Let him deal with that.

"I agree wholeheartedly and I made that very point to my father last week. I wasn't actually involved with this brochure – I only took over the running of the business recently." He looked strangely amused as he said the words. "As for getting in a professional, that's exactly why you are here. Unless you don't think you can handle it, of course."

"Oh, don't you worry. I can handle it. I've single-handedly brought more than one company back from the brink of bankruptcy."

"Glad to hear it, although we're not that badly off just

yet." He pulled up the handbrake and said, "Here we are."

Sam was forced to stew as she followed him into the building. He collected his mail from the receptionist, who turned bright red at the sight of him. They chatted amiably for a minute or so and he seemed to thoroughly charm the pants off her. He then turned to Sam and gestured for her to follow him to his office. Along the way, he was greeted by some employees, all of whom called him by his first name. Sam had learnt very early on that this was standard Finnish practice. It took her a while, at first, to realise why everyone was calling him Markku – she'd forgotten that that was his real name. Mark was just for foreigners like her who couldn't get their heads around Finnish names.

Sitting in the large and comfortable-looking leather chair in his office, he asked, "So Samantha, even though we're not quite on the brink of bankruptcy, how would you propose saving our UK export business?"

She was certain that she saw a flash of amusement on his face as he said the words and although he was one hundred per cent businesslike in every way, she couldn't shake the feeling that she was being teased.

Throughout the day, Sam tried to immerse herself deeply in the business discussion, but she couldn't stop her mind from coming back to the same thought. Why was it that you wait and wait for a decent bloke and then all of a sudden there's two of them at the same time? Like buses. Her mind thrilled at the thought of Dominic and she had to admit she was intrigued by Mark. She couldn't deny that there was something authoritative in his manner – he emanated an aura of power. But Dominic, she sighed, now that's what you call sex on legs. But she could choose only one. Talk about being like buses!

" . . . buses. What do you think?"

She couldn't believe it. Why did they keep doing that? Were all Finnish people mind-readers? Was there something in the water?

She managed to improvise, "Sorry, I was completely engrossed in your marketing schedule."

"I was just saying that we can afford to invest more heavily in the advertising campaign. I was particularly impressed with London and I was wondering how much it would cost to advertise on London buses?"

"I have no idea, but I can easily find out," Sam added this question to her ever-lengthening list of to-dos.

"Well, it's getting a bit late." Mark looked at his watch. "I was thinking, maybe you'd like to go over the marketing schedule over dinner this evening?" He hesitated, then added, "If you like?"

Sam looked at her watch, it was four-thirty, which meant that the Finnish workday had ended half an hour ago.

"What do you think, Samantha?"

"Well, I'm only allowed to invoice eight hours."

A look of regret flashed across his face. "I'm sorry, I wasn't thinking . . . "

Sam thought about the fact that she could either eat alone in her hotel or she could go out to dinner with Mark. "No, I'm sorry. I'd love to go for dinner." She quickly added, "To go through the marketing schedule of course. There is plenty to discuss after all."

"It doesn't have to be all business, does it?"

"No, I guess not," Sam said eventually.

Sam wasn't sure though. It was always easier when she had her business head on. She didn't have to think up witty and clever discussion topics. If it was business, she wouldn't have to think about how charismatic Mark was and just how nice his hands were. Talking business was much neater. Then again, where was the harm in getting to know him better? She was acutely aware of Alex's 'desperate for sex' theory. It was a good thing that he was a client and therefore officially off limits and, desperate for sex or not, it would be nice to be wined and dined.

"Shall I pick you up at your hotel later?"

"OK, that would be nice."

"Say eight o'clock?"

"Eight is fine."

He did have a lovely smile.

* * *

Sam was in her bathroom, carefully re-applying her make-up and trying to decide if she was going to mention her dinner date with Mark to Alex, when her mobile rang.

"Sam, Duncan's gone!" It was more like a wail than a sentence.

"Alex, is that you?"

"Yes, Duncan's gone!" Alex wailed again.

"What d'you mean gone? Has he left you?"

"No, he's gone to Frankfurt for a meeting with the Deutsche Bank people and he won't be back until after the weekend."

"So?"

"So, it's our six-month anniversary."

"And?"

"And he's forgotten all about it."

"Alex, I'm just wondering if you can hear yourself."

"Why?"

"Well, could you be more neurotic? Most men don't even remember their wedding anniversaries, let alone going out with someone for six months. That's not even an official anniversary, is it?"

"It is as far as I'm concerned. What should I do?" Alex whined.

"You shouldn't 'do' anything. You should just chill out. For God's sake, he's just gone on a business trip. It's not as if he's emigrating for ever."

"Maybe you're right."

"Of course I'm right. I mean it's not as if he could be getting up to anything spurious in Frankfurt. You know what those Germans are like. Especially the German bankers."

"Is that some sort of rhyming slang?" Alex perked up.

"No, I think that's merchant bankers."

"So it is. Just ignore me. I've no idea what's wrong with me."

Even though Sam had a clear view on what was wrong with Alex, she decided not to enlighten her. "So how's things apart from Duncan's German odyssey?"

"Not bad. My boss is doing my head in, though. How're things on the Finland front?"

"Oh, the usual. Brass-monkey weather."

"What are you up to tonight?"

"I'm going out to dinner."

"Woo-hoo!" Alex whistled. "Who with?"

"Mark, that Finnish bloke I told you about."

"The wrinkly guy with a 'great personality'?" Alex's voice implied the quote marks around the phrase.

"For the last time, he's not a wrinkly. He can't be that much older than me."

"If you say so."

"Anyway, he's a client," Sam said hurriedly.

"So, what about Francis? He was a client, wasn't he?"

"I didn't go out with Francis."

"No, but you bonked him, didn't you?"

"Alex, I told you that in confidence, not for you to throw into a discussion when you want to prove a point. Anyway, Francis wasn't officially a client. His head office brought me in. He was just the manager."

"Yes, but you bonked him," Alex insisted.

"Ok, I admit it. I bonked him. Is that what you want me to say? Are you sure my mother's not paying you to be my moral conscience? It's just dinner."

"Yeah, right. Don't do anything I wouldn't do."

"That leaves me loads of scope then." Sam laughed.

"Have you got enough condoms on you?"

"Goodbye, Alex," Sam said sweetly.

"Bye, Sam."

* * *

Sam was feeling really awful. Her head was throbbing. Yep, that was definitely a hangover. She lay in her hotel bed trying to make sense of what had happened the previous night.

She'd been remarkably nervous and had drunk far too much at dinner. As Mark was driving, he'd had just the one glass of wine and she'd managed to drink the rest of the bottle single-handedly. They'd not actually discussed any of the marketing plan, instead they'd exchanged travel stories. She'd enjoyed his company more and more, in direct proportion to the amount of wine she'd consumed. She couldn't really focus on the memory, but she'd been pretty sure that a kiss had been involved at some point. Exactly at which stage of the proceedings it had happened, she couldn't quite remember, but there was definitely a kiss. Thank goodness she wasn't seeing Mark today. She could deal with it later.

Her alarm went off and she groaned as her headache amplified the sound to a ridiculous level of decibels. "Shut up," she croaked, knocking her alarm clock off the nightstand.

* * *

"So to make it in condensation, why not to make this Christmas a 'Finnmeat Fantasia' Christmas?" The voice sounded triumphant. The man looked over at Sam and waited for signs of reaction to his presentation. "So, Samantha, what do you think? Do you think the idea will work in the UK?"

It was Thursday afternoon and Sam was sitting in the office of Juha Herrinen, Managing Director of FinnMeats Oy, still nursing her poorly head. FinnMeats Oy was the premier meat products manufacturer in Turku. This was the final stop on her tour of duty in Finland and she was just about ready to fly back to Manchester. Juha had been telling Sam of his plans to take the UK market by storm, with his new 'Fantasia' range of luxury meat products and all Sam had to do was give her professional opinion. He wanted to have the entire concept ready, to catch the run up to the Christmas season in seven months' time. Sam swallowed hard, wondering how on earth she could word her reply diplomatically.

"Well, Juha, let me just summarise – which by the way,

is the right word, not 'make it in condensation' – what I have just heard."

"Summarise," Juha nodded whilst committing the word to memory. "OK, fine, go ahead."

"So you have a new range of authentic Finnish pies and meat products, more tasty than anything hitherto available in the UK?"

"Fantasia, yes, that's right," Juha nodded excitedly.

"And they are all made from the highest quality . . . erm," Sam paused, drew a deep breath and struggled on, willing her stomach contents to stay put, "reindeer meat?"

"Yes, it's a Finnish delicacy," Juha encouraged, the pride oozing out of all his pores.

"And, you want to make this concept part of your Christmas exporting campaign?"

"That's right." Juha paused for a moment and added, "Now, Samantha, you must be brutally honest with me. What do you think?"

"Brutally honest?" Sam glanced over at him and he nodded, so she continued. "Well, for starters, I don't think Christmas would be the right time for beginning such a campaign. I mean . . ." Sam had run out of tactful words and Juha was looking confused.

"I don't understand."

"Juha, you want me to be honest. Well, I just don't think the UK is ready for it. We're a bit sentimental at Christmas time. Especially about reindeer. I can see it now, the wanton destruction of old Red-nose, perpetrated by the evil Scandinavians."

"Nordic people," Juha insisted.

"Same difference," Sam threw back.

"Not at all. Finland does not belong to Scandinavia. Scandinavia consists of Sweden, Denmark and Norway. We are one of the Nordic countries."

"Yes, I know." Sam had heard this geographical lecture many times before.

"Of course, we'll run a very tasteful television campaign."

"Well, in that case, you might as well go on national television, dress up in a Santa suit, sit in a sleigh singing 'Rudolf the Red-nosed Reindeer', shoot Rudolf in the head, cut him into bits and start chewing on his leg. That'll have the same effect." Sam looked over at Juha and grimaced. "I'm sorry, but that's what people will be thinking if you try to give them smoked reindeer slices at Christmas. There is no way that even the best, most imaginative advertising campaign could survive the actual slaying of a Christmas carol."

"Hmm." Juha was mulling over her words.

"Well, Juha, you have a think and we'll be in touch. OK?"

Sam got up, shook his hand and started out of his office, but was stopped in her tracks by Juha's final question.

"Do you really think I'll need the Santa suit?"

Sam was going to explain, but decided against it. She simply uttered "Let's be in touch" and dashed out of the building.

* * *

Sam had changed out of her suit and was in the process of packing it into her case when she had a flash of inspiration. She decided to leave a small portion of her suit jacket sticking out of the side of her case. In this way she could tell immediately upon her arrival whether it had been opened en route. If the material was still there at Manchester, then she would have nothing to worry about and if it wasn't then she would definitely tell someone. She hadn't quite decided if that 'someone' would be Dominic or Anne, but one of them would be told, at any rate.

By the time she arrived in Helsinki, she had dismissed the nonsensical notion that Dominic was involved in tampering with her bag. She wasn't even sure that her bag had been tampered with. Her book had probably moved during the flight. She, once more, agreed with herself that she should wait until Manchester before doing anything outrageous. She laughed at herself for being so paranoid and silly and looked forward to seeing Dominic in the lounge.

She looked guiltily at her mobile phone. She'd been very careful not to switch it on ever since her dinner with Mark. As he was a client, she had been duty-bound to give him her mobile number. She weighed up her options. She could leave it off until she got home and felt ready to deal with Mark or she could switch it on and get advice from Alex. Almost as soon as she switched it on, it rang.

"Hello?" she offered warily.

"Samantha, I don't know what you say to Markku, but he order more days from you."

It was Martti and he seemed really happy. She groaned inwardly at the news.

"Great," she uttered weakly. Kill me, kill me now.

"Keep up good work. Invoice, invoice, invoice."

With one phone call, all hope of divine mercy had disappeared. She needed to get everything off her chest.

"Corporate Finance."

"Alex, I'm in trouble."

"Bloody hell, Sam. I told you to use a condom – anyway, it's far too early to know for sure. When was it? The day before yesterday?"

"Not that kind of trouble, clever clogs."

"What then?"

"Don't quote me, but I'm fairly certain I kissed him."

"Oh, is that all? Yes, I'll get that letter faxed over immediately, Mr Smith."

"Boss?"

"That's right, Mr Smith."

"What should I do? He's ordered five more consulting days."

"When will you be back in the country, Mr Smith?"

"Late tonight."

"Well, why don't you leave things with me and I'll get back to you then."

"OK. Thanks, Lexi."

"My pleasure, Mr Smith."

The phone went dead and Sam decided to bite the bullet. She checked in with her message service. There were only two messages. One from her mother asking for an update on the man-friend issue as she was having lunch with Debbie's mother and needed to know what she should say. The second was the dreaded message from Mark asking her to call back.

"Huh, do I look stupid?" she said to the phone. "There's no way I'd be silly enough to speak to you again."

She was thinking up ways to hand over the consultancy to someone else when her phone rang once again. Lexi, Sam thought.

"That was a long one. Did he have a go about private calls again?"

"Samantha? It's Mark."

Shit, shit, shit. Sam looked at her phone as if it were the worst kind of traitor. She had to just go with it. "Yes, speaking."

"Samantha, I just wanted to call to say thank you."

Sam's mind raced. Why on earth was he thanking her? What had she done? Damn the evil alcohol. Please don't say that I slept with him, she prayed silently. I promise never ever to drink again.

"For what?" she squeaked.

"I implemented some of your suggestions today and it's amazing what a difference they've made already."

Sam raised her eyes heavenward and repeated thank you, thank you, thank you. Although maybe never ever drinking again was a tad hasty. To Mark she said, "It's my pleasure, really."

"Did Martti tell you that I need at least five more consulting days?"

"Funnily enough, I've just got off the phone to him." She dwelt on the 'at least' part. The only positive point was that he hadn't mentioned the dinner. Maybe he'd forgotten all about it.

"Anyway, I just wanted to say thanks."

"Consider it said."

"Maybe we could have dinner again, sometime? Sam, could you hold on for a second." Sam heard a short exchange in Finnish, then Mark returned to the phone. "Sorry, Sam. I have to go. We have a bit of an emergency."

Before she knew it, he was gone. Leaving her to wonder

if she was ever going to get the last word with this man.

Walking through the airport on her way to the Plus Club Executive Lounge, Sam caught a glimpse of what looked like Dominic going through the door. She was taken aback at her involuntary sharp intake of breath. She tried to remind herself that he was just a man, and nothing special, but at the same time her mind was busy pondering the curvaceous nature of his pert bottom.

"Stupid, stupid woman," she mumbled to herself as she entered the lounge.

She was confronted by a long curving reception desk, behind which sat two Finland Air employees, both trying to hold back giggles.

"Good evening, madam. Can I see your boarding pass?" said the one on the left, wiping a stray tear of laughter from her eye. She took Sam's boarding pass and made some notes on the pad in front of her. She handed the pass back with a radiant smile and added, "Your flight is on time, Ms Jordan. We'll inform you when it is ready for boarding. Please make yourself comfortable and if there's anything you require, just let us know."

"Thank you. Could you tell me if a Dominic Stewart has arrived? I think I saw him come."

Sam got no further as, at this point, the mention of Dominic's name had become too much for the other woman at the desk who almost exploded with laughter and was forced to rush off into the back room. Sam stared after her in bafflement, until she remembered the overheard conversation on the plane.

"Sorry about that, Ms Jordan." The first woman pressed her lips together, breathed deeply, coughed and continued.

"Yes, Mr Stewart is in the lounge. He mentioned that he would be waiting for you in the smoking section."

Sam smiled her thanks, sensing that any further comment would cause this woman, also, to lose control. She steeled herself and walked toward the smoking section.

She saw Dominic and as she walked towards him he turned and smiled broadly. Her step faltered slightly.

"Well, hello there!" He gestured for her to sit in the seat next to him. "Are you all checked in?"

"Yes, thank you, Dominic."

"If you could let me have your baggage receipt, I'll go and have a look to see if everything's all right."

"Here it is." Sam shook slightly as their hands touched.

"Don't worry. I'll make sure your baggage gets on our flight and I'll meet you there."

Clutching her receipt, he strode off to look for her suitcase. Sam shook her head. She was obviously in cloud-cuckoo-land. There was absolutely no way that Dominic would be interested in someone like her. He was way out of her league. He probably went out with models and people like that. Still, it would have been nice . . .

You may be surprised to know that during the flight, Dominic managed to spill only two drinks. After an initial awkwardness, Sam and he managed to relax into the comfortable banter that characterised their first flight together. This served to convince Sam that there was nothing sinister about him. They continued their good-natured argument about American sitcoms and found out that they were also originally from the same part of London. As fate would have it, they had both attended the same university, but managed to miss each other due to Sam's degree taking her out of the country during the year that they overlapped. They both agreed that Marathon was a far better name for the chocolate bar than Snickers and that Bagpuss was definitely the best children's programme on television when they were young.

Sam had just finished chuckling at his impression of the Bagpuss mice, when he stunned her.

"Look Sam, I've only just moved up to Manchester and it does get a bit lonely when you arrive somewhere new. How about going for a drink with me at the weekend? You know, showing me around the place? " He glanced at Sam, completely misunderstood her expression and added quickly. "Well, it doesn't matter. Really, forget I mentioned it."

"No, no, I think that's a great idea," Sam spluttered.

"Excellent. I'll call you tomorrow, then," Dominic grinned.

Sam smiled to herself. Thinking back to her bus analogy, she thought to herself, 'Sorry, Mark. I'm getting on Bus Number Two'.

Chapter Seven

They were both surprised to see Anne waiting at the gate for them. Still giggling over Dominic's last comment, Sam thought that she saw an almost imperceptible look of annoyance pass across Anne's face. She was snapped, quite rudely, out of her good humour by Anne's brusque tone.

"Ms Jordan, I have something for you, if you would like to follow me."

"Yes, of course, but what about my – ?"

"Don't worry about that. Dominic will get it." She looked pointedly at Dominic and gestured for him to get going.

"Of course, I'll just be off now." Dominic started to move forward, forgetting that he had put Sam's computer bag in front of his feet. He stumbled over the bag, apologised profusely and wandered off in the general direction of the baggage reclaim area. Sam and Anne both watched this performance and shook their heads, Sam in amusement and Anne in mild reproof.

"Let's get going, shall we?" Anne said briskly and clipped off in the direction of her office.

In this way, Sam, again, found herself trotting behind the efficient figure of Anne and again, she found herself wondering what delights the airline had in store for her. At the same time she was sort of hoping that Anne wasn't going to take Dominic off her case. Excuse the pun, she chuckled. As she entered Anne's office, she saw a rather large, black, hard-shell suitcase sitting forlornly in the middle of the floor.

"Well, here it is." Anne pointed at the case.

Sam almost expected her to say "Ta-da!" in the manner of a magician's assistant.

"Sorry?" Sam said, not really knowing what was happening.

"Your courtesy suitcase. Obviously, we're not admitting that any of this business was our fault and it's not a bribe, if that's what you are thinking. It is simply designed to be more efficient for the computers that read the baggage tags." Anne's own efficiency knew no bounds. "If you look here," she pointed at a smooth portion just below the grip, "you'll see that this has been designed so that when the bar-coded portion of the baggage tag is placed here, the computers will be able to read the information whichever way the bag lies. Or even upright," she added for good measure.

"Oh, I see."

"And as requested, we have placed padlocks on the front instead of a combination lock. Here are the keys." She handed Sam three keys. "Usually there are only two keys, but I had an extra one made just in case you lose the other two. I find that two keys are rarely enough." Anne seemed quite pleased with herself at this point and could even be described as looking quite smug. This quickly changed to a look of irritation as a knock on the door interrupted her flow. She went to it and opened it slightly, just enough to poke her head out. Sam heard her say something about waiting outside and trying not to break anything and assumed that it must be Dominic, with her suitcase.

"So, I can just take this, can I?" Sam enquired as Anne was sitting down behind her desk.

"Yes, of course, but I will need you to sign this form to say that you have received it." Sam had begun to sign when Anne added, "And if you could just write your home address and telephone number beside it, a number where we can contact you when abroad plus the phone number of your next of kin, just in case."

"In case of what?" Sam questioned.

"It's just procedure," Anne said brightly, and to Sam's mind, a little too brightly. "Let's get on to the subject of your next flight"

"Did you phone Pirjo then?"

"Ah yes, Mrs Hakkerainen, a very friendly lady. We had a lovely chat and managed to sort everything out."

"Lovely chat? Pirjo can't speak English very well. What? How?" said Sam remembering her last conversation with Pirjo, which caused less understanding than a comedian in a room full of Germans.

"Fairly simple really, we spoke in Finnish," Anne said offhandedly.

"Oh." Sam kicked herself for not remembering that Anne was Finnish.

"And as I said, we managed to come to an arrangement

where I book your flights here in Manchester and bill your company directly on a monthly basis. Overall, your company will probably save at least four hundred pounds per month. Your next flight is a week on Monday, and you'll be flying via Amsterdam. So if there's nothing you need to ask, here are your tickets and Dominic will escort you to your taxi."

Before she knew it, Sam had been led out of Anne's office and the door was closed, politely, in her face. Tickets in one hand and new suitcase in the other, she turned to face Dominic.

"So what was going on in there then?" Dominic asked nonchalantly.

"I was getting the top secret rundown of all the magical features of my new case," Sam chuckled. "She was acting like it's the crown jewels or something."

"Well, maybe it's really important for her. You never know, her job might be riding on getting this mess with your luggage sorted out.

Sam was chastened. "I hadn't thought of it like that."

"Well, maybe you shouldn't judge people so readily." Dominic admonished. "Let's get you through customs and to your taxi." He had obviously caught Anne's 'brisk' disease. He led a suddenly quiet Sam towards the exit.

* * *

Sitting in her office at home, the next day, Sam still wasn't 100% sure what had happened, but was quite happy that everything had been organised for her. She speed-dialled her phone.

"Hello?"

"So he asked me out. We're going to go out for lunch tomorrow."

"Samantha? Is that you, dear? Who asked you out? Is it a man?"

Sam looked at her phone in shock and clearly saw the words, Mother (Home), on the display. She slapped her hand to her forehead. She'd dialled her mother by mistake. Of all the stupid, clumsy . . . she was still a bit tired from the many flights the day before and really wasn't together enough to have THIS discussion with her mother. She put her hand to her mouth.

"Sorry, wrong number," she mumbled through her fingers and hastily put the phone down. She carefully dialled again – very slowly to ensure that there were no further mistakes.

"Corporate Finance."

"Lexi, you'll never believe what happened? He asked me out. Dominic asked me to go out for lunch with him tomorrow!"

"Look, Sam, I really can't talk just now." Alex had seen her boss walking towards her.

"This really can't wait."

Alex sighed at Sam's insistence, "Ok, Mr Smith, how can I help you? I am really busy, although I suppose I can spare a moment, but I can't talk for too long."

"Don't talk. Just listen. Where shall I take him? I want to take him somewhere hip and cool, but they're always so noisy and I want to be able to talk to him. Pretend you're talking to a client and just say yes or no, OK?"

"That'll be fine, Mr Smith."

"Giovanni's?"

"No, Mr Smith, I don't think that would be a good idea."

"Not Italian then?"

"No," Alex whispered. As her boss had wandered in the opposite direction, she decided that she could venture further comment. She whispered, "You always make a mess eating pasta. Anyway, they banned you after the spaghetti carbonara incident. I think the stain is still on the ceiling. They eventually had to knock down that wall as well."

"How was I meant to know it had a raw egg on top. It's not something you expect, is it?" But considering the Great Carbonara Fiasco, she submitted to Alex's reasoning.

"Yeah, but only you could have reacted like that." Alex, by now, was hissing more than whispering.

"OK, OK, I've got it – The Zoo," naming a relatively quiet bar/restaurant that they had both visited once before. It was one of those themed restaurants. Animal-themed décor, and apart from having to sit in cages on the backs of polar bears and giant pandas, it was fairly normal. The food was passable with a nice line in burgers and ribs and assorted 'finger food'. On the last visit Sam had found the elephant burger delicious, after she'd established that the name referred to the size rather than the contents.

"Are you sure?" Alex was doubtful. "Do you really want him to see you licking your fingers? I mean, it's hardly ladylike and romantic, is it?" she hissed.

"All right then, how about Oxygene?" Sam sighed, slowly running out of tried and tested options. "I don't want to take him somewhere I've not been before."

"Yes, Oxygene's better," Alex said in her normal voice. Sam assumed her boss must have just left the office. "Listen, Sam, don't get too excited."

"Why shouldn't I get excited? He's gorgeous." Sam was cross that Alex didn't seem to be as thrilled as she was.

"Well, you know, it might be professionally based."

"You mean he might be a gigolo?"

"No, stupid, I mean it might just be a PR thing, you know, making up for inconvenience and all that."

"That's rich, you telling me to take things slow!" Sam was irked at Alex's suggestion that she was excited. "Anyway, he just wants to see a bit of Manchester, that's all."

"Look, I'd better go. Some of us have proper work to do," Alex said good-naturedly.

"OK then. I'll call you tomorrow."

"With all the details?"

"Yes, Lexi, with all the details."

Her phone rang immediately after she hung up.

"Samantha, dear . . . "

"Mother, what can I do for you?"

"Don't pretend you didn't call me just now. I may be old, but I know how to dial 1471 and now they have that useful 'press five for ring back option'. You'd be surprised what they teach us at the Nosy Old Desperate Mothers' workshops that I go to."

Sam was stunned – her mother just didn't do funny. "Umm, mother?"

"It was a joke, Samantha. I do have a sense of humour. I simply keep it under wraps most of the time."

Sam was flustered. Her brain just wasn't equipped to deal with the sudden appearance of wit in her mother's conversation. She decided to continue the call as if it was a normal run-of-the-mill-mother-lecture-type phone call. "Er, sorry about before. I got confused," She muttered unconvincingly. "What can I do for you?"

"Tell me about it then. Who is he? I'm assuming it is, in fact, a he?"

"Of course it's a he, mother. What are you suggesting?" Sam felt as if she'd been beamed up into Bizzaro world. Her mother hinting at lesbianism! Sam had always thought that, like Queen Victoria, she refused to acknowledge that these things occurred and would prefer not to know if they did.

"Nothing at all. I was beginning to wonder, that's all."

"Well, his name is Dominic and he works for Finland Air."

"And?"

"And nothing, we're going out for lunch tomorrow. Lunch, Mother, plain and simple, not getting married, not even in a relationship, just lunch."

"What are you going to do? I have a great idea. Why don't you invite him to your house and cook for him? You're not a bad cook when you put your mind to it. It'd be much more intimate."

Sam thought about this and decided that it wasn't a bad idea, but dismissed it, rather than allow her mother to think that she'd managed to influence her. She said, "I'm not really sure what we're doing, but I'll tell you all about it on Sunday, all right?"

"All right, dear, oh, and Sam?"

"Yes."

"A pilot. Your father would have been proud of you." There was a very definite pause in her conversation. "Do be nice to him, won't you? You know how you can get sometimes. Smile a bit and try to flirt just a little and remember –"

"OK, mother, I'm putting the phone down now." Sam

was just about to correct her mother's assumption that pilots were the only people to work for airlines, but there didn't seem to be enough hours in the day to deal with the potential devastation that this knowledge would bring. Sam reflected on her mother's rare reference to her father. Her mother's favourite way of describing him was to say he'd 'passed over to the other side'. This habitually led the listener to offer sympathy. Sam never failed to be amazed at the way her mother could distort a situation to her benefit.

Whilst being factually correct, that phrasing didn't actually convey the whole story. The truth of the matter was that the day after Sam, the youngest sibling, turned eighteen and had legally become an adult, her father went out, seemingly to fetch a newspaper, and disappeared. Two days later, they received a postcard from him declaring his child-raising years (and therefore his obligation to his wife) to be complete and that he was going in search of a new life.

He reappeared, a year later, a completely different person – literally. He answered only to the name Jacqueline and was anatomically correct in every way (!). He left the country a week later to set up a transvestite outfitters in San Francisco called "Queen for a Day", where he specialised in helping those with transgender queries seek out and make-up the woman within. These days he was sharing his household with 'Fat Barry' Sanchez, an extremely hairy Mexican that he'd picked up on his travels. Still, he seemed happy enough.

Shaking her head, Sam went into her spare room to sort out her unpacking. She remembered the new case and went downstairs to get it. She placed the case next to her old one. Deciding that the two cases took up too much space in her tiny spare room, she picked up the new one to put it behind the sofa bed. As she did this, she realised that her new one was much heavier and sturdier than her old one. She tapped the side and it gave out a nice, sturdy thud. She went over to her old one and did the same, but the sound it made was much thinner. Strange, she thought. Maybe it's because one's empty and one's full. She was just about to open her case, when she remembered her little trick with her suit jacket. She lifted up the suitcase and looked for the telltale slip of fabric. It was not there. She dropped her suitcase in shock and stood staring at it for a long time, thinking that if she stared at it long enough, maybe the piece of fabric would magically appear. She wasn't sure what to do next. She'd almost convinced herself that the book incident hadn't happened, but now she had proof that her suitcase had indeed been opened somewhere between check-in at Turku and Manchester. Her mind was racing and she was pacing up and down her room, no mean feat in a room hardly wide enough to swing an average-sized cat. She walked into her office and was just about to pick up her phone to call someone, anyone, when it rang. The shrill sound shocked her and she realised just how jumpy she had become. With her heart pounding, she picked up the phone.

"Hello?"

"Hi, Sam, Dominic here. I just wanted to make sure everything was all right for tomorrow. I wanted to pick you up, but you didn't give me your address. I know I could get it from your file, but I thought that it would be rude."

"What do you mean?" Sam uttered.

"You know the sort of thing. Rooting around your file

equals rooting around your underwear drawer, not that I'd ever dream of doing that, of course. Underwear drawers are absolutely sacred in my opinion, so . . . I don't believe I'm saying this, for goodness sakes. Sam, say something before I jabber myself out of a lunch date."

Sam was still preoccupied by the fact that Dominic had rung at that precise second. He really knew how to pick his moment. Could it possibly be a coincidence? Sam wasn't sure. One thing she was sure of: she should say something or he'd think she was giving a perfect impression of a nutcase. Sam told him her address, but curiously nothing else. They said their goodbyes after arranging for him to be at her house by one o'clock the next day.

She held the phone in her hand long after the call had been disconnected. She sat there deep in thought. Two radically different thoughts were rushing round her head. He was really nervous; somewhere deep inside, a little butterfly popped out of its cocoon and started floating happily around her stomach. The second thought was a strange sense of coincidence. Could it be her subconscious was trying to tell her something? Spooky discovery and Dominic rings. She wasn't sure exactly why she hadn't told him what she had discovered. She only knew that if she was going to tell him anything, it would be face to face, so that she could gauge his reaction. I'll tell him tomorrow, she promised herself. She returned to her unpacking and pondered the weight of her new case. The sides seemed thicker too. At least this one is sturdy enough to withstand regular baggage handling, she thought. It really wasn't like the airlines to be this giving. Usually you had to stamp your foot and scream, just to get noticed. She'd managed to get a pretty decent quality suitcase out of them. I bet it was really expensive, she thought absently.

* * *

Saturday dawned grey and cold and Samantha woke up with a pounding headache. This usually happened when her mind worked too actively during the night and active it had definitely been. She had been tossing and turning all night, unable to relax. At one stage, she woke up after a dream where someone had stolen her suitcase and was holding it to ransom. She had appeared on Newsnight to plead for its safe recovery and had cried on Jeremy's shoulder. After that it had turned into a different type of dream altogether. Sam smirked at the memory, but attempted to concentrate on the matter at hand. It was D-Day and "Operation Date" was to begin.

She focussed her eyes on her bedside clock – it was just after nine o'clock. She pulled herself reluctantly out of bed, knowing that she had less than four hours to make herself presentable. She mentally went through the list of things that needed doing. Wash hair, shave legs (and more importantly, underarms), style hair in sexy manner, choose clothing, match shoes, do make-up, and last, but not least, tidy the house. She should manage it, just about, she mused.

Going to the bathroom, she looked down at the forest of hairs growing on her legs.

The advantage of working in Finland is that for eight months of the year it is so cold you rarely have to go outside without thick thermal leggings and you can get away with hairy legs. Not very sexy, but so liberating. She sighed, regretting the fact that she was too much of a baby to have them waxed. She had tried once, but

114

her pain threshold was so low that she fled the salon after the first rip.

After her shower, she spent almost an hour on her hair and just as long doing her make-up. The overall effect of this two-hour session of activity was that her hair looked sexily tousled, as if she'd just got out of bed and her face looked as if she barely had make-up on. Not for the first time she realised the irony and wished that she actually did look this good getting out of bed with no make-up on. Men have no idea, she thought.

She spent the next hour trying on different outfits, almost discarding her entire, and sizeable, collection of clothing before settling on the first outfit, a green silk dress with a low-cut bodice. She stood in front of the mirror and observed her cleavage. Who needs one of those push-the-boobs-together bras? she thought. This is what you call real cleavage.

Realising she had less than half an hour to tidy the house, she went downstairs to examine the work required. As she laid eyes on the state of her living-room, she remarked to herself that it looked more like a "lived-in" room and made a mental note to hire a cleaner as soon as humanly possible.

The problem with her job is that in the week between her visits to Finland, she is usually too tired to do the housework, so her carpet often goes a good few months between vacuumings. The last time she took the vacuum cleaner out of its cupboard, it took one look at the messy carpet and stopped working, presumably in terror. She was forced to calm it down, with the promise that she would pick up all the big bits and paperclips, before it would function.

She decided that the only thing to do was to rush outside as soon as she saw Dominic arriving and not let him anywhere near the inside of her house. This settled, she made herself a pot of coffee and heated up some croissants for breakfast.

It seemed like she'd only been sitting down for a few minutes when she saw a silver Audi A4 pull up outside her house. She rushed to the door, setting her house alarm on the way out. As she walked towards him with her most alluring smile plastered on her lips, she noticed that his eyes were firmly focussed on her cleavage. I know I'm proud of my boobs but this is ridiculous, she thought.

Dominic quickly removed himself from behind the wheel and rushed around to open her door for her; unfortunately, by the time he arrived, Sam had already got in and made herself comfortable in the passenger seat. Dominic, looking rather silly, made his way back round to the driving seat.

"Well, hello there," Dominic said to Sam's breasts.

"Erm . . . hello, I'm up here." Sam waved her hands frantically and pointed to her head.

"I know," said Dominic, his eyes fixed, "it's just that . . ." he dragged his eyes away and looked into her eyes.

"What? Never seen a pair of breasts before?"

"It's not exactly that. It's just that . . . um . . ." He leaned towards her and reached into her cleavage. Sam was just about to slap him viciously across the face when she focussed on the thing he'd just removed from her breast area. It was a rather large piece of croissant, which had got itself lodged there. Sam looked at it horrified, turned a rather dazzling fiery mahogany colour and then burst out laughing. Dominic, too, began to laugh. Together they guffawed for a few minutes until Dominic leant over and kissed her on the cheek.

"I wonder what else is down there? Some loose change perhaps?" he said and started his car.

* * *

"So what happened next," Alex said breathlessly over the phone. "Did you let him have a look?"

"Of course not! Inside I was mortified. Then we went to Oxygene like we agreed and he ordered the tomato and Parmesan salad and I had the spicy houmous."

"Sam, you know exactly what I mean. Don't make me ask twice," Alex warned.

"All right, do you want the good news or the bad news?"

"Give me the good news then – I could do with some."

Sam detected a slight edge to Alex's voice and made a mental note to interrogate her afterwards. "Well, he was wonderful."

"So what was the bad news then?"

"Well, the bad news is that he was wonderful."

"How can that be bad news?"

"It's bad news, because he's perfect. He's funny, charming, intelligent and gorgeous . . . "

"Poor you," Alex snorted, "you never did know when you were well off. Remember back in college when you dumped 'thingy' because every girl in college wanted to go out with him?"

"That wasn't the reason at all and well you know it and don't change the subject."

"I've not changed the subject. We're talking about

117

Samantha Jordan and her extremely high expectations, aren't we? If you're not happy with my interpretation, you explain properly what you mean."

"What I mean, Alex Spencer, is that he's just perfect for settling down with. I could really see myself falling for him in a big way, but . . . "

"But what? It sounds to me like you're already halfway there anyway. You might as well go the whole hog."

"I'm not sure that this is the best thing for me at the moment. You should have heard him talking about his nephews – he really loves kids."

"So?"

"So, you know I don't want the whole 'Family/Kids' thing at the moment."

"Who's going too far ahead now? Repeat after me, Samantha: One day at a time. I will not force the issue. I will let things take their course. Go on, say it for me!"

"Yes, very funny, Alexandra. You know what I mean though – I'm not sure that I'm ready."

"Not ready for what? A relationship? It's been over two years since You-know-who. You should get out there!"

"I am getting out there, I'm in the marketplace. I just don't know if I want to buy yet and this has nothing to do with You-know-who. I'm just in a place right now where I'm happy with my life and happy with me. I'm not sure I want to go back into a relationship thing."

"OK, OK, but did you snog him?"

"Of course."

"And . . . ? For goodness sakes! Blood . . . stone . . . the extraction of." Sarcasm swelled in Alex's voice.

"And . . . it was nice, very nice indeed."

"More info, please!"

"There's nothing more to tell."

"Sam!" Alex's voice was heavy with rebuke.

"Well, he was telling me about his childhood. He was born in Cyprus, where his father was based. They were an RAF family picking up sticks and moving every six years as his father moved up the ranks. He was talking about how that lifestyle teaches you not to get attached to anything or anyone. Then he looked at me with those eyes of his and said that he could get attached to me."

"Yeah yeah, get to the snogging."

"I am. You're the one who wanted more information."

"Sorry. Carry on."

"Well, I leant forward and he leant forward. He cupped my face in his hands and planted the most delicate kiss on my mouth. I nearly fainted, but I pulled myself together and . . . "

"And what?" Sam could feel Alex leaning into the phone.

"And . . . I grabbed the back of his head, pulled him really close and gave him one of my 'Frenchie specials'."

"God, you are so romantic." Alex's voice was submerged under a ton of sarcasm.

"Well, what do you expect? Listen to yourself. Anyone would think you'd never had a snog before. Or is it that Duncan is neglecting his boyfriendly duties?"

"Yeah, well, less said about him the better." Alex sighed. "So, when are you seeing him again?"

"Well, I'm not sure. I told him about my bag though."

"What did he say?"

"I see."

"You see what?"

"No, that's what he said. He said, 'I see'."

"Is that it?"

"Yes, but at least, I now know that he had nothing to do with it."

"How?"

"Because he looked really surprised – he looked me in the eyes –"

"As opposed to your breasts," Alex chuckled.

"Behave, Lexi. This bit isn't funny."

"Sorry, carry on."

"He asked me to trust him and said that he'll need to go to the London office to check a few things – he promised to call me."

"Hmm," Alex hesitated.

"What?"

"Nothing."

"No, you obviously have something to say, so say it," Sam tutted irritably.

"Well, no, it doesn't matter."

"ALEX!"

"All right, it's just . . . is that it? Trust him?"

"Yes, but you should have seen his face. He seemed completely different just for a split second. Then he spilt his wine over the tablecloth."

"He's so clumsy!"

"Yes, well, sometimes he is and sometimes he seems like the most precise person in the world. I mean, I think he does it on purpose. Like changing the subject, but without actually having to change subjects. It's difficult to remember where you were when you've had a break of ten minutes while the tablecloth is being changed."

"I have another problem with this Dominic as well."

"What now?"

"How can he afford a brand new A4?"

"I don't know if it's brand new."

"They've not been making them for long, so it's as close to brand new as you could probably get."

"Your point?" Sam was getting fractious. Damn Alex and her suspicions! She was always throwing cold water over her warm fuzzy feelings about Dominic. If Sam didn't know better she could have easily believed that she was jealous.

"Well, what's he making as an assistant customer service representative – about sixteen thousand, maximum eighteen?"

"Probably around that, I guess."

"Even if we're talking bottom of the range, there's no way a guy on his salary could afford one."

"And just how long have you been Jeremy Clarkson's long-lost twin? You don't even know the difference between a Polo and a Golf."

"I do too. One's a mint and the other's a game."

"Ha ha. Where's this knowledge coming from then?"

"Duncan's been boring me senseless about his new company car. His nose was out of joint because Justin, from US Trading, has a top of the range A4 and Duncan's only allowed a mid-range model and you know how much he gets."

"Maybe Dominic has family money?"

"Maybe, but it doesn't add up to me."

Sam had had enough of the in-depth scrutiny of Dominic's finances and changed the subject. "Speaking of Duncan, how are things with you?"

"Now who's changing the subject?"

"Well?"

"I don't know. I think Duncan is going off me."

Sam rolled her eyes and said, "Lexi, you're imagining it. You always do."

"No, not this time. He's been spending more time at his flat."

"So?"

"So, a month ago, he was here every night, now we see each other once, twice a week. He says he's busy at work."

"Well, it is getting close to bonus time – they do tend to work harder when there's a bonus on the way, don't they?"

"Yes, but it's different. I can't explain it . . . "

"Look, Alex, stop worrying. You're gorgeous and he'd be stupid if he let you get away."

"Well, I'm not exactly going out with him for his brains."

"Touché." Sam gave a wry smile. "Listen, just stop worrying and enjoy being with him when he's there. OK?"

"All right." Alex sounded unconvinced. "I'll call you tomorrow."

"Bye, honey."

"Bye."

Sam hung up the phone and decided that she'd try to change her ticket, so that she could return to London rather than Manchester. By her reckoning, she might be required there in about two weeks' time.

Ever since Sam and Alex first met, they'd been there for each other. Neither of them could imagine not having the other as a friend. Despite living in different parts of the country, or even different countries, they'd always managed to maintain contact, usually through ridiculously long phone calls. They each knew that the other was only a journey away – a journey that they would gladly undertake whenever and wherever they were needed, regardless of distance, regardless of commitments. Once, they attempted to save money on phone calls by living together. But what with Sam's lack of housekeeping prowess and Alex's scrupulously tidy obsessiveness, they managed to drive each other loopy by the end of the second week. They were forced to admit that, for the benefit of their friendship, they should maintain a certain distance. It was better that way.

Sam just didn't understand Alex sometimes. Alex was stunning to look at: tall, blonde and elegant, with piercing violet eyes. She was the sweetest, most generous person that Sam had ever known, and could often get right to the heart of all Sam's problems. Unfortunately when it came to her own life, her confidence was so low that you couldn't even limbo under it. Sam shook her head sadly and went off to look for her *Sleepless in Seattle* video.

* * *

Sam was at a loose end. She had done her unpacking the night before, so she couldn't use that to occupy her time. She had nothing more in her dirty-clothes-basket to wash and she'd be damned if she was going to do any ironing. After all, things weren't that bad yet, were they? She'd spent half an hour looking up the correct spelling of 'procrastination' in her dictionary and then translating it into French and German. She knew that she had lots of work to do for Mark, but the thought of that made her cringe. She had a great idea.

"Saari."

"Hei, Martti! Mita kuuluu?"

"I'm fine, Samantha. This must be bad news."

123

"Why?"

"You speak Finnish. You always try to – how do you say – coat me in butter when you speak Finnish."

"Coat you in butter?"

"It is English saying, is it not?"

"You mean 'butter me up', I think."

"Yes, that right, you try to butter me up when you speak words in Finnish."

"Not at all. I'm wondering about the invoicing for Fintec – how many days do I have?"

"Fintec? Let me see. We have booking for five days more."

"Well, look, I have quite a bit of information that I'm going to have to get for him. I may have to use probably three of those days working over here." She smiled – a cunning plan! That meant three days less that she'd have to be in his company and there would be hardly any point in flying her over for just two days' work. She could probably do those over the phone and –

"Oh no, Markku, he specify. He want definitely you visit. He willing to invoice separately any days you use in UK."

Damn, she thought, as she said goodbye to her boss.

"That's so typical of the luck I've been having lately," she grumbled and felt a black cloud gathering a few of its even blacker cloud friends for a rain party over her head.

Thinking of her bad luck reminded her of why she was so down. Why hadn't Dominic rung? He said he'd ring her. Why do men always do that? She absolutely and very definitely wasn't going to check her phone to make sure it was working. And she'd only checked her answerphone half an hour ago when she'd come in from the back garden

124

having hung up some clothes to dry. She'd not been out of earshot of the phone since then. In fact, she took the cordless phone from her pocket to check that she hadn't pressed the 'on' button by mistake. If it wasn't going to ring, she'd call someone. The chances were that as soon as she was in a decent discussion the call waiting would beep.

"Corporate Finance."

"Hi, Lexi!"

"Sam, will you stop ringing me every five minutes. I've already told you that I've got to get this presentation finished before three o'clock."

"Sorry, Lexi, I forgot."

"Do some washing or something. Please?"

"Fantastic idea, I hadn't thought of that. Thanks," Sam said sarcastically.

"My pleasure. Now go away and don't even think of dialling this number unless you're covered in blood and dying, and even then, think before you do!"

"Fine, just remember that your best friend status is now officially under review."

"Yeah, yeah, bye."

Oh well, there was nothing for it.

* * *

She'd just started ironing her second pile of washing when the phone rang. The only problem was, she couldn't find the phone. She walked around the room, trying to discover where the sound was coming from.

"Hello," she said, eventually finding it snuggled between a quilt cover and her Gap khakis.

"Hi, Sam – Dominic."

125

"Dominic, hi." It was about bloody time he rang, she thought. She was determined to act really cool and play hard to get.

"I've just got back from London, do you fancy grabbing a bite to eat?"

"Sure, where?" Oh, great one, Sam – that resistance lasted all of three seconds! She kicked herself.

"Somewhere in town?"

"Rose and Crown, off Deansgate. They have nice meals and the most scampi in the whole of Manchester."

"What's the lasagne like?"

Sam was taken aback. Small world – she made a mental note to tell Alex. "I have it on good authority that it's cheesy, but not too stodgy."

"Shall I meet you there or pick you up?"

"I'll meet you there in about an hour. My treat this time, though."

"Great."

She switched off the iron and went in search of a nonchalant, casual, but not too casual, outfit.

* * *

Dressed in a lilac T-shirt and Gap khakis, she let herself into her little Peugeot 306 and drove into Manchester city centre.

Sam lived in the prestigious Salford Quays area of Manchester. She'd managed to buy one of the very few houses that were renovated in the old Dockland area. She had a great view of the Manchester ship canal and was in very close proximity to the new Lowry Centre. Her neighbourhood had a nice, casual feel to it and really came into its own in the summer with the sun glistening on the water at the quayside. Drives into the town centre were usually long even though it was only a few miles. Manchester hadn't quite the traffic problems of say, London or New York, but it was getting close.

She was quite early, but she was glad of it as it would be a great opportunity to observe him, while he searched for her in the pub. She scouted out the perfect table – out of sight of the entrance, but with a good view of it from the table via a mirror. Although there weren't that many people in the pub, she staked her claim to the table by draping her jacket over the seats. She decided to be totally presumptuous and order the food while she was waiting. She didn't have to wait long. Exactly five minutes before their agreed meeting time, Dominic strode through the door. He was still in his Finland Air uniform, but even that could not disguise his sheer magnificence. Anyway, a uniform was a uniform and he really did look dashing, like some matinee idol. He moved with an almost nonchalant confidence. Both males and females followed his progress through the room, the men staring out of jealousy, the women out of pure lust. Sam couldn't believe that such a perfect specimen of manhood was there to meet her. She was in danger of swooning. She felt stupid. Modern women didn't swoon. Nineteenth century romantic heroines did. Surely it had disappeared along with corsets and hooped skirts?

Dominic finally spotted her and made a drinking gesture with his hand. Sam nodded and he turned back to the bar. After a small altercation about whose turn it was to be served, he joined her at the table, a pint of lager in one hand and white wine spritzer in the other. He'd remembered her drink of choice! Oh heaven, she thought. Of course, the white wine spritzer was her drink of choice while out trying to impress gorgeous men. When she was out with Alex, it was more or less exclusively vodka.

He leant forward to kiss her. Sam could almost feel the piercing looks of all the envious women in the bar, stabbing her in the back.

"It's good to see you," Dominic gave a shy smile. "This place is great. I didn't think any of these old-style pubs were left. If this was London, it'd be an Irish theme pub by now. You know, with faux aged wallpaper and green leather."

"Yeah, I know what you mean, Guinness on tap and your obligatory old wizened man sitting at the bar, mumbling into his drink!"

"Exactly," Dominic grinned.

"I love it here. Joe the landlord is a Cockney, like us. In fact we were all born in the same hospital in Bow." She smiled, "I hope you don't mind, but I've already put a food order in – yours was the lasagne, right?"

"Yes, and I don't mind at all. Thank you." He picked up his pint and took a very thirsty slug.

Sam was surprised to see that his hand shook as he lifted his glass. He was nervous! It was almost as if he really had no idea how gorgeous he was. Surely no man could get to his age and be totally impervious to the fact that they make Michelangelo's David look like an ugly dwarf. Sam had to pinch herself to make sure she wasn't dreaming.

"How was London?" she finally managed to ask.

"Very informative. I did a bit of digging while I was there. There's nothing too untoward. It must have just been a faulty conveyor belt at Manchester. Remember I told you that your bag fell off the belt."

"I remember, but . . ." Sam was going to ask about the

book moving and the jacket having moved as well – surely slight falls couldn't have caused those two occurrences – but something stopped her. Something told her to leave things as they were. At least until they got to know each other a little better. Dominic didn't seem too worried about it, so neither should she. It just seemed a whole lot easier to simply accept his explanation.

Their meals arrived and before she knew what was happening all tension left her body. In fact, she hadn't even realised that there was any tension until it started to ease off and she relaxed into the heady feeling brought on by lunching with an extremely good-looking man.

"How's the lasagne?" she enquired politely.

"Very cheesy and not at all stodgy. Your source was spot on. How's the scampi?"

"Plentiful, as always." Sam turned and raised her glass in the general direction of Joe and mouthed 'Fab'. Dominic simply looked confused.

"Am I missing something?"

"No, it's a private joke thing." Sam smiled over at him.

"I've been meaning to ask you – what made you become a management consultant?"

"I don't know. I didn't want to do your average nine-to five-job, I suppose. I started off as a trainer and somehow I was headhunted. Next thing I knew I was in California, training to be a consultant."

"It's not often someone drifts into consultancy."

"I guess not. I think it's the bossy, controlling side of me. Mark would call it anal."

"Who?"

"No one. A client." In one second, Mark had been

dismissed and forgotten about once more. "I like telling people what to do and seeing companies turn around. I get such a rush seeing a company thrive and being able to say, 'I did that'. What about you? Did you grow up wanting to help people keep their luggage?"

He laughed, "No, I wanted to be *Action Man*."

"What? Plastic and severely lacking in the lunchbox department?"

"No, more like being a pilot one day and soldier the next. You know the sort of thing."

"So what happened?" she asked, looking pointedly at his Finland Air uniform.

"Real life, I guess. Things are never as they seem. I'd have probably been a crap pilot."

"What about a sold –"

Reaching for his beer, Dominic somehow managed to knock over Sam's glass, spilling her spritzer all over the remains of her scampi. She jumped up, to stop the drink from soiling her trousers. Unfortunately, she was too late and a dark green stain was spreading down her right leg. To his credit, Dominic swung into action. He mopped up the liquid from the table, then grabbed some spare serviettes from the next table and rushed round to help her in her attempts to soak up the spritzer from her trousers.

"Let me!" He began wiping with his handful of serviettes.

Sam attempted to concentrate on the spillage, but found her mind filling with thoughts of his hands on her leg, starting at her knee and rising steadily up to her thigh, achingly close to her . . .

She made a squeaking coughing sound in an attempt to gather together all her resources. "Erm . . . I think I can manage now." She pushed him away in a you-can-go-and-sit-down-again-now kind of way.

He stepped back but still hovered round her. "Sam, I'm really sorry. I don't know what came over me!"

I know what came over me, she grinned inwardly, but managed to say, "Don't worry, it was an accident. It'll dry in its own time."

He raised a hand to call a waitress over to deal with the mess on the table. He looked at Sam shamefacedly. "Sometimes, I'm really clumsy, I . . ." He stopped, obviously not knowing how to explain it.

"Clumsy? You don't say."

His face showed he thought she was being serious.

"Dominic, chill. I'm joking."

"Oh." He still managed to look stricken.

"You know, next time we go out, I'm going to have to wear something waterproof."

"So there will be a next time?"

"Only if I can find something in PVC perhaps, or maybe rubber," Sam jibed.

"Is that a promise?" Dominic smiled, raising his eyebrows suggestively.

"I didn't mean it that way, you perve!" She giggled at his attempted leer.

He slipped an arm around her, pulling her close and putting his lips to her ear. Sam's entire being shivered with pleasure as his breath caressed her earlobe. "I'm getting a rush, just imagining that picture," he whispered.

He pulled her tightly against him and Sam was in no doubt whatsoever which part of him had felt the rush.

* * *

"Getting a rush just imagining that picture?" Alex's voice dripped scorn. "That doesn't even make sense – how corny! Pass the bucket, please."

"Well, I thought it was lovely. Really sexy. I had to hold on to him, just to stay on my feet. I guess you had to be there." Sam shrugged.

"Don't tell me you fell for it? Please don't say that you bonked him because he came up with that rubbish."

"I'm surprised at you, Alex – you're usually the one that says I'm too jaded and cynical."

"I'm not being cynical." Alex tutted. "'I'm getting a rush' – my arse."

"Alex! What the hell has got into you?"

"Nothing at all. So?"

"So what?"

"Did you bonk him?"

"No."

"You wanted to though, didn't you?"

"Maybe."

"So what went wrong? Did Action Man not have the requisite parts? Did he turn you down?"

"As far as I could tell, his parts were more than 'requisite', if you get what I mean!"

"So?"

"So his mobile went and he had to go."

"Went off to play pilot, did he?"

"Ha, bloody ha, you're even worse than my mother. No, there was a problem with the afternoon flight, or something."

"When are you seeing him again?"

"Probably tomorrow – I'm cooking a meal."

"Three dates in under a week? What are you cooking? Chinese?"

"No, I think I'll do Mexican."

"Mexican eh? Getting out the heavy artillery?"

"It's just a meal."

"I don't know about that."

"I do," Sam insisted.

"Three dates? Ladies and gentlemen, I think we have the beginning of a full-blown relationship. A round of applause for Sam and her boyfriend Dominic!"

Sam was taken aback by Alex's description of Dominic as her 'boyfriend'. She'd not really thought about it in those terms, but yes, she supposed he must be her boyfriend. After the call, she tried the thought out for size: 'Hello, mother, meet Dominic, my boyfriend' or 'Of course, my husband Dominic and I would love to come'.

"Hmm . . ." she mused. Suddenly she realised what she'd been doing. She must have been having a funny turn, because she'd been practising her signature as Mrs Samantha Stewart. "Next I'll be shopping for houses and looking up kids' names," Sam said in disgust, going off to the newsagent's for a copy of Country Life.

Chapter Eight

Sam was on her way back to Sainsbury's.

That morning, she had been strangely buoyant when she awoke. She'd decided that she would be cooking chicken enchiladas with an assortment of dips, tortilla chips and a healthy portion of refried beans. In her ever-efficient way, she'd written out a detailed shopping list and a timed cooking plan which told her when to start preparing and cooking the individual elements.

Sam loved cooking. At least, she loved cooking for special occasions. Everyday cooking was boring, but give her a sniff of a birthday or other celebration and she was baking cakes in the shape of penises and making a spread large enough to feed a moderately sized army.

Sam liked to cook with a precision more reminiscent of a huge military operation than a simple putting together of ingredients. She often had little bowls of chopped and sliced things lined up on her counter like little soldiers, just so she could cook à la Blue Peter. Sometimes, when no one was looking, she would even give a running commentary as if she were one of the presenters. Unfortunately, in her kitchen there were no 'here's-one-I-made-earlier's.

Upon the occasion of Dominic coming round for a romantic candlelit dinner, she really pushed the boat out. Her most impressive type of cuisine was Mexican. All her friends told her that her guacamole dip was to-die-for, not to mention her home-made tortillas. She hoped they would weave their magic for Dominic – she wanted him to be not just impressed, but über-impressed.

She spent the previous day making her house as tidy as it had no right being and polished the windows so that you could actually see out of them. She even nipped to IKEA to buy the perfect matching tablecloth, apron and candles. Overall she was pretty surprised with herself.

With her shopping list in hand, she'd driven to Sainsbury's. She'd been all the way around, queued up and paid for her shopping, when, on the way home she'd realised that she'd forgotten one very important ingredient for chicken enchiladas: the chicken. Hence her return to the supermarket. She might cook like it was a military exercise, but she shopped like an episode of *The Three Stooges*.

"I'd forget my bloody head, if it weren't halfway up my bum already," she muttered, getting out of her car. This time, she was without a list and, with only the thought 'must get chicken' running around her head, she entered the revolving doors of the supermarket.

Juggling with five bags of shopping and over thirty-four pounds fifty lighter in her purse, she struggled back to her car, cursing the fact that she was a complete sucker for a shiny BOGOF (buy one get one free) sign or a 'special offer' flash. She'd even bought some dog food, because it was reduced and on BOGOF offer. Sod the fact that she didn't even have a dog. She didn't even know anyone with a dog. Once more she accepted the fact that she was useless and should never again be let loose in a supermarket without a shopping list. Either that or she should stop cooking, thus removing the requirement for ingredients.

* * *

Much later that evening, Sam opened up a bottle of wine and surveyed her kitchen. All saucepans were in their places on the stove, simmering nicely. The enchiladas were baking in the oven and her salsa was spiced enough, maybe not to blow his socks off, but to firmly encourage their removal. Time for her to get ready – by her calculations she had exactly thirty-three minutes to get herself looking as sexy as a siren.

Tonight was definitely the night. Her lack of libidinous activity was definitely over from this day forward. She'd show that Alex with all her theories! She once more thought about the remote possibility that Alex might be right – maybe she had been choosing relationships that were doomed from the start. Maybe that was why it was important to steer clear of Mark and break the cycle. Dominic would serve the purpose nicely. Killing two birds with one stone, so to speak. It'd prove to her meddling friend that she was ready for a real relationship and she'd be able to release some of the pent-up lust which had been raging through her body for the past few weeks. And a Greek god wasn't a bad place to start. Whether Dominic liked it or not, she was going to get her fair share of action.

She'd received an anonymous gift of a family-sized (how ironic) box of strawberry-flavoured condoms through the post that morning. Unsurprisingly they were posted from Paddington, where (not so) coincidentally, Alex resided. She was determined that she was going to make use of as many of them as humanly possible and judging by her memory of Dominic's physique, she had no doubt it would be a fabulous experience.

* * *

Dominic leant back in his seat. "That was incredible."

"I'm glad you liked it."

"I can't remember when I tasted enchiladas that good."

Sam beamed, her grin spreading the entire width of her face. She'd not told him that they were enchiladas and most people couldn't tell an enchilada from a burrito. "I got the recipe from a Mexican chef I met in Texas. He even showed me how to cook them."

"Well, he taught you very well indeed."

"You sound like Darth Vader." Sam giggled, maybe she'd drunk just a tad too much wine.

"What? D'you mean, 'Obi-wan taught you well, Luke' – that sort of thing?"

"Yeah, maybe you'll show me your light-sabre later?" Sam flirted.

"Only if you're a very bad girl indeed." He smiled lasciviously and leaned forward to kiss her delicately on the lips.

At that precise second a loud beep sounded in her kitchen, completely ruining the mood. "Damn, that's the coffee machine. Sorry."

"No, I'd love one."

"Would you like dessert first or coffee?" Sam was annoyed – one minute she was the object of his desire and the next she was starting to sound like a stewardess.

"Dessert sounds good. What do we have?"

"Raspberry pavlova?" Sam asked hopefully. "It's not home-made though."

"I think I might be able to manage a little slice."

Sam immediately got up and was moving towards the kitchen when he reached out and caught her around the waist.

"Have I told you how absolutely delicious you look tonight?" he said quietly. "Maybe I should taste you?"

With that he pulled her down onto his lap and started to caress her neck gently, his kisses lingering on her shoulders and the top of her breast. After what felt like an age to Sam, his lips found hers and they kissed. Sam's heart stopped. She was glad that she was sitting down, because she would have collapsed with pleasure.

"Erm . . ." Sam's Subconscious gave a polite cough inside her mind, "Consciousness? Hello? Are you there?"

"Go. Away," her Conscious Mind said firmly.

"I would . . . only . . . erm . . . well, the lungs have requested that she breathe as they're having a bit of a job keeping her alive without oxygen."

"Will I ever get some peace around here to enjoy anything?"

Finally, Sam broke the kiss and breathed deeply.

"Bloody heaven. I'm in bloody heaven," she repeated over and over in her mind.

* * *

"'Have I told you how absolutely delicious you look tonight? Maybe I should taste you?'" Alex voice betrayed the fact that she couldn't believe her ears. "Where the hell does he get these lines from? Seventies porn films?"

"Admit it, Lexi. You're jealous!"

"Give me Duncan and his, 'Why-ay, Pet, wanna shag, like?' any day over your Dominic."

"How do you know? I bet even you'd have ripples of lust flowing through your body if you ever met him."

"Ripples of lust? Can you listen to yourself?" Alex sounded incredulous. "Are you applying for a job with Mills and Boon?"

"As I said, the little green jealousy monster is visiting, obviously!"

"Ripples of lust, my arse," Alex mocked. "So what was he like?"

Sam muttered something under her breath.

"I didn't quite catch that, Sam – did you say something about 'snow'?"

"No, I said I don't know. We didn't do it."

Alex started laughing hysterically, "You didn't?"

"No, we got as far as the sofa . . . Alex, stop bloody laughing."

"Sorry." She tried to smother her laughter.

"We got as far as the sofa – I was this close to getting his trousers off and his mobile phone rang."

"Did you . . . hehehehe . . . did you say 'let it ring' by any chance? Hahahaha . . . "

"Bitch!" Sam was beginning to smile.

"Come on, Sam! Surely you can see the funny side of it?"

"Not at this moment in time, I can't," she said with the emergence of a giggle belying her words.

"So, I bet Mr Sex-god had to leave."

"Strangely enough, yes. He had to go."

"And you had to take a cold shower," Alex eventually managed to utter through her hysterical cackling.

"You guessed it."

This was too much for Sam also and together they did a fairly passable impression of two witches overdosing on laughter potion.

Chapter Nine

Sam's life at home, in her weeks between trips to Finland, usually consisted of the same routine. Contrary to the opinion of all those who surveyed her life from afar, Sam actually liked routine. It was just that, due to an absurd twist of fate, she ended up in a job that could not actually be described as such. In a parallel universe, she was probably working in a bank with a doting husband and four perfect kids, thinking enviously about her friend Alex's glamorous life, jetting around the world. And therein lay the actual problem. From afar, Sam's life looked glamorous: flying around Scandinavia and continental Europe, with the odd trip here and there into Russia; jetting into companies, shaping their fortunes, then jetting home again. When it was put like that, Sam actually liked the sound of her job. Unfortunately, the reality was different: spending long hours waiting around in airports; living, literally, out of a suitcase, and that's only if you were lucky enough to get your suitcase in the first place; eating hotel food, commonly agreed to be the worst in the world, regardless of the country you happened to be in; having to watch stuff on television that you would normally refuse to watch, even if someone put a gun to your head, merely for the fact that it was in English. The truth of the matter was that this was Sam's reality and often, it was, to put it delicately, crap.

At dinner parties, people were always fascinated by the fact that Sam worked in Finland. They often looked upon Finland as a romantic, snow-covered, idyllic place full of galloping reindeer and Father Christmas. And so it was, the first time Sam visited there. Now, whenever asked, Sam generally gave the same answer: 'It's bloody cold – don't go there in winter if you can help it, unless you like freezing your bits off or you have a penchant for wearing so many clothes that you look like a Michelin man.'

When pushed, she could usually manage to shut people up by explaining that Finnish people like nothing better than to strip naked, sit in 100°C heat for a bit, then rush outside into -30°C temperatures and jump into a hole cut into the ice-covered surface of a lake, just for the fun of it. Apparently, it was good for the circulation. Sam was then usually asked if it was, indeed, good for the circulation, to which she replied 'It's good for catching a stinking cold, so don't do it'. At which point, they would normally nod in a strange manner, turn to their other neighbour and discuss the weather.

Sam likes her little 'home routine'. Usually she wakes late, around ten thirty, and after a little pottering in her bathroom, she goes downstairs to her kitchen to start her daily breakfast ritual: oven on, croissants in, fridge open, orange juice out, coffee machine on. Sam takes her liquid refreshment of a morning seriously. The orange juice has to be freshly squeezed – none of that 'made from concentrate' rubbish – and it had to be so full of juicy bits that you could almost chew it.

As for the coffee, she only drinks the proper stuff made from beans, which she grinds herself. In fact the easiest way to alienate her is to offer her instant. Being a creature of habit, she still drinks the same coffee that she drank in Germany when she was a student. Unfortunately, the coffee is obtainable there only. Whenever she's close to running out, she takes a weekend trip, ostensibly to visit friends, but in reality, it's for her to stock up. The words, 'we really should catch up' translates from Samspeak as 'I'm running out of whatever product is available in your area. You will be soon receiving a visit'.

After the breakfast preparations, she then takes the tray up to her office and checks on her computer for e-mails. The next few hours are spent responding to these, before she begins her preparation work for her next trip to Finland. Usually she works until about 7.30pm, at which time she settles in front of the television for a bit of box-watching.

* * *

On this particular Friday, she was woken up at nine by the telephone.

"Ms Jordan, Anne Mansfield here."

"Ugh, ergh, ugh." Sam was never very good at early mornings. She cleared her throat and tried again. "Sorry about that. Can I help you?"

"Well, I was hoping to help you with your little ticket problem, but unfortunately, we are unable to change your return destination – for two reasons really."

"Uh-huh," Sam croaked.

"Yes, firstly, the change will cost your company an additional £350 at the very least. Pirjo didn't really like the sound of that, but she said that she would be happy to discuss it with you." She paused. "Are you still there?"

"Uh-yes," said Sam.

Anne continued, "Secondly, we have been trying hard to help you and we have gone to rather a lot of trouble helping you avoid Heathrow, so sending you there would simply defeat the object."

"I see." Sam had lost the will to fight, but Anne gave her a lifeline.

"What we can do, however, is give you a complimentary Manchester to London flight the next day. How does that sound?"

Sam perked up. "Sounds great actually, thanks."

"Good. I'll sort that out for you."

"Thank you."

"Bye now, Ms Jordan."

"Bye."

* * *

It was Saturday and Sam was in a bad mood. She couldn't quite put her finger on why, but she knew in the back of her mind that she really wasn't going to get much of anything done that day.

The day dragged on until the early afternoon when her phone rang once more.

"Hello?"

"Hello, Sammy, Mummy said I naughty, I not naughty. Sammy nice."

"Chelsea, is that you?"

"Mummy shouting, Sammy no shouting. Phone Sammy."

"Chelsea, is Mummy there?"

"Mummy stairs Nanny, wee-wee now."

"Chelsea, can I speak to Mummy?"

"Sammy, I go wee-wee." The phone was unceremoniously dumped on the floor and Sam surmised that Chelsea had gone off to the bathroom. She called out for a little while, but soon realised that her sister, Michelle, probably had no idea that Chelsea had been using the phone. Chelsea had only recently learnt that the blue button on the square thingy in the living-room makes Auntie Sammy's voice magically appear and the red button makes Granny Jordan's voice appear, but the red one asks too many questions, so she'd been ringing Sam on a regular basis. Usually she wanted to complain about life not being fair or to ask Sam if she could 'tell Mummy not to shout at her', although sometimes she rang simply to enquire if Sam had seen 'Tinky-Winky' because she was having trouble locating him.

Sam detected signs of movement on the other end of the phone. She heard her sister come downstairs and she heard her mother's voice in the background telling her that all young children go through a bad patch and she and Sam were the same if not worse.

"You can always buy some new perfume," her mother said soothingly.

"I know, but it was that expensive stuff Sam brought from France," Michelle complained. "I suppose I could get her to buy some more – after all, she can afford it. Anyway, it's not as if she's got anyone else to buy stuff for."

"Think of it this way, your toilet will smell wonderful for days," her mother chirped.

"So, tell me, what has Sam been doing this time?"

On the phone, Sam's ears pricked up at the opportunity to eavesdrop on her family's discussions about her.

"Not much really, apart from the fact that she's found a man friend."

"NO!" Michelle exclaimed. "I don't believe you. He's probably an ugly git, though!"

"I wouldn't know about that. She's only told me that his name's Douglas, no, that's not it, David, no . . . Derek . . . it begins with D anyway. She seems quite smitten."

Sam fumed at Michelle's 'ugly' remark. So this was what they talked about when she wasn't around. She decided to put a stop to the discussion and shouted down the phone.

"Can you hear something?" asked Michelle suddenly. "How did that get there?" Sam heard the phone being picked up.

"Actually, it's DOMINIC!" she screeched.

"Sam? Is that you? How . . . ? Hold on, Sam – CHELSEA!"

Sam waited while her sister screamed for her child.

"How many times have I told you? The phone is not a toy. Please don't touch it again!"

"Sorry, Mummy," Chelsea apologised unconvincingly.

"Sam, what were you on about?"

"His name is Dominic."

"Dominic, eh? You old slapper! So what does he do?"

"He works for the airline."

"Sleeping with the enemy, eh?" her sister said lasciviously. "That's the best way to keep them sweet, I suppose."

"Not quite."

"So when do we get to meet this famous Dominic? Is he tasty then?"

"You are so crass, Michelle. Look, I'm going to go now," Sam sighed. Her family always had the ability to wear her out in a matter of minutes.

"All right, you old cow, but we'd better meet him soon or we might decide to surprise you with a visit."

Sam didn't have the energy to argue that she'd only known him for a few days and it probably wasn't going anywhere, because he still hadn't rung her. He'd probably gone off her by now anyway. So instead she challenged Michelle's last comment. "You'd better not. That's the only reason I moved to Manchester. Too far to come for a day-trip."

"Now, now, you don't mean that."

"Oh, don't I?"

"Listen, Sam. I'm your only sister and I know you love and adore me. Nothing you could possibly say would make me think any different."

"Yeah, you always were as thick as two short planks. Thinking's a difficult process!"

"So," Michelle went on, totally ignoring Sam's barb, "I'll expect you to turn up here with lover-boy in tow. So when will it be? Tomorrow? Next week? Soon?"

"All right, soon, I promise and by the way, I'll buy you some new perfume."

Sam left her sister wondering exactly how much of the conversation she had heard.

* * *

Sam had reread the page on her computer screen for the fifteenth time when her phone rang.

With a sigh, she picked up the receiver. "Hello?"

"Sam, hi, it's Dominic."

"I know who it is," she said frostily. "I also know what day it is."

"Look, I'm sorry. I know I should have phoned yesterday, but I've had a lot on."

"Haven't we all? Is there any particular reason for your call or are you just going to bore me with excuses?" Sam sounded cool, but in fact, she was both furious with him for not ringing and totally breathless because he ultimately had.

"I have some good news and some bad news. Which do you want to hear first?"

"Good."

"Well, I've been digging around here and I really don't think there's much to worry about. Not yet anyway."

If you were to add up all the negatives in that sentence, Sam thought, I'm convinced they could equal at least one positive. Maybe she ought to be concerned. She especially didn't like the sound of the 'not yet' part, and decided to ask, "So what are you saying?"

"I'm saying, there is a slight possibility that something may have happened to your case en route but, in all probability, I think it was harmless. Don't worry. All I would say is that if anything else happens, or there are any strange occurrences of absolutely any type during your next flight, give me a call." He paused and added, "Immediately. It is really important that you keep me informed."

"OK, but?"

"It really is nothing. Just don't worry," Dominic urged.

Sam was beginning to worry – that was the third time in a matter of minutes that he'd told her not to worry. He couldn't have been more non-committal even if he used all the conditional tenses in the grammar books. This usually meant that there was plenty to worry about but he didn't want a hysterical woman on his hands.

"If that's supposed to be the good news, what is the bad?"

"I can't get back up to Manchester until Monday afternoon and you'll be in Finland by then."

Sam's heart sank and Dominic sensed her disappointment. "We'll just have to wait until you get back. It's my turn to cook, remember? Plus, I never did get the opportunity to have . . . 'dessert', did I?"

Dominic's voice was playful and Sam blushed at the memory, but managed to flirt, "I'll look forward to it. I'll bring . . . dessert with me."

"Wonderful!" All of a sudden his voice changed and he began speaking in the same clipped tones as Alex did when her boss was around. "I'll give you my mobile number and you must promise to call me as soon as you get to Finland. OK?"

"All right, but at some point you'll have to tell me what's going on."

"Nothing's going on," Dominic's voice softened. "Look, just promise me you'll give me a call as soon as you arrive in Finland."

"I promise."

"And Sam," Dominic said quietly.

"Yes."

"Trust me. OK?"

"OK."

After he'd given her his mobile number, he once more assured her that there was nothing to worry about, then finished the call.

Immediately, Sam called Alex.

"Corporate Finance."

"Lexi, the strangest thing, Dominic called and there was something weird about the way he was talking today."

"What? Apart from him being his normal dodgy self?"

"I wish you'd stop that. He's an official of the airline, helping me sort out my luggage problem."

"I'm sorry, but you're the one who rang me and said there was something weird about him."

"I didn't say there was something weird about him. I said there was something weird in the way he was talking today."

"Why? Did he all of a sudden have a lisp or something?"

"No, I didn't mean that sort of weird."

"What do you mean then?"

"Well, if you stop jumping down my throat every five seconds, I'll tell you."

"Forgive me. Do carry on."

"Right, I wasn't worried at first, but then he kept telling me not to worry, like I should have been worried or maybe that I had reason to. Do you get what I mean?"

"Yes, and?"

"And, he mentioned that there might be a possibility of something going on, but then said that I shouldn't worry, yet."

"Yet being the operative word."

"Exactly." Sam waited for Alex to mull over the new information.

"Strange," Alex said after a long pause. "I'm sorry Sam, but I don't trust him, never have – there's something innately dodgy about this guy."

"Why?"

150

"Well, for a start, Dominic – now that's the name of a guy that should never be trusted in any circumstances, if ever I heard one."

"Glad to see that you're being strictly scientific in your assessment."

"That's just the one of the reasons. I suppose the basic reason is that I don't like him. He's been using his pretty-boy looks to get into your knickers, way too quickly for my liking. There has to be something behind it."

"Of course, I forgot. I'm such an ugly sea-monster that he really couldn't have been attracted to me, could he? Oh no, that's just suspicious, isn't it?" Sam was quite hurt by what Alex had said.

"Sam, love, you know I didn't mean it like that. It's just that something doesn't smell right about this whole thing. There's something rotten in the state of Finland Air!" Alex was attempting to lift the mood slightly with her paraphrasing.

"Great. Now we get Shakespeare."

"I can't help my intuition. You're the one who keeps banging on about trusting it."

"Yeah, I tell you to trust in it when it comes to YOUR relationships, not mine. Mine are fine, thank you very much."

"Well, it doesn't matter about when I should be trusting it. I'm trusting it now and I'm serious. He's not right."

"Alex, don't you think you're going over the top just a tad? I have absolutely no reason to be suspicious about him. None at all. He's just a normal bloke, getting on with his job."

"Listen, Jordan, you're the one ringing me, telling me that there's something weird. So don't get on your high horse just because I agreed with you."

"Are you finished?"

"Not quite," Alex continued. "If he's as good-looking as you say, then he must be dodgy. Think about all those films. Remember *Scream*? If anything weird is going on, it's usually the trusted, gorgeous boyfriend that's doing it."

"So what do you think *it* is?"

"I don't get what you mean?"

"I mean, Madame Cleverclogs, what do you think *is* happening?"

"I have no idea. Maybe he's a con man and is after your money." Alex remembered that they were discussing Sam and although she wasn't poor, she definitely wasn't rich enough to attract a gigolo. "OK, bad idea. How about drugs?"

"What?

"Drugs. I remember reading about it in *Marie Claire* or *Company* or something. There are drug dealers who befriend travellers. They gain their confidence so that they can get close enough to slip stuff in their bag!" Alex sounded triumphant, amazing herself with her brilliance.

"That is the silliest thing I've heard. Are you forgetting that it was the airline that put him on the job! His instructions are to stick close to me and my luggage! And anyway, just leaving reality behind for a second, he wouldn't put drugs in my suitcase when he was actually travelling with me, would he?"

"I suppose not. It could be something really covert. Dominic likes Action Men, right?"

"OK, I'll go with this one. Yes, he does."

"What if there is a black market for Action Men in Finland? Maybe they've been banned by the Finnish government for being too aggressive. Those sorts of countries are always banging on about society being too competitive. Dominic is probably trying to supply the AMLS with the goods."

"AMLS?"

"Action Man Liberation Society."

Sam had to laugh. "Alex, darling, you're off your trolley. Seriously, I think you've completely lost it this time."

"OK. Forget Dominic. Maybe there's a baggage-handler who is really really into fashion and knows that you're such a shop-a-holic you have all the new fashionable stuff . . . "

"Carry on, I'm enjoying this one."

"So every time you travel he has to open up your suitcase to see what the fashionable people are wearing."

"So why does the bag miss the connecting flights if he's just looking?"

"I don't know . . . he could be trying the clothes on or something. That's it, a transvestite, fashion-victim baggage-handler is trying on your clothes, gets carried away and forgets to send your bag on!"

"Oh my God, you've got it!" Sam said dramatically. They spent the rest of the call trying to come up with more and more outrageous reasons for the strange occurrences with her luggage.

After the phone call Sam sat in silence for a little while, pondering Alex's question. Did she trust Dominic? Her intuition was telling her to trust him. She should be asking herself if she trusted her intuition and that was a question that the 'pre-Phillipe' Sam would have had no trouble answering, but the 'post-Phillipe' Sam was having difficulty with. Trust.

153

She'd trusted Phillipe when he'd told her he loved her. Even when he began acting strangely, she'd trusted him in the same naïve way someone who'd never been kicked in the teeth by Love could. When he'd managed to drive away all her male friends with his jealous accusations, she thought that he must love her loads. All of this trust was in vain, when she found out that Phillipe had been having an affair with Marie Dutrest, the managing director of the company she was consulting. The worst thing was that Sam had introduced them. She'd got him the job, taking pictures for the company brochure. She'd got him the job and he'd betrayed her. When she confronted him with her discovery he laughed and told her 'of course' he was having an affair, telling her that she should not be so childish as to expect him to be faithful. He was a Frenchman and entitled to his mistresses. Yes – *mistresses*! Plural. This was when she came to her senses.

Coming sharply back to the present she wondered if, given time, Dominic too would betray her. A rhetorical question, but one which she fervently wished someone would give her an answer to.

Dominic was obviously concerned about something. She refused to believe that he would put her in danger and was sure that if there were any chance of her being in trouble, he would have told her. She had nearly slept with him; they very nearly had a sexual history, for goodness sakes! In the end, she decided to wait and see. If she didn't know what was going to happen, then she couldn't plan for it. If she couldn't plan for it, then there was no point in worrying about it. She would know soon enough.

* * *

The rest of the day passed quite unobtrusively, apart from the odd phone call from her mother. Sam had lost all the feeling of intrigue. The one thing that was worrying her was that Alex and Duncan's relationship seemed to be disintegrating rapidly. She crossed her fingers and hoped that it would last until she returned from Finland.

Chapter Ten

Sam was acutely conscious of the fact that she'd not visited her family in ages. The last thing she needed at this juncture was a surprise visit from her sister, or even more horrifically, her mother. She needed to be pro-active.

It is time, Sam thought, for a visit to the mother.

The one hundred and twenty mile drive was something that Sam faced only when it was absolutely necessary. It's not that she didn't like driving – in fact when the sun was out and the sky was blue, Sam loved it. Unfortunately, this time it would be your average northern autumnal experience, dark grey skies and raining in sheets. The drive would only be bearable if she had her travel necessities and Sam always made sure her car was fully stocked with the right equipment.

Getting into her car, Sam carried out her ritual vehicular check: Polos, four packs, check. George Michael compilation cassette, two of, check. Mobile phone, check. She toyed with the idea of taking a few bars of chocolate, just in case she was caught in a torrential flood outside Leeds, but decided against it on the grounds of improbability, plus the fact that the last thing she wanted in a disaster situation was to be found dead in her car surrounded by chocolate wrappers. She could see it now, *'Fat Bird Dies In Sugar Overdose On M62 Shocker'*. She pondered on that morbid thought and realised that she'd been having more and more of them recently. It seemed the closer she got to her thirtieth birthday, the more she seemed to obsess about her own mortality. Shaking her head clear, she started on her way.

The drive itself on this occasion seemed to drag more than ever, with only the one incident to keep her entertained. She'd been flashed near Scunthorpe.

A flash, in this context, is where a guy, sometimes nice-looking, sometimes a bit of a screamer (someone you would run from screaming in terror), holds up his mobile number for you to phone. Usually this occurs in a traffic jam or other slow-moving traffic episodes. This was not your average flash, however – this was an MM-flash, MM being the short form of 'Mercedes Man'. An MM-flash whilst waiting at a roundabout was the flash equivalent of doing an entire weekly shop in M & S.

This guy was obviously a professional. As he'd turned over his laminated sheet of paper to display the words, Phone Me! Sam had turned a violent pink and sunk very low in her seat, but not before catching a good look at his face. He wasn't bad-looking – but then she noticed that he had a child's car seat in the back. Typical! She had been flashed by a possible pervy 'married'.

She smiled. There was a time, not that long ago, when she might have been interested – if he hadn't been married, of course. Nowadays, she viewed it with a smug indifference.

She had a boyfriend who was sexier than a Hollywood superstar's six-pack. She was happy. Her mind filled with memories of Dominic and the feel of his firm stomach and suddenly, the drive began to fly by. Before she knew it, she was driving into Tealby, Lincolnshire. As soon as she entered the village, she felt her pulse slowing to a near-death pace. Each time she came home, she found it almost impossible to imagine that she had actually survived her teenage years in such a remote and incredibly boring place.

Although Sam was born in London, her parents moved out to Lincolnshire when she was thirteen in order to provide the family with a 'better living environment'. This was the worst thing that could ever have happened to Sam. Imagine just turning thirteen and realising the delights that a capital city such as London could offer an inquiring teenager and then at the crucial point being dragged away to a place where there was one bus a day going to the nearest local city, if it could be described as such. Her parents did attempt to make her into a country girl. They bought chickens, ducks and other assorted fowl. Sam even had her own lamb, Fluffy, which she took care of and played happily with right until the day when her parents decided to teach her about 'where meat comes from'. At least, she assumed that's what they intended as it wasn't very diplomatic to serve lamb cutlets with mint sauce on the very day that Fluffy mysteriously disappeared from the field beside the house. No one could ever accuse her parents of being subtle. The Fluffy-murdering incident caused Sam to turn vegetarian for over ten years until the lack of vegetarian options available in Germany turned her back into a confirmed meat-eater. So, to this day, Sam still remains a city-girl through and through. She has no interest in endless vistas of rolling green fields and she abhors all forms of insects and creepy-crawlies. In fact, for most of her years in Tealby, she'd been terrorised by the recurrent appearances in her bedroom of an infinite array of spiders. Once her mother had attempted to cure her of her arachnophobia by catching a spider and placing it in a jamjar. She then forced Sam to hold the jar, saying, 'See, darling, it's just a helpless spider'. This of course, made Sam even more terrified of the creatures than she was before because she'd actually seen one up close and personal. Sam's mother was never one for sensitivity and her tolerance of fears and phobias of any kind was virtually non-existent.

"Hi, darling, I'm on the phone," Sam's mother called from the living-room as Sam entered the house.

Sam dropped her bag in the dining-room and wandered in to greet her. Her mother put her hand over the handset and hissed. "Shoes! New carpet," then returned to her call. "Yes, Gwen, I'm listening. What happened with the beetroot after they removed it?"

Sam went back out into the kitchen and removed her shoes. Nothing much changes around here, she thought. She looked around the kitchen. As usual the floor was so clean you could conceivably eat off it, assuming there was a sudden and alarming incident where all the plates which her mother had spent the past fifty-odd years collecting were destroyed leaving nothing but the floor to eat off. Sam padded back into the living-room. Yep, nothing much changes. The doilies were still over the chair arms, presumably protecting the ten-year-old sofa from premature aging. Her mother had had a doily fetish for as long as Sam could remember. She herself was twenty-nine and had never owned a doily. When her mother was her age, she must have had a huge chest full of the things. Sam wouldn't even know where to purchase a doily. Did they still make these lacy circles of intricate design? Were they actually designed to protect chair arms or were they simply put there because they 'looked nice'? All these questions confirmed to Sam that although she was getting old, she wasn't quite old enough to appreciate that sort of thing. Sam surveyed the mantelpiece. All the knick-knacks and pottery dogs were all still there, lovingly dusted and beautifully arranged. In fact, every available surface in the room was crammed with assorted stuff which had absolutely no value whatsoever apart from the fact that they looked 'nice'. No one on the planet really needs pottery Edwardian women going out for a walk with their parasols, do they? Sam thought to herself. Her mother showed absolutely no inclination to cut short her 'beetroot fiasco' discussion, so Sam wandered slowly back into the kitchen to make herself something to drink.

Halfway into her second cup of 'medium roast, Columbian' coffee, her mother came bustling into the kitchen. She stood in front of Sam and looked her slowly up and down, shaking her head sadly.

This was the usual response to seeing her daughter after a longish absence. She would usually first assess whether Sam had put on weight and tut quietly under her breath. Then she would take in the lack of make-up and the comfortable 'driving clothes' and then commence with her if-you-only-took-a-little-care-with-your-appearance lecture. This would normally be a monologue of epic proportions customarily ending with a long sigh and 'Oh well!'. Then, seemingly to give Sam a bit of encouragement, she would proceed to relate the Marriage Statistics.

"So, I heard that Claire is getting married next month. Of course Susan got married two months ago, but that doesn't count because she found him in bed with her sister and she's getting divorced, but at least she was married."

"That's nice, mother." Sam usually found it best to humour her mother until she'd completed the ritual or Sam was seriously provoked into a proper response.

"Yes, well, Claire was never the prettiest child, and I don't think even her mother could describe her as over-endowed in the brains department . . . "

"What are you getting at?" Sam asked, knowing exactly what her mother was getting at, but the opportunity to wind her up simply got the better of her.

"I'm saying that even *she's* getting married."

"Have you ever thought that she's only getting married because she's got a really pushy, irritating mother who bangs on constantly about her getting married? She probably hates her husband-to-be and will probably spend her whole sad life wishing she'd had the courage to stand up to her bully of a mother." Sam kicked herself for allowing her mother to rile her.

"What on earth are you talking about? Mrs Goodman is as quiet as a mouse. I doubt you'd find anyone who'd describe her as a bully."

"Just forget it, mother," Sam sighed. "Anything else happen here, while I've been away? I know what a hotbed of activity this place is."

"Well, Mrs Cottman won the gardening competition, but was disqualified because she had bought her spring onions in Asda." Her mother's face was a picture of distaste.

Sam laughed and was about to ask whether the disqualification was due to the purchasing of the vegetables or the choice of supermarket, but decided against it and instead made a shocked sound.

"The chemist got a new mascara in last week and there was such a queue . . . "

"That's nice."

"I bought one for you though. Just in case you ever decide to take an interest in your appearance." Her mother sighed dramatically. "Although I suppose now you've finally hooked a man, you'll be dressing like this all the time. You'll never keep him if you continue with –"

"Mother?"

"Yes, darling."

"You've worn make-up every day of your life, haven't you?"

"Well, one must have standards."

"Well, what happened with Dad then?"

For a split second, a look of the deepest pain flashed across her mother's face and Sam felt like a mean, evil monster for throwing the whole episode back in her face.

"Well, obviously, darling, he liked my make-up a little bit too much." With that she whooshed out of the room and upstairs.

"Mother, I'm sorry," Sam called after her desperately, but she was left in the kitchen, wishing that she hadn't let her mother rile her so much. Sam had a great respect for the fact that she had overcome such a difficult situation, especially living in such a small town, but she'd never been able to tell her as much, mainly due to the constant nagging. It was difficult to tell whether her mother was upset by her comments – she was always so good at the 'brave face'.

Her mother appeared back in the kitchen dressed in her favourite Chanel suit, with the warpaint heavily emphasised – obviously she was going out.

"I didn't mean it."

"Of course you did." Sam didn't know what to say, so her mother continued, "I suppose it served me right. I'm worried about you, that's all."

"I know, but I'll be fine. I have a good job, great friends and a nice life – you've no need to worry."

"It's my job, remember." She gave Sam a squeeze of the shoulder and smiled. "Oh, by the way, could you take this over to Michelle's for me?" She picked up a plastic bag filled with material.

"Curtains?"

"Yes, Chelsea went mad with her felt-tip pens. Some idiot gave her permanent markers for her last birthday. She'll never get Chelsea's works of art off the curtains now. What are you laughing at?"

"Nothing, mother," Sam giggled. "Anyway, they probably didn't do it on purpose."

"What are you talking about?"

"The person who sent the pens. Maybe they bought them because they were really nice colours and forgot to check whether they were washable?"

"What sort of silly person would give a three-year-old permanent markers?"

"Someone without kids, maybe?" Sam uttered hopefully, remembering that she'd been the person responsible. "Not everyone has an innate knowledge of the workings of this parenthood lark."

"Yes, but even the most idiotic person knows that three-year-olds write on walls."

"Yeah, but idiotic people are prone to making mistakes."

"Don't be silly. Oh, and ask her if I can have my Delia Smith back, as well."

"All right. I'll go now, shall I?"

"Well, you might as well, I have to get going to my crafts class now, so I'll be out. Anyway, it's about time you spent some quality time with your niece – it'll be good practice?"

"Practice for what?"

"A mother can hope, can't she?" With that her mother picked up her handbag and swished out the door, telling Sam over her shoulder to remember to lock up.

Sam stood alone in the kitchen, not knowing exactly how she should react.

* * *

"Michelle? Where are you?" Sam let herself into her sister's house.

"I'm up here," a highly stressed voice called from upstairs. Sam started up the stairs. "Come on up, but mind out for the . . . "

Sam's foot squished into something soft, and definitely smelly. "Too late. What was it? I daren't look."

"It's a welcome greeting from our new –"

Before she could complete her sentence, a rather large, soppy-looking golden retriever puppy came bounding down the stairs, nearly knocking her flying.

"You've got a puppy? But I thought you hated puppies?" Rather than deal with the mess, Sam extricated herself from her shoe, picked up the animal and carried it into Chelsea's bedroom. She walked in to find Michelle painting over exuberant colourful pictures of goodness knows what. "What's going on here? Where's Chelsea?"

"I'd love to say that I've murdered her, but no, she's staying over at Tori's while I get the house sorted out."

"The place looks like a bomb's hit it."

"Close, but it's just a particularly hyperactive three-year-old who thinks she's Picasso."

"Going through a bit of a drawing stage, is she?"

"You could say that. It wouldn't be so bad, but some stupid pillock gave her permanent markers —"

Sam quickly interrupted and changed the subject. "So, a dog, eh?"

"Yeah, that was Stuart, the Wonder-Moron's great idea."

"I thought you hated dogs."

"I do. But what do you say to a child when her father goes out and gets her an 'adorable' puppy, without the slightest hint of a word to his dog-hating wife. It's not as if I could have taken it away once she'd seen it."

"Do I detect a touch of discord in the Marshall household?"

"Don't, OK? Just Don't." Michelle sighed, but attempted to mask the look of despair in her eyes by throwing a brush at Sam. "Grab hold of that and help, you old cow."

"I think I'll go and retrieve my shoe and clean the stairs first."

Although Sam was shocked at the despair in her sister's voice, she didn't feel equipped to comment on it. After all, she'd already managed to upset her mother that day – the last thing she needed was to alienate the only reasonable member of her family. So instead of talking, she did what the other female members of her family did in these situations: she put on the Marigolds and started scrubbing. Within a few hours Chelsea's works of art were obliterated and the two sisters were having a celebratory cuppa.

"So this new bloke of yours – serious?"

165

"Who knows?" Sam replied mysteriously.

"Come on, you cagey wombat. Spill the beans."

"Well, his name's –"

"Dominic, yes, yes, I know that. Get to the good bit."

"Well, he's absolutely gorgeous."

"What's wrong with him then?"

"There's nothing wrong with him." Sam didn't like the way this conversation was going. "What are you saying? Are you trying to imply that the only way I could 'pull' a gorgeous bloke is if there's something intrinsically wrong with him. Why can't anyone believe that I'm capable of pulling a stunner? Am I that revolting?"

"No, Madame Psychiatrist, stop overanalysing everything I say. All I meant was, is he single?"

"Yes."

"Has he ever been married?"

"No."

"How old is he?"

"Slightly older than me. Why?"

"Well, there must be some reason why some woman hasn't snapped him up."

"Maybe he just worked too hard and never got around to sorting out his personal life. I mean, I've never been married –"

"Yeah and we all know what's wrong with you, don't we?" Michelle giggled.

"Ha bloody ha," Sam uttered sarcastically. "No, really, Michelle, I actually do find some potential with this one."

"Do you mean he might actually be," Michelle paused for effect, "THE ONE!"

"Who knows, but it's at least possible."

"Wow. You know, I never actually thought I'd ever hear

you say those words again, especially after You-know-who."
Michelle held up her mug for a toast. "Well, good luck to
you!"

"Cheers," Sam smiled.

It was times like this that Sam was happy to be in her
sister's company. Usually there was a tense undercurrent in
their conversations.

Then, Michelle took Sam by surprise with her next
comment.

"Sam, I know Mum and I are always going on about it,
but you will think carefully, before doing anything silly,
won't you?"

"And by 'anything silly' you mean – ?"

"Getting married, yes."

Sam looked in her sister's eyes for indications of teasing,
but she was completely serious. "What's up, Michelle?"

"I dunno. Sometimes I wonder, if I had the chance to go
back, would I have done it? Don't get me wrong, I love
Chelsea to death and I would never be without her, but . . .
oh, I don't know. Sometimes when I'm peeling spuds and
Stuart's late home and Chelsea's wailing in the background,
I wonder, is this it? Is this all there is to my life . . . It's hard,
that's all."

"You're just pissed off because Stuart bought a dog
without telling you," Sam joked. As much as she hated her
mother forcing Michelle's marriage down her throat as the
epitome of perfection, there was something inside Sam that
wanted to believe it. Michelle's was the only happy marriage
she knew and it was important for her to believe that they
do happen.

Michelle smiled, but somehow it didn't quite reach her

eyes. "Get your knickers on, you old bag! We're going shopping."

"Good idea."

Together they drove into Lincoln, the nearest city, and spent a relaxing afternoon, disposing of as much of Stuart's hard-earned cash as was humanly possible in the time allowed.

Afterwards Sam returned home, happy that she'd visited her family. For the first time, she actually felt quite close to both of them. After years of feeling that she was some sort of changeling stuck in a family totally unrelated to her in every way, she started to see some similarities. She suddenly realised that her mother, with all her faults, was someone she actually admired, although all the torture in the world would never make her admit it.

Once at home, she began getting ready for her trip the following day.

She thought she'd better check in with Alex again, just to make sure that things were stable before she went. She didn't want things going belly-up when she was stuck in Finland, unable to help.

"The Spencer residence."

"Alex, give it up. No-one will ever think you're a blue-blood, no matter how posh your telephone voice is."

"Shut up, you old bag. What d'you want anyway?"

"Not much, just wanted to find out how things were going with you . . . and Duncan . . ." Her voice trailed off.

"What is this? Day One of Alex-watch? My boyfriend and I are fine, when he's around. Anyway, I'm not the one with a dodgy bloke. If I were you I'd be more worried about what your little Mr Stewart is up to . . . "

Sam tuned Alex out and wished she hadn't called at all. Alex was always the sort of person who felt that attack was the best form of defence. Dominic just happened to be the easiest target. Didn't Alex understand that people were concerned about her? Why couldn't she ask for help, before the crisis hit? It was so obvious to everyone that the whole Alex/Duncan relationship was about to explode or implode or something. Whoops, she'd not been listening. She tuned back in to Alex's character assassination of Dominic.

" . . . in my point of view."

"Erm, any more insulting things you have to say about my boyfriend?" Sam's chest puffed out at her first out-loud use of the 'B' word. "While I'm still here, that is."

"Sam, I don't mean to sound nasty. It's just that I don't trust him and you're my best mate and I don't want you to get hurt. Again. I mean he asks you to trust him and won't tell you why." The malevolence had dissipated and Alex sounded deflated. "Do you, by the way?"

"Do I what?"

"Sam, keep up. Do you trust him?"

"Why shouldn't I? I have no real reason not to trust him."

"Well, you know I don't. Have you asked Anne?"

"Asked her what, exactly? Anyway, I don't want to *get her involved* yet."

"A-ha! So deep down, you do think there's something. Why else would you have used those words."

"What words?"

"Don't want to get her involved. According to you, he's just doing his job. What's there to get her involved in?"

"Look, if you're going to be this pedantic about things,

forget it. There's absolutely nothing happening with my suitcase. Nothing at all. In fact, with Dominic's help, I actually arrived with my suitcase for the first time in yonks."

"Yeah, but you'd never suspected tampering before he was around."

"Alex." Sam's voice held a warning that Alex was walking a very fine line.

"All right. Listen. When you go on Monday, be careful and keep an eye out."

"For what?"

"I don't know, just be aware, pay attention and Sam . . . "

"What?"

"Trust no one."

"What are you on about?"

"I dunno, they always say it on *The X-Files* and, as I've always wanted to say it, this seemed like a good opportunity."

"OK, I'll call you when I get to Helsinki."

"Are you sure you trust him?"

"I think so."

"Bye then."

"Bye."

* * *

That evening, Sam took great care with her packing, deciding on the barest minimum of clothing. Although her new case appeared to be larger than her old one, she found she was able to fit far less inside. It was a bit like an inverse Tardis. She carefully noted the position of every item and closed the case. She then had an idea and rushed to her computer. She typed in a few sentences, waited for it to print, then returned to her case. She opened it and placed the sheet of paper inside. She stood back surveying her handiwork. On the piece of paper, she'd typed 'This bag is protected by MI5 and has been fitted with an anti-opening device and if opened by anyone other than S Jordan, it will self-destruct in three minutes. Please close this suitcase now.'. That'll give them something to worry about, she thought. She then placed a spare pair of knickers in her handbag and, for good measure, she put in her old rape alarm, which she'd tested briefly beforehand.

"All set," she pronounced.

She went into her bedroom, set her alarm and drifted off to sleep with thoughts of The X-files and Alex.

Chapter Eleven

Sam woke up remarkably perky, completely forgetting that she ought to be nervous. As usual, her taxi was late, so by the time she arrived at the airport she was forced to rush through the check-in process. She answered all the questions. Yes, she had packed it herself, no, she was not carrying anything for anyone else and no, it hadn't left her possession since she packed it. For good measure she added her own question.

"Can I guarantee that my bag will not be tampered with? Well, the answer to that must be: no."

The man at check-in simply stared at her as if she were completely stupid, and snorted, "Well, it's highly unlikely that that will happen."

Sam mumbled something about him not knowing who he was dealing with and wandered off in search of the lounge.

Although she had kept her hand on her rape alarm throughout her short waiting time and her flight, she was disappointed to find that nothing out of the ordinary happened. The plane landed in Amsterdam without incident and she was utterly deflated. So much for 'trust no-one', she grumbled.

Walking the incredibly long walk through Schiphol airport, she rummaged around in her bag for her mobile. Switching it on, she was informed that she had two messages waiting for her. The first, quite unsurprisingly, was from Dominic, asking if she was all right and reminding her to call when she arrived in Finland, with a final addition telling her not to worry. She was about to ring him to give him an earful about worrying her unnecessarily but decided to check out the second message instead. This one was far more alarming. It was a message from Alex, in tears, asking Sam to call her at home as soon as possible.

Sam immediately dialled Alex's number. It rang six times – Sam's heart jumped into her throat with each of them. Finally the answerphone picked up: "Hi there, you've reached Alex. I'm probably tied up and can't get to the phone, so just leave a message, will you?" There was a very long loud beep.

"Lexi, I know you're there. Pick up the phone!" She paused and tried again, "Lexi, it's Sam. I've just got your message. Please pick up."

Then Alex picked up the phone and from the resulting garbled whine, Sam surmised two things. Firstly, that Alex and Duncan had split up and secondly, that Alex was in a bad way.

"Lexi, honey, tell me what happened."

"I saw him," Alex managed in between sobs.

"Saw him where?"

"In Mezzo. He was with a woman, a-a-a gorgeous woman. She was wearing a-a-a red dress."

"Lexi, honey, it could have been anyone. A work

173

colleague, a friend?" Sam knew she was grasping at straws.

"They . . . they . . . k-k-kissed, with t-t-tongues." The pitch of Alex's voice was getting higher by the second. "I want to die. Please come. I-I-I . . ." she was unable to continue. It seemed the sobs were taking over her entire body. "I don't know what I'm going to do."

"Lexi, honey, sit tight. I'll try and . . ." Sam didn't know what she could try – she was stuck in Amsterdam. "I'll try and do something . . . just don't do anything silly, OK?"

"'kay." Alex put the phone down.

Sam's mind was racing back to the Tim affair. Alex had met Tim at a corporate do. Her bank had sponsored his football team. They hit it off immediately. For a while Alex had revelled in playing at being the perfect footballer's wife. She went along to the important matches, cheering enthusiastically from the sidelines; she accompanied him to the endless parties and a few awards ceremonies. She'd even appeared in the newspapers under the headline 'Who is the new mystery blonde in Tim Gordon's life?' Even Sam had been convinced that Alex had finally met her perfect partner. Then Tim had won a contract with Ralph Lauren and things started to fall apart. Determined to put the romance back into their relationship, Alex decided to prepare a special dinner while he was supposedly away in New York. She'd stocked up on the best food from Fortnum's and went to his flat to decorate in advance of his return. Instead of finding an empty flat, Alex had walked in on him, in bed with another man, and was devastated by it. It caused 'The Overdose Incident', where Alex had taken half a bottle of paracetamol with an entire bottle of vodka. It was something that Sam and Alex had never discussed since the night that it happened. Alex still, to this day, insists that she didn't mean to do herself any harm, but Sam knew – she'd seen the lifelessness

*in her eyes. Despite Sam's pleas, Alex had even refused to 'out'
him to the press and had threatened to disown Sam if she attempted
to do it. Even now, Tim Gordon's secret was still under wraps.*

Sam was in a panic. How long would it take her to get to
London? Amsterdam was not that far away – she could be
airport-to-door in under four hours if there was a plane leaving
soon. Alex's brother lived in Sussex, but she didn't know
whether she should call him. Especially after the Tim thing.
Alex had been so annoyed when Sam had called Alex's
mother. This time, Sam didn't want to alarm anyone unduly.
She ran to the BA transfer desk. There were two clerks sitting
behind the desk, a male and a female, both busy dealing with
customers. Sam stood in the queue for the male clerk, who was
dealing with a male customer, reasoning that men were usually
quick and to the point, especially if they were businessmen.
She looked down to see if the customer had a briefcase. He had
one of those huge square pilot's cases. Definitely a businessman.
Sam leant forward in an attempt to eavesdrop.

"Explain please, once more?"

"You need to go down this corridor until you reach Gate
thir*teen*."

"Thirty?"

"No, no, Gate thir*teen*," the male clerk explained very
slowly.

Damn, she thought, this is a nightmare. She moved over
behind the customer at the desk of the female clerk. Just as
she'd moved her bag over, the customer turned and walked
away. Sam moved her things forward.

"This is an emergency. Are there any flights leaving for
London Heathrow?"

The clerk looked at her as if she were a madwoman. But

instead of commenting, she simply turned to her computer screen and tapped on her keyboard.

"Well, there is one – it leaves in just under an hour. Are you on one of our flights at the moment?"

"No," Sam said apologetically.

"Oh. If you could just hold on one moment," the woman said snootily and returned to the tapping of her keyboard. She then began examining her nails, obviously waiting for the computer to deliver the required information. The male clerk came over and they had a little chat in Dutch.

Sam was beginning to get peeved.

"Look, I really don't have time for this. I'll say this once, take notes, OK?"

"All right, calm down, Miss."

"Listen. I am meant to be travelling to Helsinki with Finland Air in . . ." Sam looked at her watch, "one and a half hours. There has been a terrible . . . er . . . thing . . . and I must get back to London."

"Well, let's have a look, shall we?" The woman looked down at her computer screen, "I'm sorry, Miss, but –"

"No, no, you don't understand. Sorry won't do – look again."

"Well, we are completely booked," she said scrolling down her screen and Sam groaned, "in our Euro traveller, but we seem to have a few seats in Club."

"I'll take one!"

Sam got out her credit card and paid for the ticket.

"Do you have any luggage?"

"Damn," said Sam. "It's checked in for my Finland flight."

"Do you have the baggage receipt and we'll see what we can do."

"Look, I've had a few problems with my luggage, but it should be going to this flight." She pointed at her ticket.

The woman picked up her phone and began to speak in Dutch.

Sam made a decision. She looked at the woman's name-tag.

"Look, Suzanne. Forget about the luggage – I just need to get to London."

"I'm sorry, Miss, but we do need to inform Finland Air that you aren't flying, so that they don't put your bags on their plane."

"Listen, Suzanne. This is a matter of life and death – just make it quick," Sam pleaded. "Please?"

"This is highly unusual, but all right. It may be quicker if I see to it personally." The woman looked at the panic-stricken Sam and took pity on her. "You need to get to your gate – they will be boarding in half an hour. Leave it to me. I have a friend in the baggage area. He might be able to get to it. I'm not promising anything, though." She picked up the phone once more.

Sam thanked her profusely and went to her gate. She was still shaken by Alex's voice and she decided she needed something to occupy her mind. There was nothing more she could do until she reached London, so she didn't want to think about it. On the way past the Duty Free shop, Sam wondered if she had enough time to nip in. Shopping had always helped in the past, as a good diversion. Anyway she'd promised Michelle that she'd replace the perfume that Chelsea had spilt. She looked at her watch and decided that she had a little spare time, if she didn't get caught up in a queue. She looked at the cash desks in the Duty Free shop.

They were virtually empty. She could just grab the perfume and get out.

She was deciding whether or not to buy the plum Chanel lipstick, when she heard her name being called.

"Could passenger Jordan travelling to London Heathrow, please make her way to Gate 22. Passenger Jordan to Gate 22, please."

Damn! she thought. She dropped the lipstick, bought the perfume and rushed to her gate. As she arrived, out of breath and promising to give up smoking at the earliest opportunity, the passengers were boarding. She handed her boarding pass to the BA staff member and felt a tap on her shoulder.

"Miss Jordan?"

Sam spun around. "Suzanne! What's happened?"

"My friend found your luggage and has left a message with Finland Air that the bag has been removed," Suzanne said breathlessly. "It's on board this flight. Apparently your bag was under special direction – I had to call in a rather large favour. You will need to ring Finland Air, as soon as you can, to explain what happened. That's all I can do."

"Look, Suzanne, thanks for all your help. You're a life-saver."

"It's no trouble really – I just hope that everything turns out well for you in London."

* * *

Sam fretted all the way to London. When she picked up her bag in Heathrow, she wasn't sure whether to take it or leave it. In the end, she decided to leave it at Left Luggage. After all, she had all her essentials in her handbag. She could then, unencumbered, make a dash for the Heathrow

Express. Luckily, Alex lived only a five-minute taxi ride from Paddington station. She dialled her mobile.

"Lexi, honey, are you there? Don't pick up, just listen – I'm at Heathrow and I can be with you in half an hour."

Alex picked up the phone, still sobbing and her speech was just a tad slurred, "You're . . . you're where?"

"I'm at Heathrow and I'll be there in half an hour."

"'kay" Alex sniffed.

"Hold tight, honey."

Sam was on the Express when she finally remembered that she ought to be in Finland and they'd be expecting her to do some training in the morning. It was 3pm, which meant that it was 5pm in Finland – she might be able to catch Martti on his mobile. She steeled herself and rang her boss.

"Saari." Martti, her boss gave the customary surname greeting.

"Hey, Martti, it's Samantha. I'm in London. I had a bit of a family emergency and I had to fly back from Amsterdam. I would have called, but . . ."

"In London? Family what?" Martti was having difficulty keeping up with the speed of her English.

"Family emergency, mother sick. Am in London. Will call, when I know more. May be able to come to Finland tomorrow." Sam said this very slowly, sounding rather like a telegram. She crossed her fingers and hoped that her mother would forgive her for her little white lie.

"All right. Call me tomorrow. I cancel training."

Not for the first time, Samantha was glad of the relaxed nature of Finnish companies, which enabled her to call her boss at any hour of the day.

"I'll do that. *Kiitos*." Sam thanked the heavens for the fact that she had a nice boss and that she'd managed to learn the Finnish word for 'Thanks'.

"You buttering me again, Sam?"

"*Up*. 'Buttering me *up*', Martti. And no, I'm not. I'm just thanking you."

Twenty-eight minutes after her phone call, Sam was ringing Alex's doorbell. There was no reply. Alex had given her a spare set of keys, so she used them to let herself in. She went into the living-room. The floor was covered in tissues and the television was showing some special news report on the rising number of overdoses in Manchester, due to a recent influx of drugs from Eastern Europe. That won't do, she thought, and quickly switched off the television – she didn't want Alex getting any ideas. Alex was sprawled on the sofa. She looked a mess. Her face was extremely red and blotchy and her blonde hair looked like string. Sam called out and was relieved when Alex's eyes opened and attempted to focus. Sam examined the pile of tissues. She saw an empty bottle of vodka but, searching frantically, she could see no sign of a tablet bottle. She breathed a sigh of relief and, turning to Alex, scooped her into her arms and gave her a huge hug. Alex started sobbing once more.

"Lexi, love, I'm going to make you some coffee and you can tell me all about it." She started to get up but Alex caught her hand.

"Sam, you didn't have to come."

Sam smiled down at Alex and squeezed her hand. "Of course, I did."

"Thanks," Alex mumbled and passed out again.

Sam took the opportunity to tidy up a bit. She picked up

all the sodden tissues from the floor and disposed of the charred remains of the 'Alex & Duncan' pictures.

Both Sam and Alex had the habit of destroying all photos of past lovers upon cessation of a relationship. They discovered, long ago, that this was the only way to ensure that there would be no lasting reminders of past mistakes. The ritual usually consisted of setting fire to the pictures, one by one, whilst citing the faults of that particular person. Sam's favourite one was: 'Begone, Phillipe, you fart too much in bed!' It was at this time that they pledged never again to use the name of the man concerned, which is why Philippe is only ever referred to as You-know-who. Since then Alex has been out with Thingy and Whatsit. Usually they carried out this ceremony together but, judging by the debris, this time Alex couldn't wait.

After almost two hours, Sam inspected the flat and pronounced it habitable. She was incredibly impressed with the sudden appearance of her housekeeping skills. When needs must, I suppose, she thought to herself. It's surprising what adrenaline makes you capable of. Sam had heard stories of mothers whose children had been in accidents and they'd gained remarkable strength and the ability to lift whole cars to save them. Some people are able to run world-record pace on their adrenaline, if their families are in danger. Sam's adrenal secretions gave her the ability to switch on a vacuum and wield a duster.

After a cursory glance in Alex's empty fridge, she decided to get some food in the house. She left a note on the coffee table, in case Alex awoke, and wandered off to the nearby supermarket. She was in the cheese section when her phone rang.

"Where are you? I was really worried when I heard."

"Mother?"

"No, it's Dominic."

"Sorry, your voice was a little . . . um . . . high-pitched there for a moment."

"Sam, where are you?" He sounded terribly concerned and Sam felt a little flattered.

"I'm in London, at my friend Alex's house. Why?"

"Why?" Dominic almost screamed down the phone. "You should have landed in Finland twenty minutes ago. I have been frantic."

"Why?"

"Because I checked the passenger lists and you disappeared in Amsterdam, that's why! I had to call your mother, to find out where you were."

"My mother? How? Why?"

"How did I get your mother's number?"

"Yes."

"From your file. You had her down as next of kin. Why did I ring her? Well, because you went missing earlier and I was worried. I thought she might know of your whereabouts. Either your phone's been switched off or you've just not been answering it."

Sam remembered that somehow Alex's flat was the one place in Paddington where you couldn't get a phone signal, especially not on her network. She repeated this information to Dominic.

"I see. By the way, why does she think I'm called Douglas?"

"Sorry?"

"I rang your mother, tried to explain who I was and she said 'Oh, you must be Douglas'. I didn't bother correcting her."

"It's probably for the best."

"Where are you?"

"London. Why the panic?"

"I'd rather call it concern than panic," he dismissed. "What are you doing in London?"

"Alex, that's my best friend, I've told you about her. Well, she's had a bit of a crisis and I couldn't just fly off to Finland and leave her, there have been . . . problems in the past."

"What did you do with your suitcase?"

"My suitcase? I've got it, why?"

"Which airline did you fly back with?"

"BA, why?"

"Did you tell Anne about your change of plans?"

"No, why?"

"Have you got your case with you at the moment?"

Sam raised her eyes heavenwards. She was beginning to lose her temper.

"Listen, Buster, I'm standing in the cheese section in the supermarket – why would I have my suitcase with me? And if you don't start answering some of my questions, I'm going to switch off my phone."

"All right, Sam, calm down. It's a bit of a long story – I can't tell you now. I promise I'll tell you soon. Will you be going to Finland still or has your trip been cancelled?"

"Why all the cloak and dagger stuff? You're beginning to sound like some sort of spy. It depends on how Alex is, but yes, I'll probably fly out tomorrow from Heathrow. Is that of key importance, Mr Bond?"

"Well, Miss Moneypenny, it could be. I'm going to sort a few things out and I'll call you back later this evening.

Don't do anything with the case and don't call Anne. I'll sort it my end."

"OK, Mr Bond."

"Good, and Sam?"

"Yes, what now?"

"Don't worry."

Sam fumed and started shouting down the phone, but he had already put it down. She became aware of people staring at her. Remembering her surroundings, she turned to the woman at the cheese counter.

"I'll have a pound of Red Leicester, please."

* * *

"Lexi, I'm back." Sam walked into the living-room just in time to see Alex, now awake, holding a bottle of paracetamol.

"Lexi, NO!" Sam screamed and leapt across the room rather athletically. She knocked the bottle out of Alex's hands and it went flying.

"Sam, what are you doing? I've got a stinking headache!"

"Oh," Sam said feeling more than a little silly. "I thought you were going to . . . I thought . . . er . . ."

"Don't be silly, Sam, over Duncan? That two-timing little shit? I wouldn't give him the satisfaction."

Alex had, obviously, woken up in anger at the situation. Just as her relationship phases were speeding up, so too were her recovery phases. Usually she got angry on the second day.

"So tell me what happened then."

"Last night, after you rang, Duncan told me he would be working late."

"Yeah, nothing new there," Sam interjected.

"Sam, I'm telling you everything – let me get it all out, please. It's hard enough."

"Sorry, honey." Sam rubbed her arm. "You carry on. I'll shut up."

"So there I was, determined not to mope around – like you said, it's nothing new. I really wanted to go out and have a bit of a laugh, so I went next door and asked Julie if she fancied going out for a drink."

"Julie?" Sam was shocked. Alex gave her a look and she held up her hands in a I'm-sorry-please-don't-kill-me gesture.

"Yeah, I know that I've never got on that well with Julie, but that was mainly because I thought she was after Duncan. She's got this new hunk of a boyfriend and she's all right now. Anyway, we really went to town. Julie came round, we opened a bottle of wine, got all dressed up, did each other's make-up, you know the sort of thing." Alex looked at Sam, expecting a reaction.

"Oh, I'm sorry, can I speak?"

Alex thumped her with a cushion.

"You've never done my make-up," said Sam.

"You never let me."

"You never offered."

"Sam, can we finish this discussion later? I do have a tale to tell here."

"Granted, carry on."

"Well, we went for something to eat. You know that Indian place on Wardour Street? Well, we had something to eat there and afterwards we decided to stay in Soho, seeing how we were already there. We went in all the pubs, having a couple of drinks here, one or two there." Sam nodded knowingly and Alex continued, "Around midnight, we ended up in Mezzo and I saw him, brazenly sitting there."

Sam attempted to imagine Duncan doing anything 'brazenly' but decided against saying anything. She motioned for her to continue.

"He was sitting there with this woman, a redhead. She was gorgeous," Alex said miserably. "She had a few bob as well, cos I swear she was in a little red Chanel number."

"A redhead wearing red? No sense of taste."

"No, I have to admit, she looked quite good. Nice dress, nice make-up . . . "

Sam tutted in sympathy.

"Nice shoes."

"Jimmy Choo's?"

"Possibly."

"She could have been anyone – a colleague? A friend? Anyone," Sam attempted to reason.

"They were kissing. I couldn't stop staring at them. They even looked like a proper couple." Alex groaned.

"So what did you do?"

"I went over and asked him to introduce us. I said, 'I don't think we've met'. I was shaking, but I think I looked cool and calm."

"Nice one."

"Well, he didn't even bat an eyelid. He introduced us and even invited me to join them. It was at this point that I threw my drink over him."

"Excellent." Sam smiled, imagining Duncan, sopping wet and dripping.

"At least, I would have thrown it over him, if I'd had something in my glass. Typical me. I can't even make a scene properly. He didn't even have the decency to be embarrassed – he just excused himself from Amethyst."

Sam raised her eyebrows.

"Yes, Amethyst – what a bloody name! He just excused himself and took me to a corner. He told me that they had only met two weeks ago, but he felt as if he'd known her forever. Evidently, he hadn't meant to fall in love. It just happened."

"What a complete git," Sam sympathised.

"Falling in love at first sight, what absolute rubbish! You know what I think about that stupid concept. Anyway, I don't know what came over me today. I was OK with it last night. It's just that, this morning, it hit me. Not only have I been dumped, but I've been dumped for a woman with a name like Amethyst. I suppose I just fell apart."

"Just a little. You scared the life out of me." Sam squeezed Alex's hand. "So you won't be needing the mashed potatoes then?"

"Well, I don't know about that," Alex smiled sheepishly. "Will you make it with loads of cream and butter?"

"Of course."

"And you'll put loads of cheese in it?"

"Naturally."

"Yes, I need mash. Feed me mash," Alex grinned.

The rest of the night passed uneventfully. They ate mashed potatoes, pigged out on ice cream, watched all the romantic comedies in Alex's collection, smoked recklessly and reminisced over past affairs. All in all, it turned into your average 'great night in' with your best friend. Duncan had been reduced to an amusing story to tell at dinner parties. At ten o'clock that evening, Dominic rang.

"Miss Moneypenny?"

"Yes, Mr Bond," Sam said conspiratorially. Alex looked over at her friend quizzically and moved closer. Sam waved her away.

"I've sorted everything out. I've arranged for you to fly out to Helsinki tomorrow. You'll be flying BA."

"Ought you be doing that?"

"Doing what?"

"Making me fly the enemy, that's what."

"That's not important – what is important is that you don't check your bag all the way through. Check it as far as Helsinki, collect it there and then check it through to Turku."

"But that's such a hassle!"

"Trust me, it'll be better for you. I'll try and catch up with you again later in the week."

"OK, Mr Bond, but there better be a bloody good explanation for all this."

"We'll speak soon, I promise."

"Bye, Dominic."

"Bye Sam, remember . . ."

"Yes, I know. Don't worry," Sam intoned.

As she put down the phone she saw Alex staring wide-eyed at her.

"What was all that Mr Bond stuff about then?"

"It's a long story – Dominic's being really secretive and strange. It's quite fun really, like being a spy!" Sam giggled.

"Was he giving you your instructions then? What was the password?"

"Yes, I have my instructions, but there isn't a password."

Alex looked disappointed. "But there's always a password!"

* * *

After having assured herself that Alex was fine, Sam made her way back to Heathrow the next morning. Following Dominic's instructions, she checked her bag as far as Helsinki. She was having fun, getting into her role as a spy, checking behind her at regular intervals, making sure she wasn't being 'tailed'. Pausing outside the Duty Free shop, she became convinced that she had been followed by a suspect-looking man, all the way from check-in. She'd seen all the relevant detective films and knew that she should not panic or run. She wandered casually across the departure lounge and suddenly stopped to look in the window of one of the other shops. She used the reflection to sneak a peek behind her, another tip from those helpful films. The man, too, had stopped. He seemed to be hovering uncertainly behind her. If he was a spy and trying to follow her unobtrusively, he was doing a really crap job. She inched her way towards the executive lounge and slipped through the doors. She waited for the man to follow. As he entered she pounced.

"Are you following me?" she said menacingly, in the way she thought a spy might do.

"Well, yes," he said rather nervously.

"Why?" she barked.

"Well, I didn't know the way to the lounge and the gentleman at the check-in said that you would be coming here and suggested I follow you."

"Oh, sorry about that." She found herself blushing.

"I hope I didn't frighten you," he added.

"Not at all," she mumbled and skulked off into a corner.

Chapter Twelve

Sam knew she was back in normality when she saw the façade of her Turku hotel. Nothing scary here, she thought. Things never seemed to change in Finland – it's always the same routine. She saw the unfamiliar face of the receptionist and stopped.

"No Sirpa today?"

"No, she has holiday. My name is Timo and I will try help you," the young man said with difficulty. "My English, not good."

"That's OK. I should really be speaking Finnish anyway."

"Oh, you speak Finnish?" He perked up.

"No, I didn't mean that . . . I meant . . . it doesn't matter. Can I have a room?"

"Of course . . .you have reservation?"

"Yes, my name's Samantha Jordan." She looked over at Timo. "Jordan, from the Martti Saari Consultancy?"

"Ah, here it is!" He pointed at the papers in front of him. And picked up a room card. "Room 107."

Sam thought to herself that she'd never been on the first floor before. She realised that she could cope with changes in her routine at home, but all these changes in Finland were quite unsettling. She didn't think that she could cope with intrigue here.

She pulled her new suitcase after her with difficulty and huffed and puffed her way to the lift. It might be heavy, she thought, but at least it arrived with me.

As the lift doors opened on the first floor, she realised the reason why she'd never been on that floor before. It was a non-smoking floor. She groaned inwardly and hauled her suitcase back into the lift.

Timo was surprised to see her returning.

"Is there problem?" he enquired helpfully.

"Just a little one – I need a smoking room."

"Sorry, we are short of rooms. Fifth floor is normal smoking floor, but we have . . ."

"Yes, I remember. Building fixings on fifth floor."

"Yes, building fixings. Here is room on sixth floor." The young man pressed a few keys and the computer emitted loud beeps and other noises of the 'Fatal Error' variety. He looked over the reception desk at Sam and shrugged, "I not good with computer. I not change number, but I leave note for Sirpa, when she come back. She back tomorrow."

Sam thanked him and returned to the lift.

Lifting her suitcase onto the bed, she came to the conclusion that something was definitely strange about it. She remembered packing the barest minimum of clothing and yet it was heavier than she remembered. But that was a few days ago and maybe she'd not really noticed before how heavy her clothes were. It wasn't that often that she had the opportunity to transport her suitcase from the airport. Dominic was awfully worried about my suitcase, she thought. Maybe there's something inside? Maybe I ought to ring him?

Picking up her mobile, she called Dominic.

"Stewart!" came the barked response.

"Well, hello to you too, Mr Stewart," she said sarcastically.

"Sam, great," he began, but then sounded suspicious. "Where are you?"

"I'm in my hotel in Turku. Thanks for sorting out my tickets by the way. It all worked so smoothly, maybe I ought to use BA more often."

"I'm glad to hear it."

"I have a little question for you – well, it's not really a question, it's more of a statement, but I'd really like your opinion, so it's not that either. Let's just call it a 'thing', shall we?"

"Yes?" he prompted.

"Well, my case seems much heavier than it was before I left."

"And?"

Sam was very disappointed with this response. She had, at the very least, expected him to shout 'Don't open it!' or something in that vein, but all she got was an 'and?'.

"Oh, well, I thought you might be able to give me some advice, that's all."

"Open it. There's some advice."

"Dominic? What the hell's got into you?" Sam was confused and annoyed by his attitude.

"I'm sorry, Sam. I'm under a lot of pressure right now."

"What sort of pressure?"

"Nothing really, just working on a difficult project."

"So what should I do about my case?"

"There should be absolutely no problem with it. You could try opening it."

There he was again talking in the conditional tense.

"All right," she said, utterly flattened by his nonchalance. He seemed odd and she couldn't understand why. "Bye then."

She put her mobile on the bed and turned to her suitcase. She undid the padlock and, with her fingertips and her eyes half closed, she opened it. She was half expecting it to go 'BOOM', but much to her chagrin, nothing happened. To her immense displeasure, it was exactly how she'd packed it. Not a single piece of clothing had been moved. That's my bit of intrigue over with then, she grumbled.

She phoned Alex and moaned about the lack of anything exciting happening.

"So much for all that spy stuff then," Alex sympathised.

"Yeah, I know."

"So, what was Dominic talking about?"

"God knows. Maybe he just likes worrying women half to death, so he can seem like a hero."

"See, I never trusted him."

"So you keep saying," Sam pointed out. "You've never even met the guy."

"So? I don't have to meet him. I know his sort." Alex began to describe what his sort was: dark and brooding which is 'romantic novel-speak' for moody and emotionally constipated.

"That's a tad unfair, don't you think?"

"Yeah well, trust me, men are shits and they're not worth bothering about. They're like smoking cigarettes – they're great when you start, eventually they turn into a nasty habit and end up leaving you messed up inside and writhing in agony."

Sam was saddened by her bitterness. Alex seemed to be taking this latest setback in the romantic side of her life differently from in the past. Although she'd had some truly awful experiences with men, she'd never completely lost faith in the 'one true love' theory. After the tears and the depression had subsided and even after the 'overdose incident', she'd always got back out into the world with the idea that the last boyfriend obviously wasn't 'the one' and he therefore wasn't her destiny. She'd always kept faith in the fact that one day her prince would come.

This time it seemed her inner well of optimism must have finally run dry. This meant that Duncan must have hurt her more than she let on. Sam felt a strange sense of loss. Whenever she got bitter and twisted, she always relied on Alex to restore her faith in the whole relationship thing. They used to joke that they balanced each other out, Alex being the antidote to her cynicism. Now she was faced with the eternally optimistic Alex finally battered into submission by a string of useless and worthless boyfriends. Things will never be the same again, Sam lamented.

After her call to Alex, Sam realised that she still hadn't called Anne. She felt a little guilty about it, even though Dominic had said that he would sort everything out. I should ring her really, she reasoned, and picked up her phone once more.

"Hi, Anne, it's Samantha Jordan."

"Ms Jordan, may I ask where you are?" Anne sounded slightly edgy.

"I'm in Finland."

"I see. I attempted to call you yesterday when I discovered that you had vanished in Amsterdam. I tried the number you gave me, but –"

Sam interrupted. "That would be my work number – they didn't know."

"Well, they mentioned that you had family difficulties."

"Yes, I was forced to return to London."

"Is everything all right with you now? Do you have your suitcase."

"Yes, I travelled with BA this morning. Well, I thought I ought to let you know that I took it with me from Amsterdam and it's here with me in the Cumulus Hotel in Turku, safe and sound. So you're not to worry."

"That's nice. I love Turku at this time of year – so crisp. The Cumulus Hotel? Is that the one near the harbour?"

"No, I'm in the one near the market-place, it looks like a building site at the moment, but it's quite nice inside." Sam warmed to her topic. "Speaking of the harbour, I'll be doing some consulting for a company in that area tomorrow. I can send you a postcard," she offered.

"That won't be necessary, Ms Jordan. I'm just glad you arrived safely," she paused, "with your case."

* * *

Jeremy Paxman was explaining the five economic conditions which have to be met before Britain could enter the euro and Sam was nodding intelligently, thanking the powers that be that he had been seated next to her at the dinner party. She felt a tap on her shoulder. She looked to her right and there sat Dominic trying to get her attention.

"Can you hold on a sec, Jeremy's nearly finished," she said and turned back to the euro discussion.

By this time, Jeremy was sketching his thoughts on a napkin. She leant in to take a closer look.

Jeremy leaned in towards her and said, "You smell wonderful tonight."

Sam beamed with pleasure, but she noticed something strange about his voice. It sounded different. Deeper and with a very slight American twang to it. She raised her head and Jeremy had disappeared, replaced by Mark, who was explaining why it was important for Great Britain to join the single European currency.

Sam felt a hand on her shoulder once more – good, Dominic was still there. She looked from side to side; to the right, Mark, to the left, Dominic. Suddenly they both started pulling at her arms. At first she was happy that they both wanted her attention, but it was beginning to hurt. Her right shoulder was in agony.

"Mark, Dominic, stop!" They seemed not to hear her. She shouted again much louder and tried to pull her right arm away from Mark, but he held firm.

"STOP. YOU'RE TEARING ME APART!" she screamed.

Sam sat bolt upright, at least she tried to sit upright, but was severely hampered by the fact that her right arm was caught between the bed and the wall. She was disorientated so it took her a while to extricate it from its position. She was still fully dressed and had obviously dropped off whilst watching the evening film on the television. She picked up the remote control and somehow managed to switch it off just as the credits to *Rebel Without A Cause* were scrolling up the screen.

She shivered and went into the bathroom to brush her teeth. "Jeez, what a screwed-up person you are, young Ms Jordan," she murmured along the way.

Unfortunately that wasn't the only dream that Sam had that evening. In fact, she had some that were even more bizarre. At one stage, she had Dominic and Mark hitting William Hague over the head with Jeremy Paxman. Eventually, about seven-thirty in the morning, Sam woke up feeling that she'd rather stay awake all night than ever go through dreams like that again.

"SEVEN-THIRTY. . . Argh!" Sam squealed. She was late – bloody hotels, bloody non-existent wake-up calls, bloody Timo. She had half an hour before Mark picked her up and after the hissy fit she threw last time he was tardy, there was no hope that he'd be late again. At least she didn't have to stand on a street corner for him, this time . . .

She flew around the room like a whirling dervish, throwing clothes and towels over her shoulder. Exactly twenty-six minutes later, she stood in front of the mirror, showered, dressed and almost ready. She briefly flirted with the idea of not putting on any make-up – to make time for a glass of orange juice – seeing as she already had a gorgeous boyfriend and therefore didn't need to impress anyone (for anyone read Mark). However, she managed to persuade herself that she would wear make-up because it had nothing to do with impressing anyone and everything to do with the fact that it made her feel like a liberated and confident woman (and it stopped her looking like a gargoyle). Although how covering her face in oil-free, light-reflecting, age-defying foundation with AHAs managed to convey 'liberated and confident' she wasn't quite sure. Somehow she managed to be ready and waiting at the front of the hotel before Mark arrived, precisely on time as expected.

"Morning, Samantha."

"Morning, Mark."

"How are you?"

"Fine, thanks. You?"

"Excellent."

"Good." OK, he was going for business mode. So she followed suit. "What delights do you have in store for me today?"

"I thought we'd take another look at the accounts."

"Wow, you really know how to show a girl a good time!"

"Well, if it's excitement you want, there's the marketing schedule too!" He took his eyes off the road long enough to make eye contact and smile broadly.

"I can hardly wait," she smiled back.

* * *

Sam sat back in her chair and stretched her aching back. They'd been working on the marketing schedule since lunch and she thought that it was time for a break.

"Coffee?" Mark suggested, reading her thoughts.

"Yes, please. I'd love one."

He picked up the phone and uttered a long string of complicated words. Sam managed to catch *kaksi*, the Finnish word for two and *kahvi*, the word for coffee. She was guessing that by the length of the sentence, he must be asking for more than the refreshment. She tuned the Finnish out.

She had been nervous about their first meeting since THAT dinner. She was afraid that it might have made things awkward. She'd prepared an entire speech about the dinner being a mistake and that they should stick to business and avoid any further socialising and, as a last resort, she was going to explain about Dominic. To her great relief, Mark had been the perfect client, sticking strictly to business the entire day, thus making her speech redundant. She looked over at him – he was still in deep discussion on the phone. Finnish was a strange language.

On her first visit to the country, Sam had been certain that, as she was a linguist, she would have no difficulty at least getting the gist of what people were telling her. After all, most languages had a liberal smattering of Latin and Greek, didn't they? To her dismay, she discovered the hard way that Finnish was totally unrelated to any other European language. Somehow, over thousands of years, while other countries had seen their mother tongues soak up, adapt and assimilate other languages, Finland managed to stand alone maintaining its language in its near-original form. The way the people held on to it was a testament to their stubbornness.

Mark put the phone down and said, "I've ordered a small snack as well, so we don't expire from hunger. I really don't know how I can thank you for everything you've done today. I'm positive we're on the right track now. Looking at this –" he held up the marketing schedule, "I'm confident we'll crack the UK."

"All in a day's work," Sam smiled.

When the coffee finally came, Sam was surprised to see two plates of rather yummy-looking cakes.

"I wasn't sure what you liked, so I got a selection."

They both seemed to be in a reflective mood so they ate and drank in silence.

Finally Mark broke the tranquillity. "I know, let's go out tonight and celebrate."

Sam frowned. "I don't think . . ."

"Look Samantha, there's no strings, I promise. We'll just go out for a meal. Just look at it as a business meal. It's the least I can do, after today."

"But –"

"I won't take no for an answer. You'd only end up eating alone in the hotel."

It was reasoning like that got her into hot water the last time, she thought. It would be different this time – she had Dominic now. "OK," she said finally.

"I'll pick you up later. It's four o'clock now, how about I pick you up at eight thirty?"

* * *

"You would have been proud of me, Lexi."

"Why?"

"Well, I was on the mineral water all night."

"Did he try it on?"

"Nope, he was the perfect gentleman."

"So it was good?"

"Yeah, it was really great. We were in the most expensive restaurant in Turku. My menu didn't have prices in it, so you know what that means, don't you?"

"No, what does it mean?"

"It means that it was ridiculously expensive and he didn't want to embarrass me or make me feel guilty when I ordered."

"I'm beginning to like this guy. He seems much better than that Dominic. He seems steady, you know, dependable. You should get together with him."

"Great, now you're encouraging me to have an affair. I thought you'd be the last person to suggest such a thing, especially after Dun –"

"Let's not mention names, OK?"

"Sorry, it slipped out."

"'S OK. Just don't do it again. I've not mentioned You-know-who's name in over two years."

"You'll have to think of a name for your You-know-who."

"Bastard-wanker-man?"

"Be serious, Lexi. There's no way I'm saying that every time I need to refer to What's-his-face. What's wrong with What's-his-face?"

"I'd prefer Two-timing-useless-piece-of-shit, but I suppose What's-his-face will do," Alex said grudgingly. "Anyway, I wasn't encouraging you to have an affair. I was encouraging you to dump Dominic."

"Oh well, that's much better then."

"Don't get sarcastic. You wanted my opinion. I gave it to you."

"I don't remember asking for your opinion."

"Well, you've got it now."

"Cheers, thanks a lot."

"Are you meeting Wrinkle-face again?"

"Yeah, we're meant to catch up later this week."

"That should be fun."

"Yeah, right. Anyway, I'd better get going. I need all the sleep I can get, I have a consulting day with Finland Fani, tomorrow."

"Finland Fanny?"

Sam sighed, "Don't ask."

* * *

Returning from the company the next day, Sam settled on a spot of retail therapy to ease her tired brow. She walked to the market-place and started browsing in the shops. Deciding to go for her favourite purchase, she headed for a shoe shop. As soon as she entered, she knew in the pit of her stomach that she'd have an interesting time. Most people think that Finnish women are all blonde and gorgeous like the Swedes, but the reality is different. Sam had soon realised that the women came in two distinct types. The dark hair/ pale skin/ gorgeous variety and the dyed hair/ too much make-up/ Russian shot-putter variety. At this moment, in her quite delicate state, Sam would have paid rather a lot of money to see one of the latter. Unfortunately, a perfect specimen of the former approached her. The assistant was very young, extremely skinny and inevitably gorgeous, which immediately made Sam feel old, fat and ugly. She had the blackest hair and the palest face and was so petite that she looked like a porcelain doll.

"I'm looking for a pair of black boots."

"Black boots," the girl repeated dreamily.

"Yes, ones that are good for the Finnish winter."

"Winter, yes?"

"Yes."

"Having you a shoe size?" her singsong voice rose in query.

"Of course. Size seven, that would be about forty in European sizes."

The girl walked over to her elaborate boot display and picked out two different styles. "You like?"

"Yes, I like."

"I go get. Take please seat over there." She pointed to a

velvet armchair in the corner and disappeared into the rear of the shop.

Sam was just getting comfy in the chair when she returned.

"Let's be trying, yes?"

"Yes, you are, aren't you?" Sam muttered. "Sorry, yes, I'll try those." She pointed at the ones with the lowest heel.

Sam found her leg being grabbed and her foot being pushed eagerly into the boot.

"No, I don't think so. They're a bit tight."

"Yes, other ones we try, yes?"

"Yes." Sam once more found her foot being jammed into a boot. "No. I don't think it'll work. Finnish sizes seem to be narrower than UK sizes."

"I see," the assistant pondered. Then she had an idea. Sam could almost see the cogs turning in her mind.

"Have you tried losing the weight? You are very fat."

Sam's head snapped up to look the assistant in the eyes. Her Subconscious soothed her, 'Now, now, she didn't really say that. It was just my imagination playing tricks on you.'

"I'm sorry, what did you say?" Sam tried again.

"Your feet, they are fat. Have you thought of taking off some kilos? Feet get, how you say, small when you take off kilos."

Sam's fixed smile faltered. She was trying not to overreact. In the back of her mind she was sure that the conversation was just not happening. Sam stared at the woman, looking for signs of malice. There were none. The assistant, bless her little cotton socks, truly believed she was being helpful. She had sighed sympathetically at Sam whilst using the least civil and most rude words any person hoping to elicit sales commission had ever uttered.

"A lot of people have trouble getting in our shoes. The mostest of people I see are having fat feet."

"If the mostest, I mean majority, have fat feet," Sam said very slowly to ensure that the assistant understood, "have you ever considered the possibility that you might sell more shoes if you increased the width of your shoes slightly?"

"Huh?" The assistant looked blankly at Sam.

"Mostest customer having big feet, make shoe bigger." Sam enunciated every syllable. "Next thing you know, you'll be suggesting people started lopping off bits of their feet to fit your shoes."

"Lopping?" The assistant started to hop on the spot.

"No, no, not hopping, lopping with an L, like chopping." Sam started to do a rather nice mime to go with her words and the assistant was still hopping. "CHOP OFF BITS OF FEET," Sam said loudly.

Behind them there was a sharp cry of shock and they both turned to see a middle-aged woman who had obviously been watching the scene. As they turned towards her, she rushed to the door and fled with a look of horror on her face. Sam surmised that that was very probably the first, and possibly the last time, that she had ever seen a sight like the two of them in her life. Sam wouldn't have been surprised if she found out that the poor woman never left her home again.

"Oh, I never suggest chop off bits of feet," the girl said earnestly, completely unaffected by the trauma that they'd obviously inflicted on the woman.

"Thank God for that!" Sam breathed a sigh of relief.

"Blood would ruin leather."

With this Sam shook her head and decided, for her sanity's sake, she ought to get out before it got any worse.

"Erm . . . thank you. It's been entertaining," she said over her shoulder on the way out.

"English people have strange ideas," the assistant muttered to herself as Sam rushed out the door.

Sam was depressed, Finland had even managed to ruin the one, truly satisfying retail experience. Finnish women obviously didn't belong to the 'Imelda Sisterhood', an international club of women whose main motto was 'You can never have too many shoes'.

Sam needed something to help her recover from this experience and, opposite the shoe shop, she could see the very establishment that would restore her mood.

Leaving the bakery, having bought several rather naughty cakes, Sam had an unnerving feeling that she was being followed.

"Don't be sho shtupid, Missh Moneypenny," Sam amused herself with her very best Sean Connery impression. "You're jusht feeling guilty about the caloriesh." Sam looked around her once more. It's funny how you think everyone is looking at you when you've just spent a small fortune on cream cakes, she grinned. Thinking that the very least she could do was attempt to get some exercise, she started walking back to her hotel.

At that time of year, Finland was a rather difficult place to go for a walk in. The days were warmer, usually above the zero mark; therefore the snow had begun to melt. However, in the evenings, it plunged into sub-zero temperatures, around 10°C below, and the melted snow turned to thick ice. This was what made things 'interesting' as the Finns say.

"Downright bloody dangerous, I say," complained Sam, picking herself up from another stumble.

She turned the corner and saw that there were two police cars in front of her hotel. Her mind started racing again. She hurried, or rather, slid, towards the entrance.

"Sirpa, what's going on?"

"Ms Jordan, hello. Nothing much really." The stressed look on Sirpa's face said the opposite.

"Why the police cars?"

"We have a bit of a problem. Nothing for you to worry."

"Righty-ho," Sam said, still not completely convinced, but continued anyway. "By the way, I didn't get my wake-up call this morning"

"Really? There was note here in morning to place one on your phone. I put on. Maybe number in computer is wrong. I check."

"Thanks."

"We have new computer system. It make wake-up calls," Sirpa explained. "We have many teeth problems."

"You mean teeth*ing* problems." Sam corrected, wondering if Finnish people would ever get to grips with English idioms.

"Yes, here it is, 'Ms Jordan, six thirty'. You did not get?"

"No, I didn't and I definitely don't remember asking for a six thirty call. I rang down last night and asked Timo . . ."

"Timo, he not good in English. He probably make mistake. He not trained in computer. Hold, I find sheet." Sirpa disappeared off into the back office.

Sam called after her, "Look, it doesn't really matter."

"No, no, I must sort out," came the reply from the room behind the counter.

After a few minutes of rustling papers, Sirpa returned, unscrunching a piece of paper, obviously salvaged from the wastepaper bin. "Here, I find morning call sheet."

"That might not help because there was a big mix-up with the rooms last night. Timo gave me a non-smoking room so I came back and he changed the room. He said he wasn't going to change the computer. He also said that he would leave you a note."

"Silly man, he did leave me note, but he write on wake-up call sheet. I think you want wake-up call at six thirty." She held up the call sheet and Sam saw the words 'Mrs Jordan, 630'. "So, you are in room 630?"

"Yes." Sam realised what had happened. "You mean, you sent the call to the wrong room?"

"Yes, but no matter. I sorry you not receive yours. There was a call for you today, also, but he only wanted to know your room number. He said he was from airline. That means, I must give him wrong room number. I change it now, so there are no more mistakes."

Thinking the call was probably Dominic, Sam asked, "Did he leave a message?"

"No," Sirpa said concentrating on the computer. "He just asked your room number."

Sam stood in the lobby trying to make a decision. Should she go to her room or should she get herself a drink first? She needed to steady her rather frayed nerves, so she opted for the drink. It was early evening and the bar was already predominantly full of men, necking huge amounts of beer. The hotel, in all its wisdom, had called the bar "New York". Sam looked around her and as someone who had actually visited the Big Apple, noted that this bar was as far removed from that great city as you can get without falling off the edge of the earth. As she sat at the bar, she overheard two English businessmen talking.

"So, it's been a terrible day from start to finish, really," said one.

"Yes, and they say that Finland is crime-free," snorted the other.

"Relatively crime-free, I suppose. It's just ironic that I live in London, the burglary capital of Europe, and have never been broken into. I come to Finland, which has less than one burglary per ten thousand people and I have my room ransacked and money nicked."

"Sod's law," commiserated his friend.

"I wouldn't mind that, but they gave me a wake-up call two hours early as well. When I complained about it, they swore blind that I'd ordered it."

This was too much for Sam.

"Sorry, gentlemen. I couldn't help overhearing. I think the wake-up call might have been my fault. You see, there was a bit of a mix-up on the computer . . ." She stopped, her brain started to churn. "Wait a minute. If you don't mind me asking, what room are you in?"

"Well, I *was* in room one-oh –"

"Seven," Sam completed the room number for him. "What do you mean, you *were* in Room 107?"

"Well, the police are in there now, dusting for fingerprints, or whatever it is they do. They've given me a new room. I've never had a burglary before, see. I live in the burglary capital of Europe and . . . "

"Thank you," Sam said and got up.

Sam was linking the bits of stray information in her brain. She was meant to be in Room 107. Timo hadn't changed the details on the computer the night before; Sirpa had only corrected the information a few minutes ago. So, if anyone had wanted to know her room number, according to the computer, she was still in Room 107. It hit her then.

"The robbery was meant for me," she said, both astounded and terrified by the notion.

She tried to think logically. What was it about her? Why was it that people were always doing strange things to her? She thought back. Ever since she left Amsterdam to go to Alex, she'd had a strange feeling that she was being watched. Dominic had been worried about her suitcase. What was it about her suitcase? Dominic said that there was nothing to worry about. Dominic rang the hotel today, to find out her room number. She began to run through a list of occurrences since she left home. I checked my case in at Manchester, I changed flights in Amsterdam, and I went back to London. I left it in Left Luggage at Heathrow. I collected it and brought it to Turku. The only other person to know about my movements after Amsterdam was Dominic. He arranged my flight. Sam felt dizzy. There had to be something in or on the suitcase and even more frightening, Dominic must be involved. What should she do? She sat down in a corner of the bar and dialled.

"Corporate Finance."

"Alex, someone's trying to steal my suitcase."

"Who . . . ? Oh, Sam, for God's sake, would you just once in a while start off with the niceties? We don't all hit the ground running like you do. Some of us need a little lead-in sometimes."

"Alex don't be mad. I'm sorry, but it's a terrible, terrible thing."

"What was it about your suitcase?"

"I think someone's trying to steal it."

209

"Don't be so silly, Sam – why would anyone want to do that? It's not even as if your funky clothing would be fashionable over there. Finland is probably still stuck in the eighties."

"Yeah, right. Ha ha. This isn't funny. There's been robberies and everything and I have a theory."

"Oh, you have a theory – well, let me hear it by all means. Be quick though – my boss will be back in a minute."

"Now she wants speed." Sam rolled her eyes.

"Get on with it!"

"All right! Keep your lanky, greasy hair on, you old tart. I was just thinking. What if someone put something, I don't know, something valuable perhaps, in someone's suitcase in Manchester? Expecting it to end up in Finland later that same day. But then, instead of getting to Finland, the person who owns the case decides to return to London. And what if you don't know exactly where it is, so you 'help' that person get back to Finland. You find out where that person is staying and while she's out at work, you break into her hotel room and steal the case."

"You mean someone broke into your hotel room?"

"No, someone broke into the hotel room I should have had. You see, I changed rooms when I arrived and the guy didn't know how to update the computer so he left it for someone to change the next day. Unfortunately that someone misread the note and didn't change the information. It still looked as if I was in the original room."

"Shit!" Alex exclaimed.

"What if that person was –"

"Dominic!" Alex cried triumphantly. "Fantastic. See, I knew he was dodgy. I even told you. I said 'Trust no one'.

Damn, those *X-Files* are good. I mean, if you were genuine, it wouldn't enter your head to tell someone to trust you, would it?" she reasoned.

"You were right. I should have listened to you, Auntie Alex."

"But, wait a minute, why didn't they take the suitcase out in Helsinki, rather than go to all the trouble of breaking into hotel rooms?"

"Oh, I don't know. Maybe they couldn't get themselves organised quickly enough. Anyway, I picked it up in Helsinki."

"So where's your suitcase now."

"In my room, I hope."

"Where are you?"

"I'm in the bar."

"Now's not the time for alcohol, Sam! Get up to your room and check your case!"

"It's safe. They still think I'm in –" Sam remembered Sirpa. "Damn, Sirpa's changed the computer details."

"Call the police. Then get up to your room!" Alex screamed.

"OK, I'll go, but if I haven't rung back in twenty minutes, you must call my hotel and tell Sirpa to call the police."

Sam walked apprehensively to the lift. It was empty. She got in and, as the doors were closing, a large hairy arm stopped them. Sam jumped backwards as a man came in. It was the Englishman from the bar. Sam relaxed slightly.

"What floor?" he enquired.

"Sixth, please."

"I'm quite glad I'm going home tomorrow." He slurred his words slightly, obviously having had a few too many drinks. "I mean, I live in the –"

"Burglary capital of Europe and have never been burgled. I know," Sam finished for him.

"I won't be coming back here again, too bloody dangerous."

Sam flinched as the bell rang for the third floor.

"That'll be me, then. Be careful. It can be murder out there."

Sam was concerned at his choice of phrase and watched him weave his way out of the lift. She was still really jumpy and nearly had a heart attack when the lift signalled it had reached the sixth floor.

She tiptoed along the corridor and stood listening at her door for a few moments. It didn't sound like anyone was inside, so she slipped in the door card.

Opening the door, she brought herself up to her full five foot five inches and stepped boldly through.

Dominic was sitting on her bed next to her open suitcase. He was surrounded by what seemed like hundreds of thousands of pounds in small bundles of notes. Sam focussed on the thing that Dominic was holding in his hands and did something that she'd never before done in her life. In fact, if ever asked, Sam would always reply that she would never do it. Sam fainted. As she blacked out, her Subconscious confirmed to her Conscious Mind that, it was, indeed, a gun that he was holding.

Chapter Thirteen

Sam opened her eyes. She was still half-involved in a dream where Dominic was kissing her. Her brain ticked over for a little while before she sat up with a start. The air caught in her throat and she felt the pulse throb in her neck. She looked desperately around her room. She was confused – the last thing she remembered was the gun. She shook her head in an attempt to clear it.

It was definitely a gun and definitely Dominic. She checked out the room once more. Dominic was definitely not there unless he was hiding under the bed. She thought she'd better look just in case. As she leant over the edge of the bed to check, her mobile rang. The shock of the noise caused her to fall, head first, off the bed, hitting her head on the floor. She got up, wincing at the pain, and went over to her mobile.

"Hello . . ."

"So? What happened? Was your suitcase there?" Alex's voice was full of excitement.

"Well, I'm not quite sure what happened. How long has it been since we last spoke?"

"What are you on about? Half an hour ago, you said that if you hadn't called back in twenty minutes, I should tell Sirpa to call the police. I tried, but I couldn't get through to your hotel. Then my boss had a go at me for making private phone calls during business hours. I had to wait until he'd left, before I could call again, but I thought I'd better check with you before getting the police involved. So here I am. Why?"

"Well, I wasn't sure how long I was out for. You see, I came up to my room and I found . . . well, actually, I'm not sure what happened. I think I might be going mad. I thought I saw Dominic in my room with a gun and lots of money."

"Sorry. I thought you just said a gun and lots of money." Alex was convinced she'd misheard.

"I did."

"A gun! Are you sure? What did it look like?"

"Well, it was small and pistol-shaped really."

Alex didn't like what she was hearing. Sam seemed too calm, maybe she was having a funny turn. "And you're certain it was real?"

"Well, not having ever seen one close up before, I'm not certain of anything really."

"Maybe it was a mobile phone or something . . ."

"And that's not all. I think I might have . . ."

"You think you might have what?"

"Well . . . no . . . I couldn't have . . . I . . ."

"What?" Alex said impatiently.

"I might have fainted," Sam admitted.

"You what? The great Sam Jordan – fainted!" Alex started to giggle.

"Alex, It's not funny. He had a gun."

"So you said. What was he doing with this supposed gun? Where is he now?"

"I don't know. He's not here." Sam was still a bit shaky. She looked around her once more. "My cream cakes are gone though."

"Cream cakes? You've been buying cream cakes? I thought you were going to eat healthier while you were over there? Next thing I know you'll be telling me that you've been out for a pizza!"

"Alex, you're so missing the point. In fact, not only have you missed the point, you are so far past the point, you wouldn't even be able to see the point with a telescope."

"I had the point in front of me the whole time," Alex maintained. To prove it, she continued. "You were telling me that Dominic came into your room and stole your cream cakes at gunpoint!" She started to giggle.

"No, that's not what I was saying! I'm saying that when I came into the room, I had some cream cakes in one hand and my briefcase in the other. My briefcase is now under the desk and my cream cakes are gone."

Alex's only response was a burst of laughter. Sam opened the minibar. There, sitting in between the miniature bottles of gin and vodka, were her cakes.

"They're in the minibar," Sam said.

"What are?"

"The cakes."

"Sam, I'm sorry. Let me get this straight. You're telling me that you got back to your room, with your cakes, and

Dominic was sitting on the bed with lots of money and a gun."

"Yes."

"You then fainted and Dominic tidied up your room and put the cakes in the minibar."

"I didn't say he tidied the room," Sam protested.

"Whatever. Much as I'd like to believe that Mr 'I'm-a-Greek-God' Dominic is a gun-toting cream-cake-eating gangster, whichever way you look at it, it's really unlikely. I'll tell you what happened. You went up to your room, saw that there was nothing wrong, so you put the cakes in the minibar . . ."

"Go on."

"Well, after all the excitement and stuff, you were probably really knackered and you know how active your imagination gets, Miss Drama Queen. You probably just fell asleep and dreamed about Dominic, the money and the gun. It's understandable really. I'll eat all the pavlovas in your freezer if I'm wrong."

"I suppose . . ."

"Suppose nothing. Is your suitcase there?"

"Yeah."

"Go open it."

Sam went over and dragged it back to the bed. Groaning, as she lifted it up. "All right."

"Anything missing?"

"Not that I can see." Sam tipped out all her clothes to give things a closer look. She tugged at the sides of the case, inspected all the fittings and gave the elastic strap a firm tug.

"Anything different?"

"I don't think so."

"Have a look around the room."

Sam looked around her. "Yeah, what am I looking for?"

"Any stray people who shouldn't be there or anything that is in the wrong place?"

"No, there's nothing, apart from the cakes."

"Forget the cakes. Has anything moved? Anything at all?"

"Nope. But –"

"But nothing. Sam – you're imagining everything. You know how you can be so dramatic sometimes. Look, I've got work to do. You're fine now, aren't you?"

"Yes, I'm fine."

"Good."

"But what if – ?"

"What if nothing. Believe me, if I thought that the whole gun thing was in the least bit possible, I'd be flying over there to beat Dominic up myself. I still think he's the dodgiest bloke on the planet, but he's not the gun-toting type."

"You never know . . ."

"You just like being melodramatic. Take care and I'll see you on Friday. Don't work too hard and get some sleep. And don't eat all the cakes at once."

"All right, Auntie Alex," Sam said sarcastically. "See you on Friday." She ended the call.

There was absolutely no indication that anyone had been in her room, apart from the cleaning staff. Everything was where it had been when she'd left for work, but much cleaner. Her pyjamas were neatly folded and the rubbish bin had been emptied. Sam went over to her suitcase, and examined it thoroughly again. There seemed to be nothing amiss. She sat down on her bed and thought things through. I must have imagined it all, she finally admitted. I'm such a silly cow, she thought. How stupid can one person get?

* * *

Sam woke up the next morning after a fitful night of sleep containing many vivid dreams. She was now absolutely certain that she'd imagined everything the night before. But she still had an unnerving feeling that there was something strange happening, so just in case it wasn't all in her mind, she thought up a plan.

She would go to the office as normal, sneaking her suitcase out with her. After work, she would check herself into another hotel. She would pretend to be in the Cumulus, returning the next evening to pick up her room key, but she would actually sleep in another hotel for the rest of the week. She'd have to sort something out with Mark as she was due to meet with him the next day. She was doing some consultancy for a paper company in the office the day after, so she could drop the key off in the morning as the Cumulus was close to the office. As far as everyone else was concerned, she would be at the Cumulus. Only she would know the truth.

Sam packed her suitcase thoughtfully, remembering at the last moment to leave a few clothes hanging in the wardrobe. That way they'll definitely not suspect that I've left, she thought. She wasn't quite sure who 'they' were, but she knew that she wanted 'them' to leave her alone. She was careful not to think about Dominic. Her emotions, as far as he was concerned, were too agitated. She knew that, eventually, she would have to face up to the fact that he might be involved in whatever it was, but at this point, she didn't know what to think. So Sam dealt with it the only way that she knew how to with difficult problems, and pretended that he didn't exist. I'll deal with it, and him, later, she promised herself.

Sam was pleased to see that Timo was on duty at the reception desk. There were at least five people queuing up, impatiently waiting for him to get to grips with the computer, so that they could check out. This allowed her to get her suitcase out of the hotel without anyone noticing. She walked to the office and left her suitcase in Pirjo's room. She'd come up with a plausible story. She said that it had been damaged on the incoming flight and she needed to take it to be repaired after work. After dismissing Pirjo's offer to take it to the shop for her, Sam focussed on the day ahead.

* * *

Unsurprisingly, Sam's mind had not been fully on her work. But, although she had frequently forgotten her train of thought and occasionally repeated some elements, she thought it was a job relatively well done. She had begun with the five basic principles of Time Management, leading into the importance of maintaining a work diary to discover where their time was actually being used before they attempted to employ the time-management techniques. She then went into the importance of prioritisation, if they really wanted to manage their time efficiently. She then gave them two group-work exercises to illustrate the benefits of prioritisation. She thought she'd been handling the stress pretty well all in all, until a car backfired outside the training-room window during the first coffee break. Sam had thrown herself on the floor yelling 'Save yourselves'!

For their part, the participants of her training programme that day had left the training room under a cloud of mystification. They had learnt quite a lot about Time Management in the hectic modern-day business world and for this, they were grateful. Unfortunately, they had signed up for a course in problem solving. They had noticed the change of topic very early on, but were all far too polite to mention it to Sam. Despite being the world's largest per head users of mobile phones, Finnish people are particularly reticent to actually speak, especially to foreigners and in a foreign language. Give them a few too many drinks however and they never shut up. Unfortunately, the only beverages the group had had was coffee, albeit in large quantities, and caffeine didn't seem to have the same effect. The group had had a brief discussion about it, in Finnish, during the lunch break and had mistakenly assumed that she would get back to the correct topic at some point during the day.

Sam was therefore oblivious to the fact that she had been talking about the wrong subject the entire day and congratulated herself on her ability to get on with her job, despite the conspiracy surrounding her.

She took a taxi from the office to the Sokos Hotel in the centre of Turku and checked herself in under the name Alex Spencer, hoping that Alex would forgive the misuse of her name. She left a message explaining where she was on Alex's home answering machine. She then left a message for Mark, explaining that she'd moved hotels and he should pick her up at the Sokos Hotel the following morning. She'd already decided to use the noisy construction work as an excuse for changing hotels, if he asked. Finally she started to unpack once more. It was only when she had finished that she allowed herself to relax. It was then she realised that she was shaking uncontrollably. She sank down on her bed and breathed deeply. Completely unbidden, tears began to trickle down her face. If anyone had asked her, at this point, why she was crying, she would have mumbled something about tension and stress. The reality was that she was scared. She felt totally alone, with her only true ally a thousand miles away in London. Sam lay down on her bed and cried herself to sleep.

* * *

Sam was jostled awake by the hotel phone.

"Sam, exactly why is it that I find myself asking for me in a Finnish hotel?"

"Alex. Good. You rang."

"Yes, but what's wrong with your mobile? It's set to voice-mail."

"I know. I switched it off. I don't think I could handle talking to Dominic at the moment."

"Haven't you asked him about yesterday then?"

"No, I don't want him to think I'm stupid and I didn't quite know what to say to him. I mean, I could hardly say, 'Excuse me, Dominic, but were you sitting in my room yesterday with thousands of pounds, holding a gun?', now can I?"

"No, but you can see if he has anything to hide, by the way he talks to you. You know, he might seem suspicious or nervous or something . . . oh, I don't know . . ." Alex gave in to Sam's disbelieving silence, "I see your problem. Forget I mentioned it." Alex changed tack. "So what are you going to do now?"

"I don't know. I'm going to go to work the rest of the week and then get in a plane back to London on Friday, I suppose."

"Well, I won't tell anyone where you are, not even your mother. I promise. Have you told anyone else, by the way?"

"No, just you and Mark."

"That's good. You can probably trust Mark. It's not as if he'd ever be involved with anything dodgy, him being Finnish and everything."

"What's that got to do with it?"

"You know, Finnish, solid and dependable, definitely not a blabbermouth."

"You're right. I know you're right."

"I'm always right. Listen, you take care and I'll pick you up at the airport."

There was a very long silence before Sam said, "Lexi, I'm scared."

"I know, sweetheart, but there's probably nothing to worry about. Anyway, you'll be here soon and I'll look after you."

"OK." Sam put down the phone.

Sam picked up her mobile and debated whether she should switch it on. After pacing up and down the room for a few minutes, she thought it might be safer to access her messages using the hotel phone. A more expensive course of action, but probably the safest one. She had eight messages waiting for her. She settled back to listen to them. The first three were from her mother complaining that Sam never called her. The fourth was from Dominic.

"Sam, it's Dominic. Please call me."

She deleted it and pressed the button to hear the next one.

"Sam, it's Dominic. Please call. I need to talk to you."

She deleted it and continued.

"I really need to explain. Please call . . . I'm on my mobile."

The next message was even more intriguing.

"Sam, look, I'm getting really worried now. I've tried you at your hotel. Please call me. You might be in danger."

Sam considered this one and went on to hear the last message.

"Sam, I'm worried. I just need to know that you're OK. Please call me. I'm on my mobile."

This last message was the most interesting as far as she was concerned. Dominic's voice sounded so distraught that Sam had felt, for a brief moment anyway, a tiny bit sorry for him. Let him stew, she thought, and went back to bed.

Chapter Fourteen

Sam was still subdued when she met up with Mark in the morning. For the first time, Mark was doing all the talking in the car on the way to his office. A couple of times, Sam could see that he was just about to ask what was wrong, but decided against it at the last minute. Instead he was wittering on about the very important ice hockey match that took place the night previously. Sam knew absolutely nothing about sports and even less about ice hockey. Apparently Finland had played Sweden and the entire country was excited that morning, because Finland had beaten Sweden for the first time in five years. On a sporting and cultural level that was approximately like England beating Germany at football. Sam was extremely pleased that Mark was in such a chatty mood, as it allowed her to forget for a short time about the strange predicament that she found herself in.

"Listen to me doing all the talking and not asking you how you are this fine, but frosty morning."

"No, it's nice to hear that you're so happy."

"So, Samantha, what did you get up to last night?"

Well, I found out that my boyfriend was in the country and he may or may not be here to kill me for something that may or may not be in my suitcase, but apart from that . . .

"Not much," she said sadly.

"Well, I think we need to perk you up a bit today."

"I'm sorry, Mark. I . . . I didn't mean . . .I just . . . didn't get breakfast, this morning," Sam uttered unconvincingly.

"Oh well then, I'll shut up until you have some coffee inside you."

"No, you can carry on – so what's the story behind ice hockey then? Is it anything like field hockey?"

"No, not at all. You see, with ice hockey . . ."

Sam listened to his explanation of the game and pushed all the scary thoughts to the back of her mind. I'll just have to deal with them later . . .

* * *

After he provided coffee, they got straight into the organisation of the Fintec launch on to the UK market. Sam was glad that Mark too had his business head on and they'd managed to finalise all the plans. She was also grateful that Mark was so atypical of most of the Finnish managers that she'd encountered. His ideas for the launch were imaginative without being too unrealistic, cost-conscious but not penny-pinching, and ultimately showed signs of being successful. Sam just wasn't used to these things going so smoothly, especially since she was well and truly in the middle of the nightmare week from hell.

They'd worked hard together all morning and had just

finished an extremely pleasant lunch. Sam still considered it pleasant even after the discovery that the beef stroganoff she thought she'd been eating had turned out to be reindeer ragout. Surprisingly, the reindeer tasted very nice, a tad gamey, but nice, in a stringy beef kind of way.

The afternoon stretched invitingly in front of them and they settled into a relaxed rhythm, Sam coming up with the ideas and Mark providing the finishing touches.

They were such an efficient team that somehow, and approximately two hours early, they'd done as much work as it was possible to do that day, there and then. Sam was at a loss to know what to do in these circumstances as she'd never before encountered such a relatively normal Finnish manager. The last thing she needed was to be there with Mark, alone, in his office, with that enormous, hugely inviting mahogany desk, and nothing work-wise to concentrate on, especially in this week to end all weeks.

She attempted to review the launch documents, but Mark stopped her.

"Samantha, even if you spend one hundred years staring at those documents, you won't come up with anything better than what we have there. You can get back to the hotel early today."

"I have to keep improving everything. It's a bad habit of mine. I'm a perfectionist, I suppose."

"Are you this bad at home?"

"How do you mean?"

"Well, if you're like this in the office, your home floors must be clean enough to eat on."

"Funny you should say that. When I'm at home, in private, I'm a bit of a slob. As we speak, the environmental health officers are probably reassessing my house as a pigsty."

"And is there someone who has to share your pigsty?" He threw out the comment as he was busying himself at his desk.

It was such an incongruous question. There was nothing malicious or even serious meant by it. Sam knew that. However, maybe it was the reminder of home, or the oblique reference to partners and therefore, Dominic. Or maybe it was the fact that she had been so relaxed and hence off-guard. Whatever it was, Mark's question went into her very soul and unleashed a veritable Niagara of emotions and tears that she'd been keeping so carefully under wraps. All the recent events had built up so much pressure in her head that it inevitably had to come out sometime. All of those deal-with-it-later's had piled up and suddenly 'later' was now.

Sam started to cry. It was so silent at first that Mark didn't even notice. It wasn't until the huge tears began to splash on the desk, that he looked over at her face to see the streams rolling down her cheeks.

"Samantha, what's wrong?"

His innocent and unsuspecting question was like the straw that broke the camel's back. He showed no sign of the embarrassment that men – especially businessmen – feel whenever a professional woman – or indeed any woman – cried. In a second, all hell broke loose in his office as Sam wailed, letting out massive sobs of confusion and misery. Although it had been obvious all day that there was something wrong, not even Mark was prepared for the huge outpouring of emotion when it finally came. He moved around the desk and enveloped her in his arms, pulling her head to his chest. The amazing irony was that if he'd done exactly that the first time she'd been in his office, like she'd wanted him to, she would never have got so close to Dominic and therefore she'd never have very-nearly-slept with him. And she wouldn't have felt as wretched as she did now.

"Go on. Just cry," he murmured into her hair. "Let it all out."

"I don't want to go back to the hotel. I don't want to be alone."

To his credit, Mark didn't question her too closely. He listened to her pleas and very quickly she found herself being bundled out of his office, into his car and on the road to his house.

For once Sam was glad to be in Finland. Finnish people – especially those with a bit of money – liked to live in isolated conditions and pretend they were the only ones on the planet. Mark was no exception. He drove her to a huge house set beside a lake in the middle of the Finnish forest.

"Mark, it's lovely." Sam was amazed at her reaction – normally she was an out-and-out city girl. Her motto was, 'You've seen one tree, you've seen 'em all' and silence tended to scare the 'bejesus' out of her. Seeing how this time she couldn't get much more frightened, she was able to feel the tranquillity of the setting and see the splendour of it all. And, more importantly, no one would know where to find her.

"I like it also. The nearest neighbour is five miles away. I thought you might appreciate that."

"I do, thanks, Mark. I should really . . ."

"No, Samantha, you don't need to do anything. Come on."

He helped her out of the car and, keeping a strong hand at the small of her back, he led her into his home.

"You make yourself comfortable and I'll get you something strong to drink," he said, pointing her towards a large white leather sofa. "I'm not much of a drinker, so you'll have to take pot luck. You look as if you could do with a large one."

"Thanks." Sam sank down into the sofa.

Mark soon returned carrying two nearly empty bottles. "There looks to be about a glassful in each, which would you prefer? Brandy or Koskenkorva?"

"Brandy, please."

"Not up to the fine Finnish vodka then?"

"No, brandy would be good just now."

"I understand. Would you like something to eat?"

"No, I'm fine."

"Well, why don't I go and rustle something up and you can decide once you've seen my cooking."

"OK." He started to walk away. "Mark, can I put my feet up?"

He turned to her and said quietly, "You – can do anything you want."

"Thanks."

Sam drank her brandy in one gulp, kicked off her shoes, and curled up into a medium-sized ball.

Sometime later she thought she heard Mark say, "I think I should put you to bed." But she was too tired to reply.

* * *

Sam woke up convinced that she was in the middle of one of her strange dreams. She opened her eyes and saw a completely unfamiliar room. It definitely wasn't her bedroom at home and even more definitely was not a hotel room. If it was, it must have been an extremely expensive hotel room. She seemed to be sleeping under a home-made quilt and a very nicely made one at that. And, she realised with a start, she was completely naked. OK, maybe not completely naked, she was still wearing her blouse and her underwear was intact, but she felt naked. She was still too disorientated to realise that someone must have undressed her.

There came a quiet tap at the door. Here's where I wake up from my dream, she thought. The tap came again. Maybe this was real after all.

"Hello?" she offered.

"Sam, I've made breakfast. Are you up? Of course you're up – if you weren't before, you will be now. What am I saying? Can I come in?"

At first, Sam smiled, but then the memory of where she was came flooding back. She was at Mark's house in the countryside, which meant that, she took another peek under the quilt, Mark must have taken her suit off! Sam was struck dumb by this development in the continuing 'What embarrassing thing has Sam done now' saga.

After choosing her words, very carefully, she hitched the quilt up to her neck and said, "Of course you can come in – it's your house."

He opened the door and came in with a tray containing, from what she could see from the bed, orange juice and coffee. As he came closer, she realised there was more.

"I wasn't sure what you liked for breakfast, so I've made blueberry pancakes and I've got some Karelian pies – are you hungry?"

"Starved. What are Karelian pies?"

"How long have you been working here?"

"Two years, why?"

"Two years and never had them before?"

He put the tray on her lap and pointed at the strange oval pastries.

"Oh, I've seen them at breakfast in the hotel. I always thought they were rice pudding cakes. You know, sweet rather than savoury." She picked one up and started prodding it. On top of the pastry there was a layer of sticky rice onto which Mark had added some yellow gloopy stuff. "What's this?"

"That is a mixture of butter and boiled eggs. You can put anything you like on them. I have some ham and some cheese. Which would you like?"

"Ham, please." She watched him put ham on top and he passed it to her to try. She couldn't say it was an altogether unpleasant experience – the pies themselves were tasteless and the egg mixture was greasy, but edible. To be honest, she couldn't understand why they bothered with all that rice and pastry. A slice of bread was just as good. To Mark she said, "Mmm . . . not bad."

He smiled and started to leave. "I'll leave you alone – I'll be downstairs if you need me. The bathroom is down the hall and I've put some towels and a bathrobe in there for you. Just make yourself at home. Take your time though. There's no rush."

"Thank you."

"My utmost pleasure. Don't let the pancakes get cold." And he was gone.

The breakfast (including the Karelian pies) was devoured

in under ten minutes, and with a full stomach, she got out of bed and attempted to find the bathroom. She'd peered into at least four other bedrooms before she accepted that she really was in a massive house, more suited to a huge family than a single man. No one person needs this much space, she thought. If I don't find the bathroom now, I'm going back to bed. She pushed open the last door on the corridor. There in front of her was the most gorgeous bathroom she'd ever seen. The bath tub alone would put many swimming pools to shame and the shower cubicle was bigger than her entire bathroom at home. It was beautifully decorated and there were candles everywhere, which was a definite clue that there had been a woman's touch at work. She'd not even thought to ask. He might be married. That was unquestionably something she should have established before forcing herself on him in such a shameful manner. She decided to shower very quickly indeed before the woman of the house showed up to find her naked in the bathroom.

After towel-drying her hair, she tied the bathrobe loosely before emerging from the bathroom in a cloud of steam, bumping straight into a shocked woman in the process.

"Sorry. I'm really sorry. I didn't mean to . . ."

"*En ymmärrä.*" The woman shook her head.

"I'm sorry I don't understand." Sam began dredging up individual Finnish words from the depths of her memory, trying in vain to work out what the woman said. The phrase she heard was familiar.

"*En ymmärrä. En ymmärrä.*" The woman was still shaking her head as she turned and fled.

Sam stared after her, also in shock. She didn't know

how Mark was going to explain to this woman the appearance of an English consultant in a bathrobe, stepping out of the bathroom. Deep down, Sam couldn't resist a smile as she realised, belatedly, that the woman was well and truly a Finnish woman of the 'Russian shot-putter' variety and immediately frowned when she thought that she must also be a woman of the 'wife' variety. Changing quickly back into her clothes, she decided to show her face downstairs.

Very quietly opening doors downstairs, she found the woman in one of the rooms, fiercely scrubbing at a perfectly clean mirror. Through her knowledge of Alex and her habits, Sam presumed that, like Alex, this woman too was one of the 'clean obsessively to take mind off bad things' type of person. She managed to close the door again without disturbing her and endeavoured to find Mark.

She found him skulking guiltily in the kitchen.

"I think I just met your wife."

"My wife?"

"Yeah, I bumped into her upstairs."

"I very much doubt it."

"No, really, she's in the room that's painted green."

"She's in Helsinki –"

Sam's heart sank down to her stomach.

"At least my soon-to-be *ex-wife* is in Helsinki – you've probably met Mrs Virtanen. She's the housekeeper."

Sam perked up. "So why are you looking so guilty?"

"I didn't think I was looking guilty. A little shifty maybe. . ."

"Why, what have you been up to?"

"Well, you might not like it, but I thought it was best."

"Thought what was best?" asked Sam, by now alarmed.

"I've just been speaking to Martti. I told him that you

were taken ill while visiting my office yesterday and that you wouldn't be able to come in today." He paused.

"Damn, I forgot about the consultancy today."

"Don't worry. He said that he'll ask Pirjo to contact the company and reschedule. So you're free as a bird, today at least."

"That was a brilliant idea. Thank you."

"No need to thank me." He held out his hand. "Come, on. Let me give you the grand tour."

* * *

Coming out of the library some time later, Sam turned to him, visibly impressed, "I can't believe I know someone who has an actual library in their house."

"If you think that's great, you should see the music room." Opening the door, he let Sam go in ahead of him.

"Oh. My. God. Actual antiques!" She pointed to the chairs, then ran her hand over the gigantic Steinway grand piano which took pride of place in the room.

"Yep, they've been in my family for years."

"I didn't think Finland did antiques. I thought everything had to be brand-new and full of computer technology."

"Not everything. My grandmother was very partial to French period furniture."

"Is this your parents' house?"

"Not any more. They let me have it, when my father semi-retired six months ago."

"Where are they then?"

"They spend most of their time in the summer cottage or in the townhouse in Helsinki. My mother had hoped that my wife and I would start a family."

"So what happened . . ." Sam started to ask, but saw him grimace. "Look, just tell me to mind my own business."

"No. No, you're entitled to ask – I brought the subject up."

"But still . . ."

"She's American."

He said this as if it should explain everything. Sam nodded knowingly.

"We got along fine when we lived in Boston. But then we had to come back over here when my father had a heart attack. My mother wanted us to stay and she told me that I'd been messing around long enough. It was time for me to face up to my responsibilities and take over the running of the company. Portia, that's my wife, got really upset and refused to live in a mausoleum in the middle of nowhere – her words, not mine."

"But it's wonderful. So peaceful."

"Yes, but the social scene is hardly Boston. Which is why she's staying – or should I say shopping – in Helsinki until the divorce comes through."

"I'm sorry things didn't work out for you."

"Why should you be sorry? It's not your fault. Anyway, c'est la vie, que será será and all that."

They finished off the tour with a stroll in the still snow-covered gardens.

"I've said it before and I'll probably say it again, but this is amazing."

"I'm glad you like it."

"Like it, nothing. I love it."

"You should see it in the summer!"

"I'd love that."

* * *

"That's a bit heavy for light reading," Mark commented much later as he strode into the day room – which was like a conservatory but much, much bigger – where Sam had settled to wait for him while he made some phone calls and attended to other business.

"Ah, but who said it's meant to be light reading? Anyway, some people find *Das Kapital* very light."

"Who?"

Sam looked at the thick, leather-bound tome for inspiration. "Erm . . . "

"See, you can't think of anyone."

"I've got it: mad-Marxist-student-politicos!" Sam announced triumphantly.

"What, in German?"

"OK then, mad-Marxist-student-politico-linguists."

"Smartarse!"

"Talk about smartarses, I was about to ask you why it was sitting on the coffee table of your day room, looking suspiciously like current reading matter. Been brushing up on socialist theory?"

"Not really – it makes a fantastic doorstop."

"And here I was impressed by the high level of your German literacy!"

"Nope, sorry, never read it. It was a present from a friend of mine at Harvard."

Sam noticed the casual slipping into the conversation of his alma mater. "But why *Das Kapital*?"

"It was a long running joke. His nickname for me was *Commie* because of my deeply held belief in the social responsibilities of society."

"Oh yes, you bleeding-heart Scandinavians –" He was

about to interrupt, but she held up her hand, "I know, I know, *Nordic people*."

Mark laughed and threw a cushion at her.

"Declaration of war, eh?" Sam said, picking up the nearest cushion. "Prepare to die."

She thwacked him over the head. A brief, but highly enjoyable pillow-fight ensued. Laughing and breathless – and more than a little lightheaded – they both dropped on to the sofa.

"Give in?" Sam half-heartedly raised her cushion.

"Not a chance." With that he grabbed her and wrestled her over until he was on top of her.

They were so close together, not even a breath of wind could get between them. There was a feeling of inevitability about the events which were about to unfurl. They both knew that it was going to happen, it was simply a matter of how: how big (of course it mattered) and how long would it take them to get naked?

"Why-ay pet, fancy a shag, like?" Sam put on a strong Geordie accent – well, it worked for Alex . . .

"Sorry?"

"Shut up and kiss me, you beast."

Suddenly they were tearing at each other's clothes, both kissing every inch of exposed flesh. It was less a case of them having sex than the other way round. Having sex implied a tacit decision-making process. They, however, had no free will as far as this was concerned.

Sam groaned with pleasure as his mouth found a stray breast.

"Is this yours?" he asked.

Actually to Sam it came out as 'ugh, ergh, org?' as he was loathe to set her nipple free.

She wasn't quite sure what happened next – one minute she was in the throes of pure ecstasy and the next, both she and Mark were falling off the sofa and landing with a heavy thud on the floor.

"ARGH!" Sam screamed as she realised in agony that Mark was still firmly attached to her boob. "You've bitten it off!"

"I've done no such thing – see, still attached." He flicked at it with his tongue. This sent her spiralling out of control again. When she was once more in control of her senses, she detached her upper body from his and made her way down towards the zip of his trousers.

"Samantha, you do know that the breast thing was an accident, don't you?"

She looked up at him and nodded. "Uh-huh."

"Could you possibly put your teeth away while you're down there then?"

She shook her head. "Uh-uh."

"I'm just seeking clarification here – was that a 'uh-uh' meaning, 'Of course, Mark, I'm putting the teeth away now?' or is it . . . what the hell are you doing down there?"

Sam sat back on her haunches. "If you'd just shut up for one second, you'd realise that I was attempting to undo your zip with my teeth."

"And you are doing this because . . . ?"

"Cos I read it in a book. It may have been a romantic novel, but I'm sure the word penis was mentioned so maybe not. Anyway, apparently, the woman undid the bloke's trousers with her teeth, exposed his throbbing thingy and he apparently exploded with ecstasy . . . Mark, stop laughing. It's meant to be sexy not funny . . . oh, for God's sake!"

By this time Mark was nearly doubled up with laughter.

She tried to undo his trousers by the more orthodox means, but still found it difficult. "MARK! If you don't stop laughing this instant, I'm leaving." There was a smile playing at the edges of her lips.

"You. Are not. Going. Anywhere." This time the look in his eyes was serious, with just the faintest glint showing that he still maintained his sense of humour.

Sam would have loved to say that the sex was amazing, but as this was real life, she could only describe it as good, but unusual. Mark was the first man that she'd ever encountered who actually felt open enough to joke about sex. She'd been waiting to find a man who had the same attitude to sex as she had. Sam always maintained that the act itself was designed to give whatever entity that looked down from above a jolly good laugh. Human sex was your average deity's idea of a really great sitcom on a par with *Fawlty Towers* or anything *Morecambe and Wise* could come up with. And while they managed to giggle their way to a reasonable level of mutual satisfaction, for the first time in her life, Sam didn't have to smother her laughter when they had a case of 'front bottom burps' as Sam and Alex liked to call it.

* * *

Sam felt Mark breathing deeply beside her. Night had fallen and they were still in the day room, sprawled out on a luxuriously soft rug. She started thinking about what had happened and allowed herself a satisfied smile. She could hardly believe that she'd done more with Mark, three times more in fact, than she had with her actual, official . . . Sam hesitated on the description of Dominic and the smile fell from her lips. Alex would have been proud of her but, unfortunately, pride was the one emotion she simply couldn't summon up. Funny how things change. She looked across at Mark. He seemed so at ease. She'd never seen someone sleep so peacefully.

The small thought which had been lurking in the back of her brain, occasionally poking at her subconscious with a sharp implement, began to grow. It had taken a little longer than normal to appear, due to her post-coital satisfaction, but finally there it was. Soon it was so big that it completely dominated her entire mind.

"What have I done?" Sam was filled with horror. Slowly, but with ever-increasing speed, she began looking for her clothing, so casually discarded earlier. Very soon her search became frantic.

Calm down or you'll wake him, she reminded herself. Finally, she was dressed and ready to go.

"Go where?" she mumbled and Mark began to stir. She needed to get away. She looked at her watch. It was ten-thirty in the evening. She could call a taxi, but she realised that she had no idea where she was. Mrs Virtanen! Mark had told her that she lived in the cottage near the main gate. Sam put on her coat and rushed out into the night, stumbling down the driveway. Reaching the cottage, she began pounding on the door.

"Mrs Virtanen?"

The door opened a crack.

"Mrs Virtanen – taxi!" Sam held up her mobile and said, "Call taxi." She forced her phone into the poor confused woman's hand.

The housekeeper looked at Sam quizzically and said, "*Taksi?*"

240

Sam almost nodded her head off, "Yes, yes, *kyllä, kyllä,* taxi!"

The woman went back into the cottage, waving for Sam to follow. She handed back the mobile and moved towards her own phone. After a short exchange with the taxi company, she put down the phone and, looking embarrassed, pulled together her dressing gown and pointed at a cup which was sitting on a small side table. "*Kahvi?*"

Sam shook her head and tried to dredge up the words for 'no thanks'. "*Ei, kiitos,*" she eventually came up with, hoping that it was the correct term and not the slang term for 'I'm gonna murder you in your bed'.

Mrs Virtanen then sat down and seemed to weigh up the pros and cons of attempting conversation and, obviously coming to the conclusion that there was no point in even trying it, she resumed her television viewing. Twenty minutes later, there was a buzzing sound. Mrs Virtanen looked over at Sam, nodded her head and said, "Taksi."

Sam gratefully shook the woman's hand and said, "*Kiitos, kiitos.*"

She rushed to the cab and got in, saying, "*Hotelli Sokos, Turku.*" Slumped in the back seat, she switched off her mobile, steadfastly ignoring the flashing 'you have messages' icon.

She'd deal with Dominic later.

Chapter Fifteen

Sam left it until the following morning to call Dominic. She waited until she was walking through the streets of Turku toward the office.

"Stewart," came the curt answer.

"Dominic, it's Sam. I'm fine, there's nothing wrong."

"Sam. Thank God! You have to tell me where you are."

"I'm in my hotel room in Turku, why?"

"You're at the Cumulus?"

"Yes."

"Sam, don't lie to me." Dominic's voice hardened. "I really need to know where you are."

"What makes you think that I'm lying?"

"Because I'm standing in your room at the Cumulus now and unless you're under the bed, you are definitely not here. Now I'm asking you once more, where – ?"

That was as far as he managed to get before she hung up. Sam's heart was pounding. Her thoughts were racing around her mind like a meeting at Royal Ascot, but with much more crap and rather less need for a ridiculously big hat. She tried to think. Dominic was in Turku. This meant that he could have been in her room that night. She was not far from her office. If she ran, she could get there in ten minutes. With all her colleagues around her, she knew she'd be safe.

Finally, wheezing like an asthmatic hyena, she reached the office building. Her mobile rang. She ignored it. She slipped it into her inside pocket and reached for her keys. She was panting hard and her heart was pounding like a drum in her chest. She could hardly concentrate on getting the key in the lock. Somehow, she managed to get the door open. Dominic in Turku. She could hardly believe it. Dominic!

She rushed through the main entrance and into the training room. And there was Dominic, standing, mobile in hand. Someone must have let him in. Were they mad? How could they do such a thing? Didn't they know who they were dealing with? Sam stood transfixed at the sight. Then she screamed. It began silently inside her head, but soon turned into a loud piercing wail.

As Dominic leapt forward and grabbed hold of her, Martti Saari came rushing into the room, an expression of utmost alarm on his face.

"What's going on here?" Martti demanded. "Mr Stewart, is there a problem?"

"Sorry about this. I must have frightened her." Dominic was as cool as ice but was holding tightly onto Sam's arm.

Sam was amazed that Martti was so calm. Being confronted by a gun-toting maniac didn't happen every day. Although Sam had the feeling that it did to her. He obviously knew something she didn't. Talking of knowledge, how on earth did Martti know Dominic's name?

"I think I need to sit down." She suddenly felt quite nauseous.

"Yes, sit," said Martti. He pulled a chair forward.

"No," said Sam, as her stomach heaved, "I need to go to the bathroom. I think I'm going to be sick!"

Dominic had no option but to let her go, but she noted he looked nervous as he did so, as if she might take flight.

"Sam, listen!" called Dominic anxiously as she left the room. "I'll explain everything to you when you come back!"

* * *

Ten minutes later, she was back in the training room, having spent five of those minutes lurking in the bathroom in an agony of indecision. Should she make her escape? Or should she hear what Dominic had to say? With Martti there, surely she would be safe? At length she decided to confront him and demand the truth.

She had returned to find Martti and Dominic looking for all the world as if they were bosom buddies. There was much smiling and backslapping.

Martti looked over at her and smiled, "Mr Stewart telling me what happen. We cancel today your training. Mr Stewart think you need look after." He looked at Dominic. "Well, we have work doing. I leave her to you, then."

"No!" Sam finally got her voice back – but it was too late – the door had shut behind him. She stared at Dominic in confusion.

"Sam, listen. Don't talk. Just listen." He paused, sat down

next to her and reached for her hand. "Sam, I'm going to tell you what's going on, but you mustn't be frightened." Dominic paused and looked full of remorse for a moment. "I think you should sit down."

"I am –"

"Oh yes, so you are," he cleared his throat. "This isn't easy for me to say, especially when you think of our fairly recent um . . ."

"What?" She was getting worried. Dominic was usually so sure of his words that this hesitation served only to increase the tension Sam felt welling up in her body.

"You know, our recent . . . um . . . thing."

"Enough already . . . what are you trying to tell me?"

"OK. Samantha, I suppose I'd better just come out and say it."

"I wish you would."

"Sam, I am a police officer; I'm with Special Branch. I was assigned to look after you."

It was only when the air came out of her lungs in a rush that Sam was aware that she'd been holding her breath. Dominic reached into his pocket and brought out a police warrant card. Sam tried to take in the information on it, without much success. The only thing she noted was that it was definitely Dominic's picture.

"Police? But . . . ?" she stammered.

"It's a long story and I haven't got time to tell you everything now, but we have been monitoring you for a while. We suspected that your luggage was being used to smuggle illicit merchandise."

"Illicit merchandise?" Sam's head felt as if was going to explode. "Do you mean drugs?"

245

"Yes, drugs. We knew after checking you out that you had nothing to do with it, but we needed to know who was behind it."

Sam leant back in her seat, hardly able to believe what she was hearing.

Dominic continued. He knew his duplicity would anger her and his only hope was to get most of it out before it fully sank into her consciousness. "We were close to finding out when you did your disappearing act in Amsterdam."

"But how . . . ?" Sam had not managed to keep up with him. She was still trying to absorb the news that he was a policeman.

Dominic stared at her, waiting for her face to show signs that she had grasped what he had been saying. Slowly but surely, Sam caught up. Things were beginning to fit into place. This was the reason for all that not-to-panic and spy stuff back in London.

"We were following the suspects in Helsinki, expecting them to do the pick-up there, when you took the evidence back to London with you. You really put a few cats in with the pigeons then. Half of the members of the Russian gang were scouring Amsterdam for you. Not to mention half of Special Branch. Luckily, you rang me and we were able to get you back to Finland, where I could keep an eye on you."

Sam shook her head once more. Russian drug-runners? This was ridiculous. There was no way this could be happening.

"I've been so worried," Dominic admitted. "I thought they'd got you . . . or worse, I thought they'd killed you." He leant over and clutched her in his arms. "Thank God you're safe!" He looked down tenderly into her face and stroked her cheek.

Sam almost slapped his hand away.

"So why couldn't you have said something before? It's not as if we weren't alone enough."

"I almost let a few things slip."

"So all the – I hesitate to call them dates, for obvious reasons – all the 'meetings' were just part of your surveillance?"

"No, it wasn't like that."

"What was it then? Were you being paid to have sex with me? Thank God we didn't. Was that part of your 'job' then?"

"No, Sam. I meant everything I said to you. You have to believe me."

"And to think I felt guilty about . . ." she nearly said Mark's name, "about ignoring your phone calls."

"What can I say? I have no defence apart from the fact that it was a huge operation and a civilian couldn't be trusted to play along." He groaned inwardly, knowing that he'd said the wrong thing. Damn!

"Is that all I am now, a civilian? So what you're saying is that I couldn't be trusted. Well, thank you very much."

"You know that you mean a lot more to me than that."

"How do I know? I don't even know who you are any more. If I ever did."

Although Sam meant every word she'd just uttered, she was aware that she was overreacting. Just the thought of Mark earlier had reminded her that attack was the best form of defence. She backed off a little.

"So you *were* in my hotel room? I thought I was seeing things."

"Yes, it was me. We had to make sure that the evidence was still in your case. When we heard that your room was ransacked, we thought they'd got to it. Luckily, you'd changed rooms, so they got the wrong one. I went to check the case and, unfortunately, you walked in just as I found the money. I almost shot you. I don't know what I would have done if you hadn't fainted."

"Why? And why didn't you stay and explain all this when I woke up?"

"Like I said, there was no way I could have told you at that point. We had to make sure that you carried on as normal. We didn't have anything we could pin on them until they made a move for you, or rather, your suitcase."

"So you put me on the bed. You put my cakes in the minibar. You kissed me?" The words came out in a rush, she was still trying to make sense of it all.

"Yes," Dominic replied and blushed slightly at her last comment. "You looked so beautiful, I couldn't help it!"

"So, you have been following me since I arrived?" She had to keep him on the defensive. She didn't think she could handle it if he started being nice.

"Yes, but I lost sight of you, when you were at Fintec. I got a call that two of the Russian gang members had gone to the Cumulus. I was the closest, so I had to go there. We caught two of them in action, turning your hotel room upside down looking for the suitcase. We couldn't understand why it wasn't there, and neither could they."

"I'd taken it with me – I'd decided to check into another hotel, just in case you were after me."

"Well, by the time I'd finished with them, I had to get back to catch you when you left the company. I was going to explain everything to you then, but you weren't there. I waited in your room for you all night, but you didn't come back. Your phone was switched off. Where were you? We checked all the local hotels."

"I'd been using my friend's name."

"Clever girl." He squeezed her hand. "One thing I don't understand though is how you got out of the Fintec office without me seeing you? I got back there at about 3pm. You were booked in to work until 4pm."

This was the perfect opportunity to tell him about Mark, but she couldn't quite find the right words. I thought you were a 'bad guy' so I slept with the first person that asked me, sounded a little bit too forthright and anything else would have been an out-and-out lie. If she didn't mention it, it wouldn't be lying, would it? A sin of omission maybe, but definitively not a lie.

"I wanted to explain this morning on the phone, but you cut me off, so I thought I'd come here and wait for you."

"So what happens now?"

"Well, I'm not letting you out of my sight for starters," he smiled. "Let's pick up your case and get you back home."

"So is it all over then?"

"Not quite, we still haven't put all the pieces together. They had to have some people on the inside with the airline. We have our suspicions but no proof. Your part is over though, for now anyway. It's getting too dangerous for you. Once we have the suitcase, you can go home."

They made their way through the city to the Sokos Hotel, Dominic holding onto her arm, protectively guiding her through the bustle of people in the market square. It was particularly busy and Sam was getting jostled from all sides, but she didn't feel at all nervous – in fact, she was having trouble feeling anything at all. Dominic had changed his grip from her arm to around her shoulders, but Sam didn't notice this either. You could say that Sam was in shock, possibly mildly demented, but in actual fact, her mind was working furiously, attempting to come to terms with the fact that Dominic was, after all her raging suspicion, one of the good guys. The whole thing with Mark had been fully justified when Dominic was trying to kill her, but now that she knew the truth about him, sleeping with Mark filled her with shame and she felt more guilt about her behaviour than an entire Catholic congregation, before confession. The only way she could deal with the feelings was to disconnect. This often occurred when she was close to losing her grip on reality. She felt like she was in a cinema, watching all these events happening on a wide screen, with stereo surround-sound.

By the time they arrived at her hotel, Sam was almost back to normal. The lately all-too-familiar thumping of a headache returned and, with it, a brief flicker of reality. Sam embraced the pain. It was, at least, proof that she was alive and that she was not dreaming.

* * *

Sam felt Dominic's grip on her shoulders tighten and realised that they were approaching the door of her room. He let go of her and pushed her gently to the side of the door. He looked her in the eyes and placed his forefinger on his lips, motioning her to be quiet. He then stood in front of the door, drew his gun, and with one, almost inaudible, click, he opened the door. With a brief glance at Sam, he entered. Sam couldn't actually say what happened next, as she had her heart in her mouth and her eyes firmly closed, listening for the inevitable gunshot, which never actually came. What did come was a bit of a shock, when she felt a hand on her arm. She opened her eyes, gingerly at first, fearful of what she might see, and was pleased to see the strong, smiling form of Dominic loom large before her. She gratefully accepted his hand and he led her into her room. She sat down heavily on the bed and finally breathed a huge sigh of relief.

"Let's get you packed and out of here then." Dominic's voice drifted into her consciousness.

"What?"

"I said, let's get you packed and out of here. I've arranged for a flight to Helsinki." Dominic looked over at Sam's less than enthusiastic face. "Don't worry. It's a special charter, so you'll be the only one on it. You'll be going straight to the main police station there. You'll have to stay for a few days and then you'll be accompanied to London by one of my colleagues."

"Oh I will, will I?" Sam was irritated by his patronising tone of voice. "I've just about had it with you and all your there's-nothing-to-worry-about's and your you-will-do-this-that-and-the-other crap. I'm not moving until I've had all the answers I can deal with and possibly some that I can't. And if you think I'm spending another night in this damned country, you can go screw yourself, because I'm going to be on the next plane out of here if it kills me!" Sam finally took a breath and, seeing his stunned face staring back at her, realised that she'd been shouting with an incredible amount of venom.

"Look, Sam, what can I say?" Dominic began.

"Well, I'll just sit here while you try and think of something, shall I?" She picked up the remote, switched on the television and began flicking through the channels.

* * *

Dominic managed to placate Sam and convince her to go along with his plan. He thought it probable that there would be a member of the Russian gang keeping a watch on the hotel and that the only hope of keeping Sam out of trouble was to get her out of the hotel and out of the country. Sam began to pack up her things. Tired of her fussing around looking for inconsequential items of make-up and unable to impress upon her the need for haste, Dominic lost patience, grabbed her and pushed her in front of him out of the door. Exiting the hotel by the side door, they hurried down the road. Dominic was slightly behind Sam when she heard the scuffle and turned around.

She was falling to the ground when her Conscious Mind said, "Not again! For someone who never faints, she's doing an awful lot of it lately."

"I think you'll find this time it's not her fault. It seems to have been a particularly heavy blow to the head," asserted her Subconscious, shortly before there was nothing . . .

Chapter Sixteen

Sam was furious. Exceedingly groggy, seriously in agony, but furious nonetheless. How dare someone hit her over the head! She appeared to be in a windowless cupboard and as far as she could make out, she was alone. What did they think they were doing? She'd had so many blows to the head in the past few days that she was very likely suffering from a brain haemorrhage. It would serve them right if I keeled over dead, right here in this cupboard, she thought grumpily. She was lying down with her hands tied behind her back, but at least they hadn't blindfolded her. Not that that would have mattered. It was pitch black and the light visible under the door was only a dim hazy strip. There was barely enough room for her to move and the disgusting stench around her did nothing to improve her mood. The smell was a curious mixture of dead rat and sweaty shoes. As her eyes became accustomed to the dark, she attempted to sit upright. No mean feat when your hands were behind your back and your feet bound. She had almost managed to sit up when she lost her balance and fell, nose first into what seemed to be her own shoes. That accounts for some of the smell, she thought to herself. She hadn't realised her feet were so revoltingly odoriferous. I really ought to buy some of those nice-smelling shoe inserts, she began to ponder, but then mentally chastised herself for making out a shopping list while in such a ridiculous situation. Her hand touched something furry and quite squashy and she realised with a retch that she might have found the dead rat.

She lay there for a few moments trying to put together her muddled thoughts; she'd been hit over the head and thrown into a cupboard. She fervently hoped that Dominic was experiencing something much, much worse. After all, if he had told her what was going on when she'd been in London, she would never have returned to Finland. What about Interpol? Why couldn't Special Branch have sorted this out without her involvement? They didn't seem to be that special anyway – they couldn't even stop the bad guys from abducting her in broad daylight.

She gave a grunt of exertion and managed to get herself in an approximately upright position. She began struggling with the ropes. She didn't really anticipate this flurry of activity to be of any use whatsoever but she'd seen enough films to think that this was the expected behaviour for someone in her situation.

She searched around for a sharp protrusion in the wall behind her and, surprisingly, she found one. She began rubbing the ropes against it, all the while mumbling about stupid suitcases and drug-runners, not forgetting the odd rant against Dominic and his inability to protect her. She'd been sawing away for what she judged to be at least twenty minutes, without much success at all. She calculated that she might manage to cut through the ropes in about three years, give or take the odd year. The muscles in her arms and legs were aching and sore, and her entire body was tense as she gave the ropes one last jerk. Look on the bright side, she smiled wryly to herself. At least I'm getting a pretty good workout. Flex those pecs, trim those abs, tone up that pelvic floor. What the hell is a pelvic floor anyway? With a heavy sigh, she gave up the struggle and lay down to wait for them to come and get her. As her body relaxed, Sam became aware of the fact that the ropes seemed much looser. With only slight difficulty, she pulled one of her hands loose. Sam was astonished. It did work. Not quite in the way that she'd envisaged, but her hands were free nonetheless. She felt down to her feet and grasped the fastenings. Finding the knot, she got to work on it and eventually pulled it loose.

"Luckily, whoever tied this was never a Boy Scout. Call that a reef knot?" She tutted in disgust and stood up.

Right, she thought, what do I do now? She looked around for something to break the door open with. She raised her head and peered upwards through the gloom. She'd already located the door. I wonder what else is in here? She began an investigation of the cupboard. From the door she tiptoed, arms outstretched, to her left and then to her right. OK, she said, there are two shelves on the right and nothing on the left. She felt a cardboard box on the upper shelf, but she couldn't quite manage to get it down. She felt her way along the other shelf on the right-hand wall, collecting any items she managed to find. After establishing that she'd found everything, she surveyed the booty. The sum total of her assets was an old tin of paint, a paintbrush and a bottle of what smelt like nail-varnish remover. She, therefore, had the option of either painting the walls or taking off her nail varnish.

She stood there in total despair and wondered what she should do next. Her plan had been working so well up until that point that she had thought escaping would be a doddle. She took off her jacket and laid it on the floor. Sitting on it, she felt a lump under her – and remembered that she had put her mobile in the inside pocket that morning – at least she hoped that it was still Friday – what with the blow to the head and everything else, she couldn't be completely sure. She was amazed that they'd not searched her – she felt like she'd been taken prisoner by the Keystone Cops, not that she wasn't grateful for this fact. She pulled her phone out and did exactly what any woman would do in the circumstances.

"Corporate Finance."

"Alex, my God, what time is it?"

"Sam?"

"Yes, it's Sam."

"What on earth are you doing ringing? You should be on a plane to London by now."

"I know. Things got a little complicated this end. What time is it?"

"Haven't you got a watch? What is it with you, you only ever seem to ring me up when you don't know the time. I'm not the speaking clock, you know. I was just about to go to the airport to pick you up, although I don't suppose I'll bother now."

"Alex, I'm sitting in a cupboard in God-knows-where,

being held hostage by God-knows-who, and you're moaning about me not having a watch."

"What do you mean, being held hostage?"

"OK, maybe I'm not being held hostage. I know they tied me up and shoved me in here. I don't know what they want with me. I think I might be mixed up in something bad."

"Why don't you just start from our last phone call."

Sam began to tell Alex the story of how she came to be in such circumstances. Alex, for her part, listened quietly with ever-increasing concern, until she finished.

"What were you doing at Mark's house?" Alex, as always razor-sharp, had noticed that Sam wasn't being 100% expansive about Mark. Sam had glossed over the whole 'sleep with Mark and do a runner' situation, but she had had to mention that she went to his house.

"Alex, now's not the time. Can you think of anything that might help me at this exact moment."

"OK, but you know I'll need full and detailed descriptions of everything when you get back."

"Fine, but at this rate, I'll never get back. Remember, I'm stuck in this cupboard – so is there anything you might suggest?" Sam prompted.

"Have you tried the door?" enquired Alex.

"What do you mean, have I tried the door? Were you listening to me at all . . ." Sam began to rant, but remembered that she hadn't actually tried the door to see if it was, in fact, locked. She got up and stepped towards the door. Turning the handle, it opened with a loud click. "Erm . . ." Sam began sheepishly, "it seems to be unlocked."

"Told you!" Alex crowed. "Anything else I can do for you?"

"I don't think so. I'll just try to find a way out of here and hopefully we'll see each other soon."

"Try not to die before you've told me about Mark," Alex insisted.

"OK."

Sam left the cupboard. She found herself in a long corridor with doors on both sides. She tried opening a few of the doors, but they all seemed to be locked. She wasn't sure why she was trying them or what she was going to do if one was open. It's not likely to be a way out, is it, she thought. She stopped trying the doors and jogged to the end of the corridor where she saw some light. At the end of the corridor were the stairs. They led down as well as up. Now, had this been a film she was watching, she would have been screaming at the hostage character to go downstairs. They never ever get away when they go up – usually they only end up stuck on the roof dodging bullets with no means of escape. Having the actual choice, Sam became curious. Why do they always go up?

"I'll just have a quick peek at what's up there. Just for curiosity's sake, then I'll go straight down again," she muttered, convincing herself that it was a good idea.

On the second flight of stairs, she came face to face with the biggest, most muscular, man she had ever seen in her life. At least she now knew who had kidnapped her. If she hadn't been so frightened, she would have been impressed with his physique – he was well over six foot tall – actually, he looked down at six foot from a great height. He had forearms the size of Sam's thighs and was built like a brick outhouse. Sam was so shocked at his appearance that she cowered behind her hands. He stood looking at her with a hint of a confused look on his face. He was obviously expecting her to be either unconscious or still restrained. She stared at him blankly, taking in his unkempt appearance and blood-stained trousers. The man-mountain recovered first from the shock, grabbed her mobile out of her grasp and threw it to the floor, smashing it into little bits. He took her firmly by the shoulder and half carried her down the stairs and along another corridor. He walked with a severe limp, wincing and letting out a sharp gasp each time he put his weight on his right leg. Sam was dragged and carried until they finally stopped in front of a door. He opened the door and pushed her inside. It was a fairly large high-ceilinged room, bare and fairly neglected in terms of decoration. She was bustled towards a chair and firmly encouraged to sit. The door opened behind her and Sam heard a short exchange which was in an unfamiliar language that she took to be Russian. It was carried out over her head and she was loath to actually turn around to see who he was talking to. Her knowledge of Russian was non-existent, but Sam could definitely hear a female voice and, from the tone of it, it had to belong to the big man's boss. He was still to the front of her, his bulk blocking her view. As he moved away, Sam wondered what she could possibly be faced with next. One thing was certain, she wasn't going to bloody faint again, she promised herself. Emerging from behind the man was the crisp, efficient figure of Anne Mansfield.

* * *

To give Sam some credit, she did not faint. She merely stopped breathing for a little while, until her consciousness suggested that it might be a good thing for her to start again.

"So, Miss Jordan, we meet again."

The entire room took on an air of surreality. This was getting ridiculous. Anne sounded like a stereotypical 'Baddie' and this was altogether too much for Sam's delicate state of mind. The situation was so bizarre that she began to lose all sense of normality. It seemed as if the fear centres in her brain had switched off and she felt totally carefree. The room started to sway and somewhere in her stomach an involuntary bubble appeared. Very soon, Sam found herself unable to contain it and she screamed hysterically. She was no longer in control. She held her arms around herself as her stomach spasmed with mirth. She was laughing. This was not quite the reaction that Anne had expected and she nodded to the man to try and control her. Unfortunately, the sight of him looming over her caused Sam to start hiccuping.

"Dr . . . hick . . . Evil . . . hick . . . I presume . . . hick," Sam managed in between gasps and hiccups. She realised that Anne wasn't smiling, so she held her breath in an attempt to get rid of the hiccups.

"So, Miss Jordan, I gather you've been playing hide and seek with my money."

Sam exhaled deeply, "Your money? Hick! Possession is nine-tenths of the law, you know, and if you don't have it, it can't be your money! Hick!" Sam smiled at her witty comeback. "Where's Dominic?"

"You don't need to worry about him," Anne said in a quiet voice.

That cured Sam's hiccups. "Why? What have you done with him?" Sam began to panic – in all the heinous scenarios that she'd concocted for Dominic, not once had she thought of the possibility that he was dead. "You haven't murdered him, have you?" The last two words were uttered with incredulity.

"No, he got away, didn't he, Sergei?" Anne glanced sharply at the man, who began to inspect his fingernails intensely as if he'd never seen them before. "We were going to dispose of you, but we thought that you might come in handy for bargaining purposes, now that our operation has been uncovered." Anne smiled down at Sam, who was left in no doubt that she would not outlive her utility.

"I'm glad I can be of some use," she uttered sarcastically, as if she were without a care in the world. "If there's anything else I can do, you know, you only have to ask."

"Well, there was a little matter of the money. You see, we have the suitcase, but the money seems to have gone missing. You wouldn't happen to know where it is, would you?"

"Well, Anne, you probably won't believe me, but no, I have absolutely no idea where it is. In fact, up until this morning, I didn't even know that it existed. This has all been one big surprise as far as I'm concerned. First, Dominic is a copper, then you're auditioning for a part in the next Bond film and next you'll be telling me that *he* likes to paint watercolours in his spare time." She nodded towards Sergei.

"Ahhhh, so Mr Stewart is a policeman, is he? That explains a lot."

Oh, damn, she didn't know, thought Sam. "Well, I'm glad things are being cleared up for you – I still have absolutely no idea what's going on here," Sam sulked.

"Let me help you, shall I, Miss Jordan?"

"Look, I know that you're the one holding me hostage

and you have this lump of muscle over there who can probably crunch me into a thousand pieces without even breaking sweat, but if you call me 'Miss Jordan' once more, I'm likely to snap, I really will. Either call me Sam or Ms Jordan. Just don't be calling me 'Miss' any more." Sam was seriously irritated. "And while we're on the subject of Mr Universe here, does he have to lurk behind me like that? Can't he go off and do something useful, like clean out that bloody cupboard I was in – there's dead rats in there, you know!"

"All right, Ms Jordan, have it your way." Anne motioned for Sergei to leave the room, with the same dismissive wave that she'd used with Dominic in her office.

Sergei walked to the door. As he held out his hand for the handle, he turned back and spoke in English for the first time. "Would you like a cup of tea?"

"Are you mad!" screamed Sam. "I'm hardly in the mood for elevenses. You know, my grip on sanity is pretty fragile at the best of times and what with you standing there with a gun . . ." Sam glanced at Anne, who looked down at her empty hands. "OK, you standing over there like you ought to have a gun, and you asking me if I want a cup of tea," she nodded towards Sergei, "I'm pretty close to losing it. I think I'd prefer it if you would just kill me instead of acting as if we're at some kind of garden party."

"I asked only," Sergei said dejectedly. "No need to be rude." He turned back to the door and left in a huff.

"I must apologise for Sergei. For some reason, he's an Anglophile and obsessed with Emma Thompson. He's seen *Howard's End* more times than I can count," Anne shrugged. "Anyway, I digress. I was just about to tell you what has been happening. First let me introduce myself. My name is Natalia Androvitch, but I prefer to be called Anne."

"I don't know why, a nice wholesome Russian name, that," Sam murmured flippantly, safe now in the certainty that she was dreaming this entire scenario and therefore might as well enjoy herself.

"Which is exactly why I can't use it. Russia, as you know, has been in a certain amount of turmoil since glasnost and it was necessary to move abroad to expand my horizons."

"So you decided to work for an airline?" enquired Sam.

"Not quite. I work for the family import/export business. At least, I did until the British authorities, shall we say, curtailed our international activities." Anne sneered. "We were doing a healthy amount of trade with a group of gentlemen in Manchester who were providing us with some much-needed hard currency. But through the intervention of these people, we were at a loss as to the future direction of the business."

"So you decided to work for an airline?" repeated Sam.

"Yes, Ms Jordan, I then decided to work for an airline."

"Why Finland Air?"

"Because Finland has a land border with Russia, of course, and let's just say, my family are rather influential on both sides of the border. We just needed to find a way to move the merchandise from the UK to Finland."

"So . . ."

"So, we realised that if we were able to guarantee that a certain item, say a piece of luggage would regularly move between the two countries, we could . . . appropriate it temporarily for our own uses," Anne said very carefully.

"But why me?"

"We noticed that you were travelling repeatedly between Manchester and Finland, so we began observing your travel patterns. For some reason your luggage had been tardy on a few occasions so we thought that that would be the perfect cover. We felt that you would not be too concerned if our intervention caused some delays."

"So how long were you getting into my luggage then?" Sam was stunned to hear Dominic's theory confirmed.

"Only since the New Year."

"So the earlier delays . . ."

"Were nothing to do with us," Anne finished her sentence for her. "The main problem that we faced was that you recently changed your case and started flying via London Heathrow on a regular basis. We had difficulty opening your new case and we were finding it difficult to steer your luggage through customs."

Avoiding customs required an accomplice, not only in the start and destination airports, but one in the intermediary airport also. London Heathrow had a stringent hiring policy for the baggage staff and the gang had found it impossible to hire an accomplice there. Anne had acquired the job in Finland Air to ensure complicity in Manchester and Helsinki, but as Finland Air had no handling responsibilities at Heathrow, she was unable to provide the same service for the gang at that airport. They were obliged to force Sam to amend her travelling arrangements to suit their purposes.

Anne needed to be aware of Sam's travel plans and her job was to convince her to use a suitcase which aided the depositing of merchandise. Hence Anne's involvement in her disappearing luggage saga. They had been extremely pleased with the ease of this and had managed to begin trading, sending a large consignment to Manchester. Unfortunately for the gang, Sam had decided to disappear with the considerable payment.

"We really hadn't thought of the possibility that you would not complete one of your journeys. Silly really, but everyone makes mistakes!" Anne shrugged. "Anyway, we were trying to find you in Amsterdam, when you rang and told me your whereabouts. Very thoughtful of you, by the way."

"My pleasure," Sam said, remembering her little discussion with Anne about the beauty of Turku and the relative merits of the various hotels. I can't believe I offered to buy her a postcard, she thought to herself.

"You've caused quite a bit of trouble for poor Sergei. He blames you for his thigh."

Sam raised her eyebrows quizzically and Anne continued, "Gunshot wound."

"Oh," said Sam, still none the wiser. She was busy trying to remember how these things ended.

She thought back to all those thrillers that she'd watched at the pictures. Usually in these cases, when the Heroine is being held hostage, the Bad Guy (or Gal) tells all their evil plans. Then the Hero arrives, just in time to save her from being tortured.

Sam stared at the door, willing someone to come through. It opened to reveal Sergei brandishing a cardboard box full of metal items.

Thanks, Sam groaned inwardly, I actually meant someone of the Good Guys variety.

Sergei started removing gnarled and vicious-looking instruments out of the box, excitedly chattering to Anne in Russian. Sam was starting to worry. This is the part when

Anne leaves me alone with Sergei, for him to start torturing me, she thought. She glanced back at Anne, who had a weary look on her face.

"I must be going now. Sergei will – look after you," she smiled. "I'll be back to see if you have remembered any more information when he's finished. Sorry, I meant to say, when you're finished."

She walked briskly out of the room and locked the door behind her, leaving Sam with the huge mass of Sergei. He was still engrossed in his inspection of the box contents. Sam's knees were bouncing away in agitation. Finally, he turned and approached her.

"Would you like a cup of tea?" he said, placing a small table in front of her.

"Do I need a cup of tea?" she asked hesitantly.

"Well, it makes easier." He was faltering with his language – obviously they hadn't said these words in *Howard's End*.

Sam was desperately hoping that he hadn't seen any other of Anthony Hopkins' films, especially not the one with the Lambs and all that Silence. She nodded her head meekly.

Sergei turned back to the table and started to work on something. Sam watched his back, imagining all manner of nasty things. Think. Think. What would a secret agent do in such circumstances? An agent would probably pull out some of that exploding chewing gum or find a knife in his shoe. Unfortunately for Sam, she had neither. Odd noises emanated from the other side of the room and this only made her more nervous. It appeared her fear mechanism had returned and she felt the adrenaline course through her. She was on the edge and knew that she would soon be tipped over. She tried to calm herself and placed her hands, palm down, on the table in front of her. She looked like a swan, serene above the table, but underneath her legs were jittery and frenetic. The noises stopped and Sam braced herself. Sergei turned towards her with both hands full of metallic objects. The light bounced off the side of the large object in his right hand, temporarily blinding her. Sam recoiled, her knees catching the table sending it flying forwards, hitting Sergei forcefully on the shins. Sam was by this time by the door cowering behind her hands. She heard a moan and a heavy thud and then silence. She felt warm liquid flow to her feet. She prayed silently that it wasn't blood. She couldn't bear it if it were blood.

Letting her hands fall to her sides, she surveyed the scene. Sergei was lying on the floor with the table resting on his upper torso. He had blood on his forehead and his skin was turning a violent lobster red. There was steaming water everywhere and for the first time, Sam clearly saw the object which had obviously caused his injuries. There was an old-fashioned, round-bottomed kettle on the floor near his head and there, in his left hand were the remains of a cup and some tea leaves.

Sam was horrified; she'd killed a man. She gingerly approached his prone form and poked him with her toe. He let out a groan. He was regaining consciousness! She looked around for something to tie him with but, finding nothing suitable, picked up the kettle and whacked him once more over the head. And this is for the one you gave me in the street, she thought triumphantly, hitting him again.

Satisfied that he was still alive after the second blow, Sam went over to the box that he had brought in. It contained nothing more dangerous than a few old pieces of cutlery and household implements. Next to the box was a camping stove on which he had evidently been boiling the kettle. Sam felt stupid and elated at the same time. Her overactive imagination had spurred her into action, when the poor chap had only been making her a cup of tea.

Suddenly she heard the sound of a key turning in the lock. Sam seized the camping stove and rushed behind the opening door. Sadly, she didn't even look to see who it was before bringing it down on the head of the figure entering.

It was Dominic, now also lying spread-eagled on the floor next to Sergei. Aghast, Sam rushed to his side, hoping that she'd not done too much damage. She held his shoulders and attempted to shake him awake. Finally, after much man-handling, Dominic stirred.

"You hit me," he muttered. "I came to save you, and you hit me." He got to his feet with a groan.

"How was I supposed to know it was you? I haven't got x-ray eyes, you know," she protested. "Anyway, you were too late to save me. I saved myself. A girl can't wait all day to be rescued, you know. New millennium, new women." She pointed at the still unconscious Sergei.

"What on earth have you done to him? Why am I wet?" Dominic looked at the pools of water surrounding him. "Were you attempting to drown him or something?"

Dominic couldn't be sure, but Sam seemed to have a slight manic quality about her. She was flushed and breathing heavily, her eyes glassy.

"It's a long story," she said with a glint in her eye. "Shouldn't we be getting out of here? Anne might . . ."

"It's all right," Dominic said in the most soothing voice he could muster, having so recently been clouted with a camping stove. "The cavalry is here. She's been arrested along with the rest of her family. But you're right. We should get you back home." He took her hand and led her out of the room.

Once outside, he escorted her through the swarms of police who were milling around the building, all the way to his car. Opening the car door, he eased her inside. She was shaking uncontrollably now as everything was beginning to sink in. She dared not even hope that she was safe, as she'd been through that feeling too often in the past few days, only to be plunged into further misadventures. She simply sat in the passenger seat, limp and spent. Seeing four policemen carrying Sergei out of the building, she realised clearly for the first time just how much danger she had been in. The mental exhaustion set in and tears started to course down her cheeks. Dominic started the car and Sam's eyes drifted closed.

She awoke to his smiling face, hovering nervously in front of her.

"We're here," he said cautiously.

"Where?"

"Turku Airport. Your plane awaits, madame," he smiled.

"Can I go home? Will you be coming with me?"

"Yes, I'll be coming with you as far as Helsinki. Then we'll put you on a flight home."

"No, London. I need to go to London," Sam said shaking her head dreamily. "Alex will be waiting for me." Sam's eyes flew open. "Alex!" she exclaimed.

"Don't worry. She's been told that you are on your way back," Dominic reassured her. "She'll be waiting at Heathrow. Come on. Let's get you on board."

He escorted her to the plane. It was a small eight-seater aircraft. Dominic fluttered around her like a butterfly, doing up her seatbelt and getting her settled down, before sitting beside her.

Sam nodded off to sleep again and woke feeling much brighter.

"We'll be landing in a few minutes," smiled Dominic.

"So what happens now?" Sam enquired .

"Nothing much. I have some administrative stuff to do and then I can go home too."

"So do you do this sort of thing often? You know, guns, drug gangs and all that?"

"Too much for my liking. I've just about had enough of it all. I'm ready to retire, I think." Dominic glanced at Sam out of the corner of his eye, trying to gauge her reaction.

"I see," Sam eventually said.

"I really want to get out of the force and maybe start my own consultancy business. You know, security alarms and such. I'm getting too old and tired to be running around making the world safe from evil," he grinned. "You know, I have been thinking about this for a while now. I was in my dentist's office a few months back, and I saw an old copy of one of those country magazines. I've always fancied living in the countryside. You know, two-point-four kids and a wife at the Aga stove. I dunno, it really made me think about my life."

"What do you mean?"

"I mean, what have I got to show for my life? I'm nearly middle-aged and I have no kids and no responsibilities."

Sam actually thought that this sounded rather good, but instead she uttered hastily, "I know. Life goes quickly. doesn't it?"

"Most of my friends from university have it all. Wife, kids, job in the city, you know the sort of thing. I just think it's my turn. You might think it sounds silly, but sometimes I even think of names for my kids . . ."

They were descending into Helsinki, so, what with the noise of the engines, Sam couldn't hear him but she thought heard him say, ". . . Elliot and Jade."

The plane landed with a sharp bump and taxied towards its parking spot. Sam glanced out of the window and saw people amassing around a car. The door of the plane opened and three policemen entered.

"It's bedlam out there," one of them said to Dominic. "We should try and get her out of here."

Sam looked to Dominic, not quite understanding what was going on.

"The media seem to have found out about the arrests," he said. "It seems that everyone wants to talk to you. Are you sure you're up to this?"

"I'm sure I'll be fine," Sam said uncertainly.

Dominic gripped her hand and led her to the door. They emerged from the plane to a hail of calls and Sam's name being shouted by various reporters. She was blinded by flashbulbs and the throng felt as if it was going to suck her up and spit her out. In the jostling, Sam's hand was ripped out of Dominic's firm grasp. The police, who were trying to protect her from the crowd, bustled her into the waiting car. She looked back in time to see Dominic being swallowed up in the hordes of reporters.

Chapter Seventeen

Sam closed the oven door. Wiping her hands on her apron, she turned to the pile of potatoes and began peeling them. Who'd have thought that she could be happy living in Surrey? She gazed around her spacious kitchen and sighed in contentment. She looked out of the window to see Dominic returning from his walk with three of the dogs. Out of the corner of her eye, she saw a black cat jumping onto the work surface where the apple-pie was cooling. She shooed it away, telling it to go find some mice to play with. She had no idea why she was peeling so many potatoes, but she put them in a huge pan anyway. She heard the back door being opened.

"Don't you dare come in here with those dirty boots. I'll kill you if you get mud on the carpets, Mr Stewart."

"I'm taking them off now, Mrs Stewart." Dominic padded into the kitchen after removing his muddy boots in the utility room. "So, how long will dinner be?"

"About half an hour. Do you want to set the table?"

"The kids can do that – I have plans for you." He caught her in his arms and held her tight. Sam felt safe and blissfully happy. A warm feeling spread through her, emanating from the security of his strong arms.

They must have stayed in that position for ten or so minutes before a young girl of about six years came running tearfully into the kitchen followed by a boy approximately two years older.

"Mummy, Mummy, Elliot won't let me play with the computer."

"She's got grubby fingers. I don't want a sticky mouse," he complained.

"Now, now, children, play nicely. Dinner is nearly ready. Why don't you go get yourselves washed and help set the table?"

As the two children left the room, the girl pinched the boy on his leg.

"Ouch. Jade! What did you do that for?" He rubbed his leg. "That's it. You're dead!" Jade ran screaming away from his grasp.

"Dominic, sort them out, will you?" Sam pushed him towards the kitchen door. "I have things to do."

Twenty minutes later, the dinner was ready. Sam arranged the food in large bowls and placed them on the as yet unlaid table.

"Can someone please set the table?" she shouted up the stairs. There was no movement so she walked tiredly back into the kitchen to fetch the cutlery.

"Dominic, kids, dinner is ready," Sam shouted when she'd finished laying the table.

Dominic came down the stairs holding a baby in his

arms. He was followed by a three-year-old, then a five-year-old, then Jade, followed by Elliot, who was in turn followed by two more children and strangely, yet another two followed them. They couldn't possibly be all hers, could they? Sam twisted around in a panic and briefly caught sight of her face in the mirror. She saw an unrecognisable image reflected in it. Deeply lined and fully bagged under the eyes, she'd aged considerably. How could that have happened during such a short space of time? She was suddenly exhausted. Catching sight of the ever-increasing stream of children emerging from the stairwell, she shrieked. The room began to spin dizzily . . .

* * *

Bathed in sweat, Sam woke to find herself in a plane. One of the cabin crew approached her.

"Are you OK?" she enquired, concern etched on her face. "You seemed a little distressed."

"Where am I?"

"We're just over London. The captain is just about to put on the seatbelt sign. We will be landing in about ten minutes."

Looking out of the window she saw the familiar sight of the city.

"Are you sure you're OK? You have been through rather a lot. Would you like a drink of something? You're looking a bit peaky"

"No, thanks. I'm fine, really."

"I'm just going to get you a brandy. You really aren't looking well."

The stewardess turned and disappeared up the aisle, returning very quickly with a glass of brandy.

"There you go. Have a slug of that and you'll feel better."

"Thank you." Sam sipped the alcohol and felt its warming properties calm her considerably. "It'll probably be a nightmare here, won't it?"

"Not at all. You'll be met at the gate and taken to customs. Don't worry. We won't let you be mobbed. I heard Helsinki was crawling with paparazzi. Bet you're glad to be home after all you've been through."

"I don't want to sound stupid, but how did you know –" Sam wasn't allowed to finish her sentence

"It's been in all the papers. Plus we had a special briefing about making sure you had a relaxing flight back. That lovely policeman was especially adamant that we were to take care of you. It seemed like he'd taken quite a shine to you, you lucky thing. Now he's what I'd call sexy."

"Yeah, right," Sam managed weakly.

"It's really a fine state of affairs, isn't it? You never know who could be doing something dodgy these days, do you?"

Seeing as she didn't allow time for Sam to answer her questions, Sam assumed that they were all rhetorical.

"You know I always thought there was something dodgy about that Anne – I met her once in Manchester, you know . . ." She was happy to chat away and Sam was happy to let her.

Chapter Eighteen

Sitting in the comforting mess, which was what she'd turned Alex's living-room into, Sam put down the newspaper. The headline screamed *"Superwoman Stops Suitcase Smugglers"*.

"Alex, look at this. They've found out all about me. My entire life is here in the papers. They've even spoken to my mother. Oh God, this one's an exclusive."

"Oh no!" exclaimed Alex, appearing from the kitchen with a plate piled high with mashed potatoes. "What's she saying?"

"'We're all still in shock'," Sam read aloud. "'My daughter has been extremely brave and we're all proud of her. We're just happy to know that she's safe . . . blah, blah, blah'."

"Well, that doesn't sound too bad."

"Wait, wait . . . here you go. 'Of course, being unmarried, she's had to learn to take care of herself'. Can you believe that? Attacked, kidnapped, I mean, I could have died and she won't leave it alone." Sam looked at Alex and rolled her eyes. "She just can't help herself."

"Does she say where you are?"

"No, but apparently I'm hiding away in a secret location!"

Alex looked around her flat. "That sounds more exotic than it is. And it's hardly secret – I've had to take the phone off the hook – they just don't stop ringing. I'm glad I got that new mobile or we'd have been completely incommunicado." Alex had taken time off work to help Sam get herself together. "There you go!" She passed Sam the plate and disappeared back into the kitchen.

"We're incommunicado anyway. Have you managed to get a signal on that thing yet?"

"You have to stand over by the back window," Alex shouted from the kitchen.

Sam picked up the mobile and wandered over to the window. She looked out and to her relief, the hordes had subsided. "At least they've stopped hanging around outside."

Sam had been at Alex's for two days, during which time the media circus had become almost unbearable. Her entire family had been harassed mercilessly by the press. They'd even managed to locate her father or should that be mother number two? Anyway they'd found Jacqueline and she'd used all the publicity to plug her shop.

"Why must I have the two most embarrassing parents on the planet?"

"I dunno, lucky I guess," Alex smiled. "You could have done worse. You could have been stuck with mine. At least yours are sentient human beings."

Sam replied with an eyebrow raise à la Roger Moore.

"OK, your father is at least."

"Sentient maybe, but hardly typical father material any

277

more. Anyway, yours aren't that bad. A bit stereotypically middle class maybe . . ."

"Yeah, the Stepford parents. The highlight of their day is making cups of tea and warming their slippers in front of the fire."

"See what I mean? Normal."

"Whatever. I need to nip out to the shops – will you be OK?"

"Yeah, sure. What could possibly happen to me here?"

"Best not to tempt fate. This is you we're talking about. Trouble seems to find you . . ." Alex picked up her purse and left the flat, leaving Sam alone with her thoughts.

Sam had wanted to speak to Martti to tell him that she needed a few weeks off work. She decided that it was better to get it over with, so she picked up Alex's new mobile phone and dialled.

"Saari."

"*Martti, hei, mita kuuluu?*"

"Ah, Samantha, still putting butter up me, I see."

"For goodness sakes, Martti, this isn't *Last Tango in Paris*, you know. I'll say this once more and definitely for the last time. The phrase is to butter someone up."

"So, Samantha, you are still buttering me up, then."

"Yes, I mean no, I'm not trying to butter you up. I'm just trying to get some time off."

"No problem, you take few weeks off."

Sam found herself thinking longer term and before she knew it, she found her mouth opening and a completely unexpected sentence found itself being said. "Actually I was thinking about handing in my notice." It wasn't until she said it that she felt how right it sounded.

"No, I cannot let you do! I give you sabbatics?"

"What is that?" Sam tried to think of what that could mean.

"Sabbatics – you know, when you take time off work to do something. Usual for year."

"Oh, you mean sabbatical?"

"Yes, right. You take sabbatical for a –"

"Two."

"OK, two years, but I want you back. You still work for Saari Consultancy. You remember."

"OK, thank you for being so good about it."

"My pleasance. You go relax, Samantha." She sensed that Martti was smiling. "By way, I talk Markku, yesterday. He try find you. I tell him I not know where you take yourself."

"If he calls again tell him I will call him."

"You call him, OK fine. Take care of you."

"I will – and thanks, Martti. *Kiitos*."

"Butter me up! Goodbye, Samantha."

Samantha wasn't ready to hear Mark's name. She'd talked things through with Alex, many times, but she still didn't know what she would say to him. And Dominic, well, Sam had not heard from Dominic, apart from a brief message passed on by Alex's local police station, promising to get in touch when he arrived back in London. For her part, Sam simply couldn't face ringing him.

She had used the time since she last saw him to think. Like Dominic, she too had thought deeply about her life and realised that there was something missing. Even though her life was seemingly full to the brim with potential life-partners, she somehow felt unsatisfied. It takes a near-death experience to clear out all the rubbish floating around the mind. Her entire life was in sharp relief and for the first time, she could see the path ahead of her clearly. She had made a decision, but this decision was so private that she hadn't even told Alex. She had a plan, in fact the plan had started to form while she was sitting next to Dominic in the plane. Hearing him talk about his life and how it was time to go after the things that truly make you happy. She felt ready to talk to Dominic. Sam picked up the phone and tapped in his number.

"Stewart."

"Dominic, it's Sam. Are you still in Finland?"

"Yes, I can hardly hear you – I'm on my way to court. Is there something wrong?"

"No, nothing's wrong, I just wanted to talk to you. I need to talk to you."

"Sam, I can't hear you. I have to go, but I'll be back in London tomorrow. Can we meet up then? I have something really important to ask . . ." There was a loud hissing on the phone and the connection was broken.

Sam put down the phone and heard Alex's key in the lock. Dominic had something important to ask her. Deep down she knew what that would be and she felt her chest constrict. Alex had gone straight to the kitchen and Sam tried to concentrate on the excited babbling of her voice.

"So I have *Sleepless in Seattle*, some popcorn and some Ben & Jerry's Ice Cream. Everything we need for a serious night in."

"I don't know if I'm up to watching the video," Sam uttered wearily.

"I know I'm being a right old pain, but I want to hear everything again. From the beginning. Last time you told me, we kept on getting interrupted and then you were so tired, you kept forgetting where you were. And I was so patient leaving you to rest yesterday, but you're loads better now so . . ."

"I can't believe you want to hear it again."

"Go on, Sam," Alex wheedled. "It's so romantic, you being kidnapped –"

"Me being kidnapped is romantic?"

"OK, maybe not that part, but him coming back to rescue you. Talk about romantic!" Alex was still chattering.

"Talk about change of tune. Are you the same person who said that anyone with a name like Dominic just couldn't be trusted?"

"I know I didn't like him and all that, especially when he got away from them and left you all alone."

"You called him the dodgiest git on the planet at one point. I'm certain of it."

"Yeah, yeah, how many times do I have to say I'm sorry for that. How was I to know he was an Action Man in his spare time. And to save you from certain death! He has style, I'll give him that."

"Certain death? Don't be so dramatic. Sergei was only going to make me a cup of tea." Sam smiled at Alex's excited face.

Alex had sat down on the sofa, with a large spoon and a full tub of 'Chubby Hubby' Ice Cream, expectantly waiting for Sam to continue.

"Well . . ." Sam began.

Dominic had had a trace put on Sam's mobile phone, from the time he had lost sight of her in Turku. This meant that whenever she'd used it, they'd been alerted to her presence. This was how Dominic knew that she was on her way to the office that Friday morning. As the Cumulus Hotel was only around the corner from her office, he'd managed to get there before her. Luckily, the trace was still active when she had called Alex from the cupboard. They had managed to use the signal to pinpoint her whereabouts. The police were then able to surround the building and capture the gang.

"That's fantastic," Alex breathed.

"Yeah, but I'd already knocked out Sergei, by then."

"Still, he didn't know that when he came into the room, did he?"

"I suppose . . ." Sam put a handful of popcorn into her mouth and chewed pensively.

"So when's he coming back then?"

"A couple of days, he reckons."

"When did you talk to him?"

"While you were out. He says he has something important he needs to ask me."

Alex shrieked "Ohmigod, you don't mean he's going to ask you . . . "

"I doubt it."

"Why not? I bet you he is. He obviously loves you."

"Whatever it is, he'll be here soon."

"Yeah."

"A couple of days."

"That'll be nice." Alex's voice belied the fact that she was desperate to say something, but didn't know how to bring it up.

"Yeah, it will. Go on. Ask away, Lexi me old pal."

"What?"

"You have something to ask, so ask it."

"It's nothing really."

"Just ask."

"OK." Alex took a deep breath. "So when are you going to tell Dominic about your horizontal shuffle with old Wrinkle-face?"

"Can you possibly forget that I told you about that?"

"Not possible in the slightest, sorry. It's too good as potential blackmail fodder." Suddenly serious, Alex looked at Sam. "You'll have to tell him, though."

"What he doesn't know won't hurt him," Sam said hopefully.

"That's not fair. They always find out eventually. We always did, didn't we? And you of all people know how much it hurts – remember You-know-who."

"I know. You're right. I will tell him. Not just now though, eh?"

"All right. Although, I can't believe that you actually did it. You had sex with a Finnish bloke . . ." Alex shook her head sadly.

"I can't explain it either. You'll just have to put it down as a lapse of judgment in difficult circumstances. Although I was thinking about it today and he was really really nice. Not once did he try to find out why I didn't want to go back to the hotel. He let me stay at his house . . ." Sam started to list all the things that he did for her.

"He let you bonk him senseless. Yeah, Sam, he was really selfless," Alex said sarcastically.

"Has this whole Dominic thing not taught you anything about judging people before you get to know them?"

"I like the guy, but he's not a saint, Sam."

"I'm well aware of that." Sam was quiet.

Alex decided to get her on to a more lighthearted subject.

"Who'd have guessed that Finns were so relaxed about

sex? Remember that German bloke I went out with? The one who worked on the American base as a translator?"

"No."

"You have to remember. It was just after I'd gone out with Randy, the American soldier."

"No, but I remember Randy. Randy by name –"

"Randy by nature." Alex joined in with Sam and giggled at the memory.

"What did he use to say?"

"When?" said Alex.

"You know, just before he came, what was it he used to say?"

"Erm . . ." Alex started guffawing and then, in her best Southern States accent, "Look out, mama, the F16's coming!"

"That's it!" Sam had to hold her stomach to avoid hurting herself, she was laughing so much.

"I remember he had the smallest dick I'd ever seen."

"Yeah, more of an F1$\frac{1}{2}$ than an F16!"

By now, their screeches had become so high-pitched that they were attracting the attention of the local canine population.

After a few minutes spent calming themselves down, Sam had a brainwave. "I remember now, your German was called Jorg – or something like that."

"No, it wasn't Jorg . . . it was Jürgen." Alex smiled at the memory. "What was it you used to call him?"

"I don't remember any more."

"Neither do I . . . erm . . . it had something to do with Jokes."

"I can't believe you can't remember the names of the blokes you've been out with!"

"Neither can you."

"I'm not the one he went out with."

"I've got it." Alex beamed. "Yoking Yorgon."

"That's right! I remember now. He couldn't pronounce his J's. He looked like Arnold Schwarzenegger without the steroids and talked like him too." Sam started imitating his accent, "'It vas onlee a yoke, Samanta.' How could I have forgotten. What about him?"

"I was going to say that he was the last guy I slept with who had a sense of humour about sex."

"Yeah." Sam was wary about coming on to the Jürgen subject. It had been another disastrous Alex-ism.

This used to be Sam's secret way of describing Alex's way with men. She'd almost forgotten about the term and it was only now when she remembered how Jürgen had screwed Alex up that she was reminded of it. Alexism is the very refined art of finding a complete no-hoper, wastrel, bastard of a man and persuading yourself that he is the best bloke on the planet. The interactions tended to be very short-lived, but extremely intense, usually ending in a spectacular manner.

"Why did I stop going out with him?" Alex was trying to recall the nature of their break-up.

Sam was in two minds about reminding her of the cause of their split, but took a chance that as they were in a light-hearted mood it couldn't do any harm. "He started having an affair with a prostitute."

"Oh yeah," Alex sighed, suddenly subdued. "I wonder what he's doing now?"

"They got married and had five kids remember?" Sam reached over and squeezed Alex's hand.

"Yeah, right." Alex looked at Sam and smiled a smile

285

that didn't quite reach her eyes. She murmured nostalgically. "It was fun while it lasted though, wasn't it?"

"As I recollect, you did have some fun stories. I remember you telling me about the time you two tried to have sex in the back of a *Trabbi*." The memory of Alex's leg sticking out the front window of the tiny East German *Trabant* car made Sam chuckle.

"We used to giggle . . . oh I don't know, it was fantastic, Fanny-farts-a-go-go!"

"ALEX!" Sam choked on her food, finally having to spit popcorn out in front of her.

Laughing, Alex got up and went in search of a cloth to clear it up. Sam began making a half-hearted attempt to pick the bits off the coffee table. Then, as she was wiping down a magazine, she saw a sheet of paper beneath. It was a list of children's names. Two of which were underlined and surrounded by little heart-shaped doodles. Sam looked at the paper, startled. Alex returned to find her staring into the distance. She snatched the paper away from Sam.

"Oh, don't look at that. I wanted to surprise you. I've decided on some names."

"I can see that," Sam blurted. "Why those names?"

"I don't know. They just sound right, I suppose," Alex shrugged. "Not that I'll ever get to use them in my present state of singledom."

"Talking about singledom, or rather not singledom for very much longer, how's Debbie getting on with her wedding plans? It's got to be soon, hasn't it?"

"Yep, next week. And they've not found a new house yet."

"Why? Are they moving?"

"Yeah, he's been given the North-West, so they can't stay in Lincolnshire. Been looking for months apparently."

"What about the thing itself? You heard any details?"

Sam knew that Alex was the font of all wisdom as far as weddings were concerned.

"She's having ice sculptures. Apparently, she hates them, but her mum's insisting on it."

"And they say that it's the bride's day."

"Not with her mum, it's not. She's worse than yours."

"No one is worse than mine."

"You wanna bet? Her parents are blowing almost twenty-five grand on it."

"And, don't tell me, she'd be happier to get it over with in a registry office."

"Yep. I dunno why though – weddings are meant to be beautiful. Mine definitely will be. When I've finally found the right guy of course."

"So tell me, have you got it all planned then?" Talk about stupid questions!

"Of course, this is me we're talking about!" Alex exclaimed.

They both sat back on the sofa and Alex began to explain her plans for the perfect wedding, the perfect house and the perfect husband. Smiling to herself, Sam allowed the rush of details to flow over her.

* * *

Sam woke early the next morning to the sound of Alex shrieking.

"Sam, you simply have got to see this!"

"What time is it?" Sam croaked from the spare bedroom.

"It doesn't matter what time it is. Get a load of this."
Alex rushed into the bedroom and threw the tabloid onto
Sam's chest.

Sam looked down to see the headline, *Footballer Gay
Gordon's Secret Life* and smiled, "Well, it looks as if Tim's
little secret is all out in the open now. I told you that you
should have gone public when you found out."

"I couldn't have. It wouldn't have been right."

"You could have earned yourself a tidy little sum."

"Yeah, well, I was a bit indisposed at the time, if you
remember."

"Yeah, sorry." Sam grimaced at the memory and changed
subject quick. "So how did they find out then?"

"His chiropodist found out Tim was going to get married.
Apparently, he couldn't in all conscience allow it to
happen. He didn't want the poor woman to suffer."

"The same chiropodist?"

"Yep."

"Hell hath no fury like a foot doctor scorned, I suppose."

"I've had them on the phone already this morning. As
if your story's not enough, they're after me now." Alex
groaned. "I've no idea how they found me. I went out with
him years ago. Are these people psychic? They're certainly
superhuman."

"They had a picture of you, remember, quite a few of
them actually. They probably did their research back then
and filed it all away."

"We're a right pair, aren't we? Both of us hiding out from
the press." Alex started thumbing through the paper.

"God help us if they put the two stories together!" Sam
laughed.

"That'd be hilarious." Alex chuckled.

"Well, at least it's knocked me and my parents off the front page."

"Only as far as page three, I'm afraid." She held the page up for Sam to read.

"*Luggage Woman's Trannie Father Speaks Out?* I don't believe this. Are they totally incapable of keeping their mouths shut? I've only just managed to persuade my mother that I'll never keep a husband if I'm splashed all over the press and now I'm on the tit page. I give up."

Alex got up. She seemed to have come to a decision. "That's it. I'm sick of hiding out. Let's both go out shopping."

"I can't face it, Lexi. You go. Do me proud."

"Aww, c'mon, Sam."

"No, really. I have stuff to organise."

"Oh, yes, your big day. OK, I'll scout around for some nice dresses while I'm out." With that Alex lifted herself off the bed and headed towards the door.

"Don't forget the headscarf and the dark glasses, Lexi love," Sam shouted from her bed.

"Good idea."

Sam heard the door opening and the barrage of calls and flashbulbs. She smiled. Good on you, Alex. Sometimes Sam was astounded at Alex's courage.

Sam dozed for a while longer and then dragged herself out of bed and into the shower. An hour later, she was sitting on the sofa, wondering where she should start. She'd been thinking all night about what Alex had said about Debbie. Maybe she ought to get in touch with the blushing bride. She had a few things to sort out herself. There was a lot of organisation to do and Debbie might just be able to help. It was a big step for Sam, but she had absolutely made up her mind that she would go ahead with it.

First things first though. It was time to talk to her mother. She picked up the phone and dialled.

"No, Chelsea, not there, please, darling. Hello?"

"Hi, mother, how are you?"

"Samantha, thank goodness you rang. I've been going out of my mind with worry. Alexandra said you wouldn't be answering the phone and –"

"We have a mobile now, I'll give you the number later. I have something important to tell you."

"Can it wait, dear? Chelsea's just gone into the other room with paints. I should really check up on where she's painting."

"No, it can't wait. I think you'll want to hear this."

"All right. Go on then."

"Are you sitting down?"

"No, should I, darling?"

"You might want to."

* * *

Debbie, although totally frazzled by her wedding preparations, was ecstatic to hear from Sam. The phone conversation had been extremely beneficial to both parties and Sam was relieved that she'd been able to cross one major item off her to-do list. She looked down at the remaining items. How difficult could this be to organise? She was a management consultant for goodness sakes! While she was deciding her next step, the mobile rang, shattering her thought process.

"Darling, I've just had the most interesting conversation with a journalist."

"Did you have to, mother?"

"Did I have to what?"

"Give them an interview – I thought we'd talked about this."

"Calm down, dear. I didn't tell him anything. In fact, he didn't even want to speak to me – he wants to talk to you."

"Well, I'm not –"

"Before you 'go off on one', which I think is the current term for it, I think you might be wise to think about his offer, especially in light of your recent revelation. He says he'll make it worth your while."

"How much?"

When her mother mentioned the figure, Sam had to sit down and take a few calming breaths.

"You can't be serious."

"Deadly serious, darling. It's a world exclusive apparently. I have his number if you need it."

"Too right I'll take it. By the way, have you had any luck with the Travel Agent?"

"They have a couple of things, but she's getting back to me in a little while with the details. I'll let you know."

* * *

Sam let herself into Alex's flat. She'd spent the afternoon in a solicitor's office and was thoroughly exhausted. Alex looked up from the early evening edition of the *Evening Standard* and smiled from ear to ear.

"They're really going to town on Tim."

"See, that's what you call karma – what goes around comes around."

"Yep. By the way, I have a couple of messages. Your mother says Martinique, whatever that's supposed to mean.

And a Mr Jameson asked if you could call him with your decision."

"Great. Thanks, Alex."

"What the hell's going on, Sam? Even your mother has started talking in codewords."

"All in good time, young lady."

Alex's face fell. "But I'm your best friend . . . "

"I'm sorry, Alex. It's top secret at the moment. I'll let you in on it soon, I promise."

"But, by rights I should be helping. God knows when I'll get a chance to do this for myself."

Sam sat down and looked at Alex's crestfallen face.

"Can you do me a favour tomorrow morning? I need some things from the shops and I don't think I can handle going myself."

"You're going to trust me to do shopping for you?"

"If I can't trust you, who can I trust?"

"Exactly what I've been saying all along."

Chapter Nineteen

Sam put down the phone. She was immensely pleased with herself. She'd just negotiated with a tabloid to sell her story for an obscene amount of money. There had been talk of a book deal and she had had public relations experts enquiring about her representation. Life was good. Her plan was coming together. All she needed was . . .

The phone rang again, interrupting her thoughts.

"Hello, Spencer residence," Sam said playfully.

"Sam, it's Dominic. I'm back and I really need to see you. Will you meet me tonight?" His words came out in a rush.

"I can meet you earlier than that. How about meeting up in about two hours?" Sam calculated that that was all the time she needed to sort everything out.

"Great – where will we meet then?"

"Same place as before?"

"Fine! See you then."

She was still staring at the phone when it rang again.

"Sam, it's Mark. You left a message."

"Mark, yes I did. Thanks for ringing . . . "

The conversation they had was stilted, tense and difficult. Sam tried to explain her actions after *that* night. She didn't really know how to explain. She told him about Dominic and how she had panicked, but even she knew that it was a lame excuse for what she had done. She let him in on her plans, adding the hope that they could still remain friends. He wasn't happy, but there was nothing Sam could do about that. She'd made her decision and even Mark couldn't make her change her mind. It was unfortunate, but deep down, she knew she didn't want to lose him forever. When it came down to it, Sam was glad that Alex had bugged her mercilessly until she'd left him a message. Alex had reminded her that it wasn't fair to leave someone without a proper explanation.

Sam hung up and dialled Alex's mobile number, "Alex, I need your help. Can you come with me to meet Dominic?"

"Are you sure you want me there? I don't want to be sitting there like a gooseberry while you two get smoochy."

"Where are you anyway?"

"Outside the door, trying to find my keys. Let me in!"

Sam got up and opened the front door, to see Alex with at least six bags full of clothes.

"That's the last time I'm going shopping for you," she moaned. "The list of instructions was so complicated it took me and two assistants ages to sort everything out. I think we've got everything though. Did you ring that chappie who rang last night?" She flopped down on the sofa, exhausted.

"Yep, everything is working out perfectly."

"So tell me what all this is about."

"Not yet. Please say you'll come with me. I'm meeting him in a couple of hours. I've got to decide what to wear."

"OK, but this plan of yours better be worth all this."

Out of nowhere, Sam said, "I've sold my house."

"Is that what you've been up to? That's what you were chatting about to your mother last night?" Alex looked incredulous. "Isn't that a bit previous? What if he doesn't ask you to marry him? I mean, he hasn't actually asked you yet, has he?"

"It's all right, Alex. Stop worrying. I'll just buy another one, somewhere. I know what I'm doing." Sam began gathering up the bags.

"Where have I heard that before?" Alex said suspiciously, knowing that this was always a precursor to another one of Sam's great adventures. "I remember, that's what you said when you got the Finland job, and look where that got you!" she shouted at Sam's retreating back.

* * *

Dominic was nervous. He was about to do something that struck even him as more than a little absurd. He was going to propose to a woman he hardly knew, but in some ways felt as if he'd known forever. He wasn't altogether sure that it was the right thing to do, but it felt right enough for him to want to give it a try. He had had enough of the danger involved in his job. He wanted to slow down and smell the flowers. He'd handed in his notice the day before and had begun the process of setting up a security consultancy. He had already received two offers of large contracts for his fledgling company. His future was all set. He just needed one more piece to slot into the puzzle and Sam seemed as good a person as any to give it a try with. In his excitement, he'd arrived far too early. He was in such a state that he'd just knocked over his wine for the second time. The waiter was resignedly cleaning up once more when Dominic saw Sam arrive. He was slightly disconcerted to see her followed by a tall, elegant blonde woman with an irritated look on her face.

Alex was scowling; she didn't quite understand why Sam had dragged her along to meet the famous Dominic. She muttered something under her breath.

"Stop whingeing, Alex. There he is!" Sam grabbed her arm and dragged her across the room.

"Hi, Dominic! This is Alex."

Sam turned to Alex to see her transfixed.

Alex's heart was sinking. This was the man. Her perfect husband. The one that she'd described in perfect detail, to Sam, the night before. Sam hadn't even hinted at the resemblance. And Sam was going to marry him. She couldn't believe her bad luck. She gazed at him and stretched out her hand.

Dominic's head was moving between Sam and Alex as if he were watching a tennis match. He was bewildered. He looked at Sam, whose face wore an inscrutable smile. He turned to look again at Alex, whose face had fallen. He saw her hand outstretched and grasped it firmly. Immediately their eyes met, a shot of electricity ran up both of their arms.

Sam was enjoying this. She had known that this would work. She sat down at the table and sat there for a minute in silence.

"Don't you think you ought to sit down, the pair of you," she hinted.

The spell was broken. They looked, as one, at Sam. Dominic was the first to react. He blushed all the way down to his shirt-collar and sat down hastily. Alex walked around the table to her seat, glancing guiltily at Sam. She wasn't sure what to do next, so she picked up her napkin and began carefully arranging it on her lap, reluctant to catch Sam's eye.

"So, you're Alex?" Dominic managed when his voice returned.

"And you're Dominic," Alex said shiftily.

"I'll just leave you two to get acquainted. I need to go to the little girls' room," said Sam.

She got up and walked in the direction of the toilets, glancing back briefly to ensure that they had begun their conversation. She was ecstatic – finally one of her plans had worked beautifully. As soon as she'd seen the names on the sheet of paper in Alex's flat, she knew that her idea was right. She'd been so shocked to read 'Elliot and Jade' underlined, that at first she hadn't realised the implication. They were the same names that Dominic had told her on the plane. She couldn't be sure that they would be attracted to each other, but she had a feeling in her water that they would. The introduction today confirmed it. They were perfect for each other.

She looked at her watch. She had two hours, and so much to do. She went to the bar and asked for some paper. She began to write, the words flowing out of her. She was thinking so fast, her hand could hardly keep up with her thoughts. She finished the letter and gave it to the hostess with the instructions to take it to table five in twenty minutes and give it to the blonde lady. That should give her time, she thought. She picked up her handbag and left. She had a meeting to get to.

* * *

They were alerted to the hostess's presence by the delicate 'ahem'. She smiled at Alex and handed her a letter. The letter was written in Sam's messy scrawl. Alex began to read.

Dearest darling Alex,

I'm really sorry, but I have to leave. I have to meet some journalists. It seems I have a story for them. They want to pay me a huge amount of money, so who am I to argue? I realised when I was in Finland that I have a life to live and I have decided to live it. I'm not ready to settle down now and I don't know if I'll ever be. I've never really wanted to be little wifey at home, you know that. I want some adventure and excitement. I want to find my perfect place, the way that you've always known yours and I can't do that in England or even in Finland with Mark. I love you more than you know. You've always been my rock, protecting and comforting me, and I think it's time for me to share you with someone else. Dominic was not my 'Mr Right', so I can't marry him. I was hoping you could break it to him gently, but I'm sure you'll find a way to help him get over the disappointment!

I'm going away for a while. I'm not sure where, but you know I'll be in touch as soon as I can. Don't worry. It won't be forever. Take care of Dominic. He's very very special. It's funny. He came to me to help me find my luggage and, because of him, I've managed to lose the luggage of my past. My time with Mark has taught me that I can be open to new relationships. I just need to clear my head and decide what I want to do with myself.

Don't forget to send me an invite to the wedding. I'll be thinking of you and will miss you like crazy, every day. Think of me and remember that I will always be

Your best mate

Samantha

PS. I think Sam is a great name. Unisex too!!!!!!!

* * *

Alex was in tears by the time she'd finished the letter. She handed it to Dominic and ordered the best bottle of champagne in the house. By the time the bottle arrived Dominic, too, had finished and absorbed the letter.

He picked up his glass, held Alex's hand in his and said, "A toast. To Sam, may she find the life that she wants."

"To Sam," Alex agreed and smiled at Dominic. "And to lost luggage."

* * *

Sam stood in line at the check-in. She was running really late, but she'd finally finished her interview with the newspaper. She clutched her handbag tightly to her chest. Inside was a slip of paper that gave her her freedom. A cheque for two hundred and fifty thousand pounds. What with the proceeds from the sale of her house, she had enough to get by for a few years. It wasn't going to keep her in luxury forever, but it would at least buy her a new beginning. Her mobile began to ring.

"Hello?"

"Sam, it's Debbie. I've just been speaking to my solicitor and everything's set. We're exchanging contracts next week, just before the wedding in fact."

"Fantastic. My solicitor in London has all the details if you need anything. Is there anything else I need to do?"

"I don't think so."

"Great. You have a fabulous time and don't let your mum get you down. It's your day remember."

"Yep, I'll try to remember that. Are you sure you can't come?"

"You know I'd love to, but I'm flying off in about an hour."

"You have a great time, yourself. And, Sam, thank you."

"For what? You're the one paying over the odds for my house."

"You know what I mean. We were in such a panic, and along you come like a knight in shining armour. I don't know what we'd have done . . ."

"Actually, it's Alex you should be thanking – she's the one who told me about you needing a house."

"There's my soon-to-be-hubby now. I've got to go. Take care of yourself, won't you? And come over for dinner when you get back. You know the address!"

"No probs. Bye."

Sam smiled. Sometimes she just got lucky. Everything had been going so well that she knew that things could only get better. Then her phone rang again.

"Hello, the new and improved Samantha Jordan speaking."

"Samantha, it's Mark again. I've been thinking about what we discussed earlier and I have thought of an alternative."

"I don't understand."

"Remember, when we were talking earlier, you said that you needed to have some time alone to decide what you wanted out of life."

"Of course I remember. You asked if I would go and live over there in Finland."

"Yes and you said that you couldn't, not yet, and that you needed to get away."

"Yes, but what was that you were saying about alternatives?"

"Remember saying that you couldn't give me any answers and it wasn't fair to keep me hanging on and that the only alternative you could think of would be for us to be friends and stay in touch. Well, I don't want to be friends."

"I'm sorry you feel that way." Sam's voice sounded harder than she felt. To her immense surprise, she felt remarkably sad.

"No, you don't understand. I want you to marry me."

"Mark, we've been through this already . . ." Sam sounded calm, but the marriage proposal had set her trembling.

"No, we didn't explore all the options. I can't leave Finland for at least eighteen months."

"So you said before, and I don't want to live in Finland. I need to get Finland out of my system."

"I know, but I've thought up a way to compromise."

"OK, I'm listening."

"My marriage proposal is valid for two years."

"I don't understand."

"I don't want your answer now. You have two years to make up your mind."

"But what if I find someone else? What if you do?"

"If that happens, then we weren't meant to be together. Let's let Fate decide."

"Why two years?"

"I told Portia about you and she refused to sign the divorce papers. It seems that she doesn't want me and she doesn't want anyone else to have me either. We now have to remain separated for two years, at which point I no longer need her consent to divorce her."

"I see." Sam tried to think. "I don't know."

"What have you got to lose? I'm not saying that you can't contact me for two years. What I'm saying is that in two years if you don't want to marry me, we can simply agree to be friends. And if you decide before then that you want to be with me, you can come whenever you want."

"Why are you doing this for me, Mark?"

"Because I love you, stupid. Remember the saying – if you love someone, set them free – well, you're free to go and I won't stop you because I know that you will come back to me eventually."

Sam was at the front of the queue and the clerk was coughing politely. "Mark, I have to go."

"Remember Sam, two years. You know where I am. I love you." He put down the phone.

Sam smiled. She'd still not managed to have the last word. She handed her ticket to the woman at check-in. She was more confused than ever. At least Alex's future was set. She thought sadly about leaving Alex. She knew that Dominic would take care of her, but still . . .

"Miss Jordan, will you be checking in any luggage today?"

Sam pictured the bags she had packed at Alex's flat that morning. She'd been running so late that she hadn't had time to collect them. She was annoyed, but maybe it was better this way after all. Sam suddenly smiled. She thought about Alex and Dominic and about Mark and had a feeling that everything would be all right. She looked down at the woman and grinned.

"No, I have no luggage."

Epilogue

Sam breathed deeply as she descended the steps from the aeroplane. She inhaled the air as she would a fine wine – the bouquet was just as expected. In all the islands that she'd visited so far, the overtones were the same: aeroplane fuel and sea salt. It was through the undertones that she could distinguish the individual Caribbean countries. Fried chicken, that was Jamaica. Burnt sugar, Barbados, and Martinique was distinctly floral. But here? Sam sniffed once more. She detected a faint note of, she breathed again, just to make sure – bananas, that was it! Definitely a hint of bananas. So there she was in St Lucia, a true banana republic. She fervently hoped that the country's politics didn't live up to this description. So far the bureaucracy seemed straightforward. The landing card was basic and simple – where have you come from and where will you be staying while you are here? Unfortunately, Sam had absolutely no idea how to answer the latter question.

Sam stepped forward handing her passport and landing card to the official.

"Where will you be staying?" He looked up at Sam and added with a distinct glint in his eye, "And what's your phone number?"

Sam held back a smile and said, "I don't know where I'll be staying yet, so no phone number. Is it necessary for me to know if I want to enter?"

"No, not at all," he winked and murmured, "but it is necessary if you want me to phone you and show you the best night of your life."

Sam laughed out loud. After months of Caribbean travel, she was well used to such remarks. She grinned slowly and carefully formulated her reply.

"That's big talk. I sincerely hope you can back it up with action. Let me have your number and I might give you an opportunity."

The official scribbled a number on a spare piece of paper and handed it to her tucked inside her passport.

Another thing Sam had learnt was that there was no point in being indignant about such things over here. All Caribbean men feel that it's their duty to at least have a pop at pulling any half-decent-looking female – hell, any female, half-decent-looking or not. She'd got used to it and accepted her fate with pleasure.

After flashing a wide smile, she was waved straight through customs and she exited the airport building. She was immediately surrounded by the obligatory twenty or so taxi drivers.

"You won taxi?" they all called in their laid-back Caribbean drawl. They jostled her, offering to help her carry her bags. They observed her curiously, rephrasing the words in their heads as they took in her single, moderately-sized rucksack.

In the past six months, she'd managed with a miniscule amount of clothing. In Martinique, her first port of call, she'd been able to swap her designer trousers and shirt, as well as her wonderfully chic Bally shoes, for a sundress, swimsuit and battered pair of second-hand sandals, not really a fair swap, but she'd been happy with it. Since then, she'd extended her clothing range to include another sundress, two swimsuits, a pair of shorts, a sarong and a pair of long trousers. Add to this a pair of comfy trainers and Sam had a large enough wardrobe to last her for as long as she needed. As Alex had pointed out during one of the short phone-calls they'd had since Sam began her travels, this was quite a departure from the Ms Shopaholic who could spend a couple of thousand pounds on clothes without blinking, not to mention her collection of shoes.

After waving away the pushy taxi drivers, Sam sidled up to a man who'd been sitting quietly observing the throng.

"I need to find somewhere to stay."

"You won go to Castries?" the man mumbled, referring to the capital city. "Tourist like Castries."

"No, no tourists. I'll stay down here in Vieux Fort. You know of a good guesthouse?"

"English?"

"Why not?"

"Come." The man picked up her rucksack and ambled towards his car. Sam followed unhurriedly.

Once in the car, Sam strapped herself in tightly. Another thing she'd learnt on her travels was that, although road rules do exist, no one took much notice of them and the males found it particularly necessary to overtake on totally unsighted corners. Sam closed her eyes, definitely a pre-requisite if she wanted to prevent her heart from jumping up to her mouth at every turn, and started the conversation.

"So where are we going?"

"Missus Bryant, she has house. She make it sweet. You like."

"Is it far then?"

"No, not far." That was to be expected. Nothing over here was too far or took too long. It was all a matter of perspective.

A little way up the road, the driver turned to Sam. "You on vacation?" He said the word as if it were much longer than the original word. Vay-kay-shun, each syllable was strung out as if on a line to be dried.

"No, I'm on a new life. Sort of." Sam smiled.

"You won new life? What wrong with your old one?"

Sam wasn't quite sure how she should answer that one, so she simply shrugged.

* * *

Not long after her arrival in St Lucia, Sam was summoned to do her duty. Alex and Dominic were married in a beautiful church near Aylesbury. The wedding was picture perfect, in the way only a wedding planned with military precision could be. Not surprising when you realised that Alex had been planning it since her early years. The bride wore white and the groom wore a look of pure devotion for his wife-to-be. Sam had even agreed to wear pink, even though it clashed horribly with her newly cut and dyed copper hair. They had all agreed that Maid of Honour was too dull a name for someone so important and Sam had never liked the idea of being a Maid, so Sam was the Best Mate and made a stirring Best Mate's speech at the reception.

She eventually managed to hand in her notice at work. Martti only agreed to it when she promised to do some work for him on a freelance basis. The Fintec launch had been a fantastic success.

The introduction of their products to the UK market brought the company name to the most influential of lips. Fintec caused a stir large enough for Mark to be invited onto all the main television programmes such as Working Lunch and even Newsnight, where he had caused a stir of his own in the hearts and minds of women up and down the country. The Sun had described him as 'The thinking woman's crumpet' and the Financial Times had described him as being in the top ten of 'Finland's richest and most eligible men – as soon as his divorce comes through'. The name Fintec even made a Tony Blair soundbite.

Alex had sent Sam all the newspaper clippings as well as all the articles and pictures in Hello magazine of Mark with all his new-found famous friends. Alex had continued to moan at her on a regular basis to 'get her fat arse over to Finland and marry Wrinkle-face, before he is snapped up by one of the gorgeous women that accompany him to the A-list parties'.

Sam had been totally gob-macked with how well everything had gone and she was astounded when he publicly attributed the entire success to her guidance and organisation. Mark had even sent her a letter via Alex, which had stunned her with the news that if she ever got bored with Caribbean life, she could always open up her own consultancy, seeing as he was being bombarded with requests from other Finnish companies for her services.

Sam thought about what had happened since she'd left England. She couldn't even begin to describe what Mark had done for her in that time. The thing she was most pleased about was what he hadn't done. Being a man of his word, he hadn't pushed for her to make a decision. He hadn't even tried to glean her contact details out of Alex. He'd simply sent his letters via Alex until she'd eventually sent him her contact details.

After the wedding, Sam returned to the Caribbean. Six months later, she was offered a great opportunity and in a fit of spontaneity, she finally settled down on St Lucia. She had not settled on her special someone as yet, but was having fun making up her mind. She had, however, found her special place. She had used her money to buy Mrs Bryant's small guesthouse in the south of the island, near Vieux Fort, chosen specifically for its distance from the bustle of the package hotels in the north. She had three guest rooms and a beautiful stretch of golden, sandy, and more importantly, private beach. She had spent her time honing her household skills and preparing meals for her guests. A strange career choice for a 'modern-day career woman', or so her mother thought, but she was enjoying herself immensely. Mark had steered some of his more well-known clients in her direction, so she made enough from her little venture not to have to worry about money.

At the opening of her guesthouse, she'd invited him to the party. He had declined in such a beautiful and gracious manner that Sam had almost given in there and then and agreed to marry him. Mark had however reminded her that if she agreed to marry him, she had to be certain that she wanted to spend the rest of her life with him. He'd had one failed marriage and was determined that he would not have another. This made Sam more confused than ever as every other day she changed her mind. In terms of decisions made, she had come to the conclusion that she was more than fond of him and definitely wanted to be more than friends. After a year of experimentation and travelling, she'd finally asked Mark to visit her because she'd missed him. She was still waiting to hear his answer.

* * *

Sitting in the office of her hotelette, as she liked to call it, Sam smiled, thinking about the life she now had. Even after four months she could hardly believe that this house belonged to her. She looked up from the book she was reading and glanced at the fax machine on the desk in front of her. It had burst into action, spewing out a page of handwritten script. She got up and wandered over to it. Seeing Alex's handwriting, she laughed out loud. It had been nearly a year since she had been to their wedding and she didn't need to read the fax to know what it was going to tell her.

Sam picked the fax out of the basket and held it up. It consisted of one line, written large and in capitals. It read:

GET YOUR BAGS PACKED, YOU OLD COW.

I'M PREGGERS!

Sam was in the process of composing her reply when she received another fax. Smiling broadly, she scrapped what she was writing, wrote a new reply to Alex and sent it through the fax machine.

* * *

Dominic arrived home from his office. His business was booming and security was a growth area, especially in London. His ex-colleagues had been supplying him with a steady stream of custom and his international contacts had got him into some major blue-chip customers. He was still glowing from the great day that he'd had.

He'd been having breakfast that morning, amazed that he had a wife as perfect as Alex when she announced that she was expecting their first child. This had made him so ecstatic that he was certain that his life just couldn't get any better. He'd driven to his office where he'd been given the news that he'd been retained by a large banking concern, to secure their offices worldwide. He'd been pinching himself all day just to make sure he wasn't dreaming. After all, this was when disaster had been known to strike. He was certain that just before the *Titanic* had struck the iceberg, the captain had probably been saying that it was the best day of his life and how things couldn't get any better.

On his way back to their house in Aylesbury, he'd stopped off at the jeweller's and picked up the most incredible eternity ring which he was going to present to Alex that evening.

Parking his car, he thought he heard a strange noise coming from inside the house. His mind started racing. He heard the noise once more and this time he was certain that it was a female cry, almost a screech. It was Alex. His heart pounded as he let himself hurriedly in the front door.

"Alex, where are you?"

"I'm in the kitchen," Alex's voice sounded strangled.

Rushing into the kitchen he found Alex at the table, crying, and clutching her stomach.

"What's up? Is it the baby?" Dominic was frantic.

Alex was unable to speak. She had something in her hand. She decided against even attempting to utter an explanation – she simply handed him the paper.

Dominic read the text and looked down at his wife, seeing that she was actually crying tears of laughter. "I don't understand . . . ?"

Alex burst into giggles once more and stood up to give him a hug. The paper floated to the floor, whilst he was taking her into his arms.

It read: CAN'T COME FOR A FEW WEEKS. MARK IS BRINGING JEREMY PAXMAN TO STAY!!! LOVE SAM

THE END